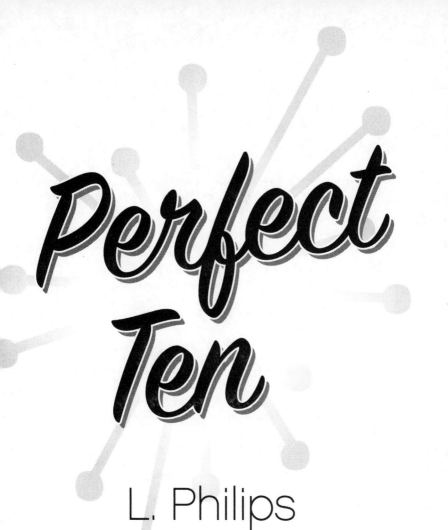

Perfect Ten

L. Philips

Viking

Viking
An imprint of Penguin Random House LLC
375 Hudson Street
New York, New York 10014

First published in the United States of America by Viking,
an imprint of Penguin Random House LLC, 2017

LIBRARY OF CONGRESS CATALOGING-IN-PUBLICATION DATA
Names: Philips, L.
Title: Perfect ten / L. Philips.
Description: New York : Viking, published by the Penguin Group, [2017] |
Summary: Sam Raines performs a love spell with his Wiccan best friend after breaking up with the only other gay guy at school and finds himself pursued by three seemingly perfect suitors.
Identifiers: LCCN 2016030972 | ISBN 9780425288115 (hardcover)
Subjects: | CYAC: Dating (Social customs)—Fiction. | Gays—Fiction. | Wiccans—Fiction.
Classification: LCC PZ7.1.P517 Pe 2017 | DDC [Fic]—dc23
LC record available at https://lccn.loc.gov/2016030972

Printed in U.S.A.
Book design by Nancy Brennan
Set in Melior LT Std

1 3 5 7 9 10 8 6 4 2

Brent—this book is for you.
It's always been for you.

One

"... and so I'm thinking maybe before the holidays, when his parents are picking up his sister from college. We're thinking of doing it up right, you know? Hotel room, hot tub, champagne . . . I know it's clichéd, but it's also kind of romantic, right?"

We're walking home from our school, Athens High, and Meg is rambling, as Meg often does. And as I often do, I'm zoning out completely. Until she says that.

"Wait. What?"

She stops walking and stares at me, so I stop walking and stare back.

"Sam, did you hear anything I said?" Her hands go on her hips like my mother when she's frustrated with me, but with Meg, it's nowhere near as effective. "Great Goddess. I wish you gave me half the attention you give to your imaginary friends."

I manage to stop myself just short of rolling my eyes. "They're characters. Not imaginary friends, and come on, Meg. I'm sorry. What were you saying? You and Michael?"

"Yeah. Sex. While his parents are away. Clichéd first time but hopefully with good room service. What do you think?"

"What do I think? Oh, that is a whole can of worms, Meghan Grace."

"Enlighten me." Meg fishes a pack of Marlboros out of an inside pocket of her black skull-and-crossbones hoodie, the one she never goes without. It's got these little devil horns sewn onto the hood so that when she puts it up she looks positively demonic. Or at least she thinks she does. But her wholesome face and stick-straight strawberry-blonde hair kind of lessen the effect. She slides a single cigarette out of the pack and lights it, and I can't help but notice that the Zippo she's using has the Sacred Heart of Jesus on it. It looks like something an old sailor would have tattooed on his sagging bicep, and don't even get me started on the irony of Meg using such a thing.

"You know I'm not exactly Michael's number one fan," I say.

She inhales deeply and blows the smoke in my face. "Because you won't give him a chance."

"Because apparently you're smoking for him now, for one."

I pluck the cigarette out of her fingers and throw it to the ground, crushing it with my Adidas. We both cough.

"No, I'm not," she sputters.

I narrow my eyes at her.

"Okay, not *for* him. He just looks so cool doing it sometimes. You know? Like some old-time movie star, leaning up against a wall, brooding and sophisticated . . ."

I sigh loudly and start walking again. "Yeah, a brooding and sophisticated candidate for lung cancer. And it's such a bad idea."

"Fine." Meg takes the pack of Marlboros out again and hands them to me, as if she doesn't trust herself to dispose of them. "I just wanted to try them once."

"I meant about the hotel room," I say, and pocket the pack. I'll ditch them in the first trash can I see.

"Why?" Meg loops her arm through mine and guides me in the direction of Saint Catherine's Cemetery, which is one of six in Athens that, legend has it, make a pentagram if you connect them on a map, with Saint Cat's in the center. Meg loves that, as she loves all things spooky, and all things witchy. Our freshman year, after a particularly heinous fight in which her über-Catholic parents threatened to (a) send her to a convent, and (b) perform an exorcism, Meg ditched Catholicism for good and took up Wicca. It was kind of a genius power play on her part, because as adamant as they are that she be a virtuous Catholic, they're even more scared that they'll cause her to sink deeper into the dark side. She's got them in that perfect rock–slash–hard place position where they're too panicked to punish her much. So as long as she keeps it quiet and doesn't break curfew, they get by with vague disapproval and guilt trips.

Anyway, the cemetery is also the shortest way to get to our houses from school, as it's right in the middle of our neighborhood. I don't know why, but some construction company in the seventies thought it would be a good idea to build a subdivision around a cemetery. I bet a lot of weird stuff seemed like a good idea in the seventies, but I digress.

"Come on, Sam," Meg prods. "What's so bad about Michael?"

"You mean besides the smoking and the horrible cliché of losing your virginity in a hotel?"

"I've already owned up to the cliché, Samson . . ."

"You just caught him texting another girl a few weeks ago."

She pouts prettily. "He explained that. It was nothing."

"And the time before?" She opens her mouth to protest, but I go on before she can. "I'm just saying, why would you want to with him?"

She unlinks her arm from mine and gives me a shove that has a little more force than I expect. "I don't know. Why did you want to with Landon?"

At the mention of my ex-boyfriend–slash–other best friend, I feel myself tense. "I was in love with Landon."

"And I love Michael."

"But Landon and I were different."

She crosses her arms over her chest and kicks hard at an innocent pebble in her path. "Oh yes, and you and Landon were the exception to every rule. Michael and I couldn't possibly be that perfect. No one can live up to the Sam and Landon standard of epic and tragic romance."

"That's not what I'm saying. And we weren't that tragic."

"Darling, you two were practically Brontë characters. You broke his heart and now here you are, two years later, and you haven't even had a crush on someone since, have you, Sam?" I don't answer, and there's a tense pause between us before she adds, "Exactly two years, actually."

"You know, I could have gone through the whole day without thinking of it, but thanks for that reminder," I say acidly.

"I'm sorry," she says, and I know she means it. "He brought it up to me at lunch. He's the one who remembered. Not me."

I don't know how any of us could have forgotten it, least of all me. October tenth, two years ago, I ended my relationship with Landon. He didn't speak to me for almost six months. Meg didn't speak to me for three days, the longest we'd gone without talking since I accidentally decapitated one of her Barbies when we were seven. Hell, I wouldn't have spoken to myself if I could have gotten away with it. I absolutely loathed Samson Raines for a long time afterward. But now Landon is my friend again. We worked everything out. He and I are fine. All three of us are fine.

Fine, fine, fine.

"I wish he didn't remember," I say, and Meg shifts our arms so she can squeeze my hand. I sigh. "Bygones. Anyway, we were talking about you and Michael, and not my love life, which is totally unfair to bring up by the way, because I don't exactly have any options, do I?"

"There's always Archie," she says, smirking. Archie

Meyers is the only other gay boy besides Landon and me at Athens High, but he's not even a blip on my radar. It's not that I'm shallow, but there is absolutely nothing attractive about Archie. Between the buck teeth, the acne, and the IQ that must top out in the double digits, I would have to be drunk out of my mind to even consider it. Even then it would be a stretch.

But then her smirk droops thoughtfully. "No. Wait. I heard the other day that Archie's dating some guy he met at a Dungeons and Dragons meeting over the summer . . ."

I turn my head slowly to Meg. "Seriously? Even Archie Meyers has a boyfriend?"

Meg makes a clicking sound with her tongue. "There's a whole big world of boys out there, Sam. Someone perfect for everyone, I think, even the D and D playing sort with buck teeth."

"Then I'm sure there's someone out there for you who isn't a total douche like Michael."

That sets Meg off on another tangent in defense of her boyfriend, effectively taking the attention off of me. I only half listen as I walk her to her large brick house on the corner, and nod automatically when she suggests I call after dinner to work on homework together. I pat her family's statue of Saint Francis on his bald head as I walk away, but I don't go home. Mom won't expect me home for a while, and Dad is in New York, yet again. Instead, I walk past my house and back toward town, toward Landon's.

I was in seventh grade when my dad got published. He'd written for literary journals before, and had a few short stories in collections from small presses, but that was the year the big stuff started. Dad had always been sort of an artsy type of writer, not interested in a bestseller or in prose that didn't border on the poetic, and *Backyards of the City* was no different in that regard. What was different was that it caught the attention of important people who deem certain books to be important and give those books important awards. He's since published five books, all to the same critical acclaim, that bring in a steady enough income that he only teaches one class at the university now, and just because he wants to. We remain in the sleepy little cottage-esque house my parents moved into before I was born because, as my parents say, it has a well-used, vintage charm—a motif that runs through all of the Raines family purchases.

Landon's house, by contrast, is big, old, and grand. It looks like something that should be on the front of a Victorian Christmas card, replete with a horse-drawn sleigh and a man in a top hat. It's solid brick that's been painted white, and has six large columns in the front to hold up its massive front porch, black shutters that were meant to actually work at one point in time, and a red door for a bit of flair. Inside, valuable antiques mix well with his mother's latest Pottery Barn finds. All of it is impeccably tasteful, impeccably tidy, and it's always made me feel a little intimidated.

Landon doesn't ask questions when he opens the door, just starts up the ornate staircase to the second floor. His parents aren't home. They never are. I know his father is a lawyer but I've never really figured out what his mother does, besides shop at Pottery Barn. She's busy, that's all I know. And whatever it is that she's doing must be more important than spending time with her only child. Their "hands off" parenting thing seemed really cool for a while when we were dating, but now that my dad is away a lot, I know the truth of it: it really sucks.

When we get to his room, I glance around, noting any subtle changes. There are a few new books on his shelves and his desk looks in slight disarray, like he's actually using it for once, but for the most part his room is spotless as usual. He claims the housekeeper cleans it every day but I don't know if I buy that because I've seen him straighten the books on his shelves one too many times. Regardless, his bedroom feels warm, comfortable. His bed is huge and fluffy, the sheer curtains over his windows let just enough sunlight in, and the desk, bookshelves, and overstuffed armchairs make it equal parts library and living space to me. In short, it's heavenly, and I'm a little jealous of it.

I take off my jacket and toss it on a chair before opening one of his windows. He digs through the bottom drawer of his dresser, finds the old pencil box where he stores his stash, and we both park ourselves on his bed while he rolls a joint. He lights it and offers me the first hit, and I take it with a smile.

"You know, if we're not careful, we might make this a habit," I joke, because it already is a habit. My voice is tight with smoke.

"We could have worse ones," Landon says in wise response.

I lie back, head resting on one of the ninety pillows on his bed. He joins me, and for a few minutes we pass the joint back and forth in silence, staring at the fancy swirls in his ceiling.

Pot was something Landon discovered without me, and he introduced it to me last July. It's not like I'm some sort of Goody Two-shoes or something, I'd just never had the opportunity to try it before. Since then it's just sort of unspoken that we smoke together every once in a while, when we both sense that it's needed, and it's also unspoken that we never invite Meg. It's not that she'd disapprove or even that she wouldn't be fun to have along, but this is our thing, our time. Sam and Landon time.

"So what's up?" he asks, knowing something is.

I groan. "Meg says she's going to have sex with Michael."

"Ugh, why?" There are three things I can always count on Landon for: his support, his intuition, and his hatred of Michael Jenkins. Landon laughs, low and throaty. "Not if he were the last man on earth."

"Not even then," I agree, then chuckle. "And speaking

of the last man on earth, Archie has a boyfriend."

"Yeah, I know. Rumor has it, said boyfriend is actually attractive too."

And Landon would know. There's nothing Landon doesn't know about everyone at Athens High. Gossip is his superpower.

"How is that possible?" I ask, and Landon shrugs.

"Maybe Archie is like Clark Kent. When he takes off his glasses he's suddenly way hot."

I shake my head. "Very doubtful. Even then . . . he'd still have to meet someone. Like, have the ability to come into contact with actual other boys who would be interested."

"Apparently Dungeons and Dragons is as good as Grindr. Who knew?"

Chuckling, I take the joint from Landon's hand. "Permission to be utterly shallow?"

"Permission granted, soldier."

"I find it incredibly insulting that Archie Meyers has a possibly hot, steady boyfriend who shares his interests, and I, Sam Raines, who is not completely unfortunate looking—"

"Of course not. I dated you, and I have incredibly high standards."

"—can't find someone to even have a crush on, let alone an actual relationship. I mean, it's been an embarrassingly long time since I've been kissed."

"Since me," Landon says, and the absolute confidence in his statement makes me cringe and get a little angry too.

"Well, yeah," I say, and already hate how defensive I sound. "But it's not like you've been making out with anybody. You're in the same boat as me. The same small, drifting, utterly solitary boat."

Landon doesn't say anything, but his skin goes so pink it's near fuchsia. And Landon only blushes when he's guilty about something. He doesn't get embarrassed, or even ashamed, really. Just guilty.

"Wait . . . you *have* kissed someone?" There's a pause, then Landon sits up and looks at me, dark blond brows stitched together. He nods. Just barely. "You didn't tell me."

"Should I have?" Landon asks, and I honestly don't know how to answer. It's not like I expected to be his only forever, and I'm not sure how I'd handle that conversation, really. But now I feel like he's springing this on me, and knowing that he's been with someone else makes me feel even more alone, if that's possible. I take a deep hit to numb the feeling away.

I shrug, and Landon continues to look at me with a scrutiny that nearly makes me angry. Then he shifts and drops his head onto my chest and wraps an arm around me, and there's a rush of nostalgia and relief all at once.

"Sometimes I'm not sure about our rules," Landon mumbles against me. "We're a bit complicated."

"Understatement of the decade."

He's quiet. I hear him blow out smoke. I can almost hear the thoughts in his head. Then he mumbles, "I should have told you."

"Maybe," I say, and because I'm being totally honest,

I add, "I don't know. But now I feel like even more of a loser for not having someone."

"You're not," he says so easily that I know he believes it. "But you want someone?"

I don't know how to answer, exactly, so I watch for a moment as smoke sucks out the window and into the twilit sky. I'm sure his snobby neighbors love that. I should be getting home soon, but there's still a little weed left and I need the numbness right now almost as much as I need air.

Then I decide to keep being honest with Landon because (a) he probably knows the truth anyway, and (b) I don't like keeping things from him, and I'm a little sore that he's kept something from me.

"I want to be with someone. But not, you know, just anyone. I want *someone*."

He nods against me. "I know."

And of course he knows. He knows me; he knows my history. Our history. He knows that I almost had what I'm looking for with him, until we screwed it up beyond repair.

He moves, nuzzling into my neck. "So Grindr isn't an option."

I laugh, which, combined with the weed, makes me feel pretty good, like maybe this day isn't a total loss. "Not an option. So what do I do? Dungeons and Dragons?"

"Maybe Archie knows someone." Landon laughs, then sobers. "I don't know, Sam. We've got one more year in this abysmal place, then we can take over the world.

Guys will be falling at our feet, all gorgeous and sexy and, you know, gay. But until then . . ."

"Until then we just wait it out? Is that what you're saying?"

"What's one long, miserable, lonely year?"

I stare at him and mumble my reply. "On top of two already? Awful."

Just then my phone lets out a shrill ring and I curse. I'd forgotten all about calling Meg. I sit up; Landon immediately curls into the space I left behind. "Hey, Meg."

"Hey. Did you do your calculus yet? I can't get number fourteen."

I look over at Landon, whose gray-blue eyes are watching me with amusement. "Not really. I'm at Landon's."

"Ugh, are you two hanging out while I'm stuck doing homework? I hate you."

"Not really," I lie. "He's reading one of my new stories."

"And talking about his deep longing for romance," Landon says, loud enough for Meg to hear, and I swat at him.

"Put me on speaker," Meg orders, and I do, and she addresses Landon directly. "Do you know anyone, Landon? Sam is clearly miserable."

"Thanks a lot!" I interject, but they talk to each other as if I'm not there, as if it wasn't that Meg called *me.*

"Well, it has been two years," Landon says, smirking at me. Then he mouths to me, "Exactly two years."

"Is there a dating site for miserable, desperate, gay seventeen-year-olds?" Meg asks, and instead of defending myself against Meg's insults, I mouth back to Landon, "I'm sorry."

Landon shrugs my apology away, then says what we've learned to say to each other over the past year and a half, low enough that Meg can't hear over the line. "Bygones."

"No website I know of," he says to Meg, louder. "eHarmony is mostly for adults. Straight adults. And Sam's already ruled out Grindr."

I roll my eyes at my friends' conversation.

"Well, I have an idea, but you're not going to like it."

Landon and I both lean over my phone and say in chorus, "Tell me."

"We could do a spell."

Landon covers his mouth to stop a laugh from escaping while I say, "Meg . . ."

"Don't give me that 'Meg . . .' crap, this shit works. Trust me. I've been doing this for years now."

Landon, composure regained, pipes up. "And how, exactly, has magic worked for you, oh wise mage? Or, I'm sorry, it's magic with a *k*, isn't it? Magic-k?"

"The *k* is silent," Meg says irritably. "I passed my chemistry test last week because I said a spell for intelligence."

"You also studied a week for it," I say. "Next."

I hear Meg blow out a breath. "I cast a love spell the night before Michael asked me out."

"And that brought you a real prize, didn't it?" I mumble, and Landon elbows me.

"Well, I was happy with the results, but if you want

we could be more specific." I hear some papers shuffling, the sounds of books being closed, then opened. I can picture Meg at home at her pre-Wiccan-era pink desk, pulling out the spell books she keeps hidden from her parents' strict regime. "I think maybe . . . ah, yes. Here it is. Let's do this."

Meg reads out a section of a witchy manual, about doing a spell to find a soul mate. "It suggests making a list of qualities you want in a boyfriend. You know, to give the spell direction."

I look at Landon, who is trying so hard not to laugh his face is purple. "Well, directionless magic could be a real problem, I suppose. Sort of like Santa Claus without Rudolph."

"Or Frodo without Gollum!" Landon says.

"Very funny," Meg says. "I know you two are godless heathens, but don't you think it might help to believe in *something* greater than yourselves?"

Landon leans close and whispers, "Did a witch just call us godless heathens?" and I feign shock.

"I'm just saying, putting some positive energy out into the universe could really help you, Sam. You get back what you put out there."

There's a brief pause where Landon seems to be considering Meg's words, and I'm trying to figure out why he's considering. Then, to my utter surprise, Landon says, "Maybe she's right. At the very least, this gets you started, you know? Gets you out there, looking."

I stare at him. Landon and I are not religious in the

slightest. My parents are atheists, his only went to church when it looked good for his father's political career. We bonded over our mutual disdain for organized religion, and our mutual love of concrete, rational things, like science and facts and stuff. We are both amused by and a little in awe of Meg's zealotry sometimes.

So now I'm feeling a little betrayed, and a little angry that he thinks this would be good for me. And if I'm being honest, maybe I'm a little angry that he doesn't have a reason to feel as pathetic as I do because apparently there's been someone—or several someones for all I know—for him. It's like a double whammy of jealousy and self-pity.

"You really think I should do a magic spell?" I ask him.

He shrugs. "Like I said, you can always wait it out. Or you could do something."

"We know you're lonely, Sam," Meg says, and my ears burn.

Landon's arm snakes around my waist, and maybe it's his touch that reminds me how great it can be to have somebody. Maybe it's the idea giving me feelings of hope and possibility, things that I haven't let myself feel in a while. Maybe it's the strong weed. But something pushes me toward saying yes, and I do.

Meg squeals. "All right. I promise you, Sam, the Goddess always listens to me. She won't disappoint you. You've got an in with Her."

Landon cracks up then, and I laugh too, but Meg's

voice drones on, oblivious. "So you'll make a list then? Qualities that you want? Oh, and you'll have to write your own spell. That makes it even more personal. And we can do it Friday night, Sam! It's Friday the thirteenth! Great Goddess, it's perfect. We can even do it at Saint Catherine's, where the energy is strongest."

"Excellent," Landon agrees, with so much sincerity that he actually might be for real, and I kick at him. He's totally turned on me.

"Wait, Meg," I say. "Slow down. How many qualities? Like, twenty?"

"Hmnn. I think that's too many. Kind of greedy, and we don't want the Goddess to think you're greedy."

"Right, of course," I say. "Wouldn't want the flying spaghetti monster to get the wrong idea about me."

"Samson," Meg warns, "if you're not going to do this right, I won't do it at all. You can't be disrespectful."

"She's right, you know," Landon says, eyes sparkling with mischief. "If you're going to do this, don't half-ass it, Raines."

I am completely outnumbered. I sigh. "I'm sorry. You're right. So what, like, ten? Ten things I want in a boyfriend?"

"Yes. I think that's perfect." I can almost hear her smile. "The Perfect Ten! This is going to be fabulous, I can feel it. Can you feel it?"

I can't feel a damned thing, but I'm used to being a bit perplexed by all of Meg's feelings and intuitions and senses. "Oh yeah, I can feel it," I lie.

Meg lets out another squeal and says good-bye, and I stare at the phone for a moment in silence, wondering what I've just gotten myself into.

"Am I crazy?"

"Nah," Landon answers. "Magic or not, I think it would be good for you. Wasn't lying about that. Plus it will make you think about what you want. And that can't be a bad thing, right?"

"I guess not." I pick at a loose thread in my sweater, a vintage find from my dad's closet. "Hey, Landon. I know it's none of my business, but who was he?"

Landon cocks his head at me. "No one special, Sam. And it's always your business."

"But you didn't tell me. And I guess I just . . . I just thought that you've been lonely this whole time like me. It's kind of weird to think that you haven't been."

He waits a few ticks, then says, "What makes you think I'm not lonely?"

We smile at each other then, silent words flowing between us for a long moment, then Landon squeezes my knee. "Let me drive you home."

••••••••••••••••••••

"So I've been thinking that you need to write your spell in Latin," Meg says as we arrive at our lockers the next morning. "Since that's what you study and all, it will give the spell an even more personal touch. And Latin is such an old language. Lots of energy built up in it."

I glance around for Landon, hoping he'll save me from Meg's nonstop spell planning, but he's nowhere to be found, the jerk.

"Fine," I agree. I can manage a spell in Latin. Meg takes French so it's not like she'll be able to understand it anyway. I could write about sea monkeys for all she knows.

"So have you finished your list?"

I toss my book bag on the floor next to locker number 75 and spin the combination. "Not even close," I admit. In addition to not having much time to even think about the list last night, it was surprisingly hard to come up with the qualities I did manage to write down. Honestly, it's all so embarrassing that it's hard to even think about. Like I'm so pathetic I'm resorting to religion I don't even believe in. And even if, by some Wiccan miracle, the thing works, is the Perfect Ten even going to want some loser who had to use magic to get a date? It might be easier to adopt thirty cats and start wearing mumus around the house now, and cut to the chase.

"Show me."

I take out my English notebook and hand it to Meg, looking her over as I do. She looks cute today, less goth than normal, and with a pair of skintight jeans and a low-cut V-neck shirt, she's showing off all her endowments nicely. I catch a few of the boys checking her out as they walk by, and I'm really kind of jealous.

She looks up at me, wrinkling her nose and sticking out her lips. It's her Not Good Enough face.

"What? It's a start."

"Not much of one."

She hands the notebook back, and I look down at what I've written:

Perfect 10

1. Sexy
2. Talented

Yeah. Creative, isn't it?

Regardless, those two things are important to me. I want a guy who's going to make my palms sweat and my heart drop into my stomach every time he walks by. I want him to send my whole body into shudders and shivers when he touches me. I really, *really* want to want him.

Number two is equally important. My boy needs to be interesting, and good at something. I mean, I won't complain if he happens to love literature like me, or loves to write like I do, but what his interest is doesn't matter. Hell, he could be fascinated by medieval jousting or taxidermy for all I care. Just as long as he has something, because it's essential that I'm not his only interest. That was the problem with Landon. I mean, it's not like Landon was a loser or something, but it was like he had no life outside of me. And it may sound awesome to be the center of someone's universe, but in reality it's bad. Really bad.

I shake my head to clear the thoughts of Landon and take my notebook back. "I've got until Friday night. Don't panic."

Meg stops rummaging through her own locker, number 77, and lays a hand on my arm. "Just take it seriously, okay, Sam? I know you don't believe like I do, but if the Goddess answers you with someone, you want that list to be good, you know? So think hard about what you want. Sexiness and talent are fine, but what about brains? Michael says the most attractive thing about girls are their brains."

"What would Michael know about brains?" I mumble, slamming my locker door shut, and wouldn't you know? Michael appears at Meg's side, cramming his tongue down her throat before saying hello to either of us.

"Raines. Good to see you."

He constantly calls me by my last name, and he's always slightly formal with me, as if he thinks this is how civil, grown-up men should behave.

Douche.

"Why, hello, Michael," I say, slightly breathless and batting my eyelashes. He swore up and down to me that he wasn't at all uncomfortable with my sexuality when we first met, the way people who are uncomfortable with my sexuality usually do. So whenever he's around, I up my queerness a few degrees. "You look so handsome today."

That's a lie. The guy is wearing cargo pants and a Cleveland Browns T-shirt. He's tall and thin, so he's got that going for him, and if he just dressed decently at least he wouldn't look like a total schmuck next to Meg's prettiness. Do yourself a favor, Michael, and pick up a *GQ* once in a while.

His skin turns red but he ignores me and kisses Meg again. "See you before last period, babe?"

"Of course."

They make out again and I look away so that I don't vomit all over the hallway. Once they break apart, Meg and I walk to the Foreign Language hallway, where she'll have French and I'll have Latin.

"He tries to be nice to you, you know."

I shrug. "It's not me he has to be nice to. I'll like him when he stops being a lying, cheating bastard."

Meg says nothing, even though I can tell it's taking quite an effort to keep her mouth shut. Finally, when we get to Madame Vinson's classroom, she orders me to work on my list in Latin class.

"But we're conjugating—"

"Work on it, Sam!" she hisses just as the bell rings, and hops over the threshold that separates hallway from classroom. Tardiness is detention in Athens High. I jump over my line too. "And put some thought into it, please?"

A noncommittal nod is the best promise I can give her. "Coffee after school?"

She rolls her eyes as Madame Vinson taps her on the shoulder, giving her the evil eye. Vinson doesn't permit English in her classroom. "*Oui!*" Meg answers.

And of course I don't pay attention in Latin, which means the twenty sentences Mr. Ames assigned to translate will be a real bitch tonight, but I do come up with one more item for my list, thanks to Michael's lack of fashion sense:

3. Style

Two

We go to the Donkey, which is the only respectable place in Athens to get coffee. Sure, there's Brenan's and Perks and the Starbucks stand inside the college bookstore, but those places are for people who wear North Face and Uggs and have daddies who send them an allowance check each month. In other words, they're for the spoiled college kids. The Donkey is the only place in town that doesn't burn their beans and has a crowd that's a little more alternative. Any night of the week you'll hear some great musicians or poets on the little stage in the corner, catch someone reading Kafka or laboring over a political science thesis, or overhear a deep discussion on the merits of legalizing marijuana.

Yeah, the place stinks like patchouli and unwashed hair, but I love it.

Meg and I sit on stools at the bar and the barista—a guy named Ted—sets our usuals in front of us before we can even order. Meg gets out her latest book on Wicca, which I initially thought was about gardening because the title is *The Garden Path*, but Meg assures me it's about the magickal properties of herbs or some other nonsense. I get out my Latin and start to work. We'll work side by side for a few hours in the coffeehouse before going home. It's not that I don't want to go home. My parents are really quite awesome, even if we don't always talk about everything in my life. But they're cool about me and who I am, and love that I'm different.

It's Meg who doesn't want to go home. Ironically, she's the one whose parents don't approve of her "lifestyle." In their eyes, she'll never be as perfect as her younger sister, Catherine, who declared she wants to be a nun last year, or her older sister, Margaret, who already has three children with her über-Catholic husband, like every dutiful servant of the church should. Even her brother, John, who nearly failed out of college, ranks higher in the family because he still attends Mass every weekend. I guess his soul is still pure or something, even if he can't get a passing grade in chemistry.

So I indulge her. Nearly every day, unless Michael has a day off from his job at McDonald's and she ditches me for him, we sit here until the coffee, the homework, or the excuses run out.

I don't look up from my translations until I hear Meg suck in a breath and a pointy elbow lands squarely in my ribs.

"Ow! What was that for?" I hiss.

"Look."

I look where she's looking, in the direction of the entrance, where two boys about my age enter. One's thin with spiked-up hair and a great smile and the other . . .

The other is drop-dead gorgeous. He's small, with icy green eyes and thick black hair that falls into his face as he moves. And the way he moves makes me want to quote Byron.

I watch in what I think is a discreet manner as they shed their jackets and claim a table by the window. They're both wearing green-and-gray ties, with gray sweaters over them that have the same emblem embroidered on the chest.

I turn back to Meg. "Holy Cross High School?"

She nods, mouth agape. "Maybe I should have let my parents send me there."

"Yeah," I agree, snorting. "Although something tells me I have a better chance with these boys than you do."

"Oh I don't think so. The blond one checked me out as they walked in."

"Well, you can have that one, I'm more into—" I stop my teasing short because the beautiful one is standing right next to me at the bar. *Right next to me.* And holy shnikes, Batman, he even smells good.

Ted—stupid Ted with his stupid easy excuses to talk to cute boys—offers the boy a big smile and says, "What'll it be today?"

The beautiful boy replies, "Spearmint tea for me. Triple espresso for Brad."

"I'll bring it out to you," Ted promises, but the boy doesn't move. I dare to look in his direction and see that he's staring down at my homework. Meg elbows me in the ribs again.

I clear my throat and the pretty one flushes. "Sorry, I didn't mean to be nosy. Your homework caught my attention. I sort of love Latin."

"If I'm doing this wrong, please tell me. I was distracted today during class." I shoot Meg a scathing glance for good measure, because now it's all her fault if the beautiful boy thinks I'm stupid. Her eyes are wide and she's nodding at me, urging me to keep talking.

"Well, actually, if you want to conjugate this . . ." I don't have any clue what else he says, because at that moment he reaches for my pencil and our hands brush. I almost yelp when his skin touches mine.

He corrects my homework for me and explains it, but then Ted delivers his drinks. In a rush to keep him there, I pick up my notebook to ask about another translation, and he sees my English notebook underneath. Before I can cover it up, he's read all three items on my list.

"Eyes," he says to me, and I'm too busy willing myself to shrivel up and die to fathom what he's talking about. Another sharp elbow lands in my side.

"Huh?" I ask. Oh Sam, you're an idiot.

"For your list, which . . . I assume isn't homework." The beautiful Catholic-school boy smirks at me from behind his cup of spearmint tea. "The windows of the soul. Nice eyes should be on your list."

"Hey, ready?" Suddenly the other boy is there, and

he gives me a disdainful glance before slipping his hand into his boyfriend's. He's maybe a 5 or a 6 on the hotness scale, while the pretty boy is easily a 9.8. It's totally off balance, but I'll give him one thing: he's got beautiful amber eyes that seem to be lit up from within, especially when he looks at his boyfriend.

"Yeah, let's go."

"Thanks for the help . . . um . . ."

"Nic," the pretty boy says. "And this is Brad."

"I'm Sam, and this is Meg. Thanks for explaining the Latin. I'm usually really good at this, honest." Meg jumps to my defense beside me, echoing my claim.

Nic just nods. There's a bit of laughter behind his eyes like there's no way in hell he believes me. "Good luck with the rest of your work." He winks, which just about gives me a heart attack, then he and his boyfriend leave the Donkey without looking back.

"What the hell, Meg?" I ask, turning slowly toward her. "What the *hell*?"

"Should have gone to Holy Cross," she mumbles into her cappuccino.

"Why? Why are there pretty gay boys at a Catholic school in Nelsonville, the biggest hick town this side of the Hocking River, and none in Athens?"

"Isn't there a law about that? Murphy's law or something?"

"A law about how all gay boys will be wherever Sam Raines is not?"

"Something like that." She snorts, then pats my hand. "So . . . what have you learned?"

I think for a beat. "I have a Catholic-school boy kink?"

"Besides that."

I think hard, remembering the pretty boy, taking in the details. "I want someone with nice eyes. And that hair. Meg, did you see his hair?"

Meg is busy pulling my list out of the pile of homework in front of me. "Yeah, I saw his hair. So . . . nice eyes and good hair?"

"Thick hair," I amend. "Something I can run my fingers through."

She scribbles these things on the list in her loopy handwriting, then looks back to me impatiently. "And what else have we learned?"

I'm clueless, so I shrug. I have no doubt that whatever I'm meant to have learned has something to do with signs from a goddess or the mysteries of the universe.

She lays her hand over mine and pats it like she's explaining something to a small child. "We've learned this isn't impossible. There are plenty of boys close by, now we just need them to come to *you*."

·····················

Perfect 10

1. Sexy
2. Talented

3. Style
4. Nice eyes
5. Thick hair

I stare at my list. I'm in Latin class. My homework was perfect and I even understand it now that I look over the slanted letters Catholic Boy printed to replace my mistakes. Mr. Ames isn't much for grammar today, though, so he's lecturing on the Colosseum instead of actually teaching the language. That's just fine with me. I have to work on my list. I need five more things, and I have only one day left to come up with them. How had I thought twenty would be a reasonable number? Clearly, zeroing in on things that would make Mr. Right, well, *right* is going to take a while.

"Sam."

Rachel Gliesner taps me on the shoulder and I reach back automatically for the note she's going to hand me. Rachel sits between me and Landon in the middle row in Latin, and has since freshman year. Thank goodness she's a sweet girl with a sense of humor, because she's probably passed a million and a half notes between us over the years, and I'm sure that as sweet as she is, she probably wanted to wring both our necks while we were dating.

I open the note. Landon has scrawled, *After school?*

I scribble, *Coffee with Meg. Come with?* and hand it back over my shoulder to Rachel. Seconds later the note is returned to me with a simple smiley face drawn on it.

Typical Landon.

I met Landon freshman year. He'd gone to West Middle School because he lives in the snobby part of town, so I hadn't met him until my middle school and his merged into Athens High.

It was sort of a mutual, easy thing. I'd told everyone I was gay by the time I hit eighth grade, and it wasn't a secret for him either. So naturally the rest of the school pushed and shoved until we found each other, and we started dating by the time Christmas break rolled around. We didn't even really ask each other out, it was just assumed after we kissed (that happened at Jack Grossman's Christmas party, which was in his basement while his parents hovered nervously upstairs, but it was the first time any of us had been to a real party) that we were together.

Landon was my first kiss. And here it comes: Landon was my first everything. *Everything*, if you catch my drift. That's the truth of it and it might also have been our biggest mistake.

Once we were together we fell in love hard and fast, and we couldn't keep our hands off of each other. To be blunt, the hormones were a-*raging*. When sex happened, it caught us completely by surprise. Don't get me wrong, even though sex ed is clearly just for straight people, it's not like we didn't know what we were doing. My parents, in their usual fashion, had bought me books about gay sex, and Landon had done his fair share of "research" online (read: porn). We knew the mechanics, how part A fits into slot B, et cetera, but we were totally, completely, utterly unprepared for how it made us feel.

By then we were fifteen, it was the summer between our freshman and sophomore years in high school (simultaneously the best and worst summer of my life), and to be honest, I figured there must be something wrong with me that I couldn't handle it. We're guys, after all, isn't this what we were supposed to do? Shouldn't it be no big deal?

But as it turns out, it *was* a big freaking deal, because it made everything else so intense. Sometimes that was nice. Every kiss became a promise of something more. Every time he said "I love you" I felt invincible. But on the flip side, the bad stuff blew up too. The smallest disagreement became an enormous fight. The tiniest doubt grew into suspicion and accusations. The weight of our feelings settled on us and began to smother. It was too much, too fast, and we were underprepared and too young.

That's right, I'll say it: we were too young to have sex. Write that down in the books, ladies and gentlemen. A teenager admitted he was too young for sex. Go ahead. Throw your Abstinence Club party. Don't forget the streamers.

Of course we didn't figure that out then. We were both too stupid/stubborn/in love to really get what was going on. All we knew was it felt like we were slowly suffocating each other.

I broke things off with him on a bench on College Green, one October afternoon. It was a cowardly move on my part, because my dad was going to New York the next day, and Mom and I were going with him, and I wouldn't be home for a week, but it was the only way I could go through with it.

Landon didn't talk to me for six months. I think—and I don't mean to sound vain about this—that it was harder for him than it was for me. As jealous and possessive as I was about him, he was ten times worse about me. I would hear things—through Meg, who was good friends with him too, or from random people at school—about how he wasn't coping well. But one day he showed up on my doorstep with a single rose and simply said, "Sorry I've been distant. I've been processing."

Of course I wanted to dive in and analyze things, but it seemed he was already done with that part. Before I could say anything else, he said, "It was too intense. Way too intense."

And that was that. No analysis required. We'd both arrived at the same conclusion, and there was nothing more to talk about.

....

It's always different when Landon joins us at the Donkey. Not a bad different, just different. We talk more and work less. Meg sets aside her witch book, I abandon the short story I've been writing, and we let Landon tell us the latest gossip. The thing about Landon is that he's really easygoing and really quiet when he wants to be, so people tend to talk around him, even the teachers, under the false impression that he's not listening or he doesn't care enough to tell anyone else. He's always got a variety too, since he floats between cliques at our school and fits in with all of them equally well. He's like a walking *Us Weekly.*

When he's done, Meg fills Landon in on our latest: the status of the list and the voodoo she's researched that will go along with it. Landon's intrigued, to say the least.

"So what do you have so far?"

I pick up my short story and reveal the list to him. He scans it and snorts as he gets to the last item on the list.

"Thick hair? Well, I guess that means I'm out." He chuckles, running a hand self-consciously through his blond hair, which is baby fine and falls around his head in chunks that alternate between limp and sticking straight out. Yes, I was once very attracted to this boy, but that was eons ago and I wasn't really thinking with my brain. Thick hair isn't the only item on the list Landon falls short with, but the one he has a shot with is his eyes. They're a pretty shade between gray and blue, and huge.

"You should have seen the boy that inspired him to put thick hair on the list." Meg's practically swooning as she talks.

"Tell me," Landon says, and gives me his full attention. I tell him all about the Catholic-school boy, unafraid to share every detail, and he hums his approval when appropriate. It's times like these that I'm really thankful that Landon and I became friends after the breakup. Meg is always great for girl talk, but Landon truly gets where I'm coming from.

Meg gets up to go to the bathroom, leaving me alone with Landon for a few minutes, and Landon doesn't let the opportunity go to waste.

"You're actually hoping this spell will work, aren't you?"

I laugh a little, staring down at my list. "You know I don't believe in this shit."

"I know, but that's not stopping you from wanting it to work, is it?"

I look up at him. "It would be nice if it did. That's all."

"I understand that completely," he says. Then, "Hey, Sam? Can I be there tomorrow night? For this little black magic ritual, I mean."

"Meg says it's actually white magic, whatever the glittery hell that means, so don't let her hear you call it black. And of course," I answer. "Want to make your own list? I'm sure we could do the spell for two."

Landon smirks at the offer, but there's something a little off in his eyes. Distant.

"Nah, I think I'll wait and see how yours goes first."

"I see. You're letting me be the guinea pig."

"There's a reason why royalty always had people taste their food."

We're laughing at that when Meg sits down with us again. "What's so funny?"

"Nothing," Landon says. "I was asking if I could be there when you two perform magic."

"No."

Meg's answer is so quick and final that it takes both Landon and me a moment to recover. I get there first. "What? Why not?"

"Because," Meg begins, using the tone she always uses when she thinks we're being idiots, "this spell is about your future, Sam, and Landon is a part of your past. You don't want his presence interfering with that. It's bad juju."

"I thought you said this wasn't voodoo?" Landon asks me, and Meg glares at him.

I sigh. "He's part of my future too, Meg. As a friend. Just like you. I want him there." When she says nothing, I pout. "Please, Meghan Grace?"

"Don't call me that. And fine," she relents. "If you want him there, it's your call. But you have to follow my instructions exactly. I don't want his presence mucking this up."

"Yes, great voodoo priestess!" Landon says, and Meg, finally laughing, wads up a napkin and tosses it at Landon's face.

....

Going home from the Donkey is better when Landon's there, because he has a car and Meg and I don't have to walk. It's a Honda Civic that's seen better days, nothing in comparison to the Mercedes and Audi that his parents have in their garage, but it's a car. They told him when they bought it for him that he'd have to work to get a car like theirs, just like they did. It was supposed to teach him responsibility or prove he wasn't totally spoiled or something, but he never had to pay a cent for it regardless.

I have permanent shotgun in his car so Meg doesn't even try to call it. I promise I'll call her later when Landon drops her off at her house, and we drive off. We head to my house, where my mother welcomes him with so much fanfare you'd think he'd been off fighting in a war.

She pushes muffins (lemon poppy seed, still warm from the oven) our way, then makes herself scarce, but not without ruffling Landon's already messy hair on her way out. Landon helps himself, and through a mouthful of muffiny goodness says, "Your dad home?"

I shake my head and pull on the fridge door, removing two Diet Cokes from the inside. We pop them open and settle onto stools at the kitchen counter. "New York again. Probably until the end of the month. I think he's even doing a couple of book signings."

And because Landon knows Allen Raines, he chuckles. "I bet he hates it."

I laugh too. "Mom and I are bracing ourselves for the Fame Stifles My Creativity rant when he gets back."

"Which isn't much different from his son's English Class Stifles My Creativity rant."

I lean across the counter so I can get closer to his face when I stick my tongue out at him. Landon ignores me in favor of another bite of muffin, then picks up his phone. I peer down, nosy. He's checking the weather for tomorrow's big event.

"Gonna be freezing in a graveyard at midnight," Landon says with a slight wince.

"I just hope it doesn't take forever. You know how Meg is with this stuff."

"Yeah, didn't she meditate in the woods for five solid hours last summer?"

"According to her." I grin at him and polish off my muffin. I take another from the plate. "We'll just have to rein her in. The spell I wrote is short, anyway. And the list itself is only ten words. Or it will be, when I'm done."

Landon recites the list from memory. That's another one of Landon's skills. Near photographic memory. That's why he can pass all of his classes with minimal effort. Of course he gets minimal grades as well, but Landon isn't one to do any work he doesn't have to do.

"Sexy, talented, style, nice eyes, thick hair . . ." He sniffs. "That's only half of Mr. Right. You need five more."

I groan. "I know. Help me think."

"Hmm." Landon takes a long swallow of Coke and muses. "What about a sense of humor? You're pretty funny sometimes. Mostly unintentionally. You should have a boyfriend who laughs at your jokes."

"Gee, thanks," I say, but consider it. "And shouldn't he make me laugh too?"

Landon shrugs. "Sure."

"So that would be two different things, right? He

should be funny and he should find me funny."

"I don't know, that's kind of cheating," Landon says. We eye each other.

"I think it's two different things."

"I think you're just lazy and don't want to come up with more. Come on, Sam, this is your future you're talking about. Don't half-ass it." Landon's eyes are twinkling and I know he's mocking me, but he's also got a point.

"All right, all right," I grumble. Regardless, I pull my notebook out of my bag and write it down. "Sense of humor. Got anything else? I mean, what would you want?"

Landon thinks. "I don't know. Someone attractive. I'm shallow like that."

I look down at my list. "I already have sexy on here. I can't put attractive."

"Why not? Being attractive is totally different than being sexy."

"And yet you wouldn't let me use sense of humor twice," I say. "Why is it different?"

"Think about all the ugly, old rock stars that date hot models. Mick Jagger, for example. Sexy, but not attractive."

I ponder this, humming lightly. "Okay, I can buy it. And that gives me seven. Just three more."

"What about rich?" Landon asks. He's halfway through his second muffin and he uses what remains to point at me. "I mean, if you can ask for anything, why not ask for a guy who can take you in his helicopter to New York for a weekend?"

Point taken, I mull it over, and oddly enough, it's

Landon that my thoughts turn to. Landon, and all the nice things in his house, the nice cars in the garage, the plethora of books in his bedroom. It's all awesome, but like his car, he's never had to work for any of it. He's never had to make an effort. And because of that, he doesn't really have any goals.

"He doesn't have to be rich," I conclude, inspiration hitting me. "But he does have to have ambition. I don't want a guy who doesn't have goals."

Landon nods, eyes narrowing. "I like it. You're brilliant, Sam. Just two more things now," he says, taking my notebook from me and writing *ambitious* under *attractive* on the list. "Think, Sam. What else?"

My thoughts are picking up speed and I feel giddy, and a little lightheaded. Ha, maybe the magic is working already.

"What about fun?"

"Fun," Landon repeats, as if the word should be so much more than it is.

"Yeah, I want to have a good time with him. He should be fun. Don't you think?"

"I think it's kind of lame, but we're desperate at this point." He gives me another smirk but adds it to the list. "One more. Let's dig a little deeper than *fun*. Dream big, Raines."

I think hard about the things I consider important in my life, things like bands I love, or writers I admire, politicians I agree with. "I want him to like the same things I like," I tell Landon.

"Okay, so . . . you want him to have the same opinions you do?"

"No, not really. That would be boring. I just want him to have good taste. I don't want him to think that *The Hangover* is a brilliant film or that pop music actually qualifies as music, you know?"

Landon's dusty-blond brow arches. "So you want him to be an indie snob like you?"

"I want him to have taste," I say again, as if saying it louder and slower will clarify.

"Good taste," Landon repeats to himself as he adds it to the list, and, praise Jesus (or the Goddess, whatever), I'm done. He tears it out of my notebook and hands it to me. It's like this:

Perfect 10

1. *Sexy*
2. *Talented*
3. *Style*
4. *Nice eyes*
5. *Thick hair*
6. *Sense of humor*
7. *Attractive*
8. *Ambitious*
9. *Fun*
10. *Good taste*

As I scan the list, I hear Landon chuckle softly. I look up. "What's so funny?"

Landon shakes his head, eyes sparkling with humor. "It's just that a guy with all of these things? As rare as a unicorn, my friend. I'm pretty sure it might actually *require* magic to find someone like that."

"And you will be so jealous when I do."

Landon only chuckles again. "I suppose I will. So you're ready?"

"Yes. List is done, spell is done. Now all we need is the cemetery and a bunch of superstitious bullshit."

Landon's smile is devilish, and if this were two years ago, I'd have a hard time not kissing that smile. Hell, I'm having a hard time now. "And don't forget the most important thing, Sam . . . a witch."

Three

The witch sits across from me, gnawing on Cheez-Its, practically bouncing up and down with excitement on the cafeteria table bench. Today is *the* day, Friday the thirteenth, and all Meg can talk about is the positive energy in the air and how perfect the night is going to be for my spell. She eyes me, mouth full of orange bits, and says, "Don't you feel anything, Sam?"

"Hunger," I say, picking up my sandwich, which is my mother's specialty: chicken salad with cranberries in it and a kick of horseradish. With the crusts cut off, of course.

Meg sighs a deep, disappointed sigh. "Aren't you excited at least?"

"I am, actually," I say through a bite of chicken. "And nervous. Really nervous for some reason."

Her eyes widen and she breaks into a squeal and I immediately regret my decision to be honest. "You're nervous because you want it to work! I knew it! You want to believe. And you will, you'll see. I'll have you doing rituals with me in no time."

"Whoa, slow down. I don't want to form a coven or anything." I shrug. "Just hoping for a boyfriend."

"Speaking of . . . let me see the list."

I slide the list in her direction and she reads, mouthing along with the words. Finally, she looks up, nodding. "It's good. I can almost imagine him, can't you? Someone tall, dark, and handsome perhaps. Broad shouldered, muscled. A deep, sexy voice and eyes you can sink into . . ."

I wave my hand in front of her face, highly amused. "Earth to Meg. This is *my* future boyfriend, remember? Not yours. And I said nothing about being muscled."

"Maybe you should have," she mumbles, then giggles at herself. "How about the spell?"

I grab my notebook and turn it to the page where I've scribbled the spell. It's a mess, currently. Like what most of my first drafts look like until I clean them up for the final, with words and even whole sentences scratched out, but it's there in its entirety.

Meg slides the notebook back toward me. "I actually don't want to see it. Whatever you say is personal and completely up to you. I don't want my influence all over it. Just wanted to make sure you had it done."

"It is, except I don't know how to start it."

Meg cocks her head. "What do you mean?"

Before I can say any more, Landon slides in next to me and scoops up one of my celery sticks like a master ninja. His lunch period is different from ours since he's in band (and don't let him hear you make a band geek joke; he can get vicious about it), so he's skipping out on rehearsal to visit. I push the rest of the celery toward him and he eats ravenously.

"One o'clock is way too late for lunch," he says. "I'm a growing boy, for pity's sake. What are you two up to?"

"I'm teaching Sam how to be a witch," Meg replies earnestly, then turns back to me. "Go on, Sam. What were you saying?"

"I'm saying I don't know how to begin the spell. Like, is it like a letter? Dear Goddess, please grant me three wishes?"

Landon snorts. "Is Meg's goddess a genie?"

"You know what I mean. What do I call her? How do I start?"

Meg's smile for me is a little smug. She's truly enjoying her mentor role. "I'll begin for you. You'll see. As for what to call the Goddess . . . She goes by many names, Sam. She's got a very long history. But if I can make a suggestion?" I nod. "Since you're asking for something regarding love, and you wrote your spell in Latin, why not call Her Venus? The Roman gods are probably the ones you're most familiar with."

I look at Landon to see if he agrees and all he does is take another bite of celery. "Don't look at me. The only goddesses I'm familiar with are Marilyn Monroe and Beyoncé."

"And you," Meg goes on before either of us can laugh at Landon's joke, "I don't like it that you'll be there. Not one bit. So you have to be quiet the entire time. No jokes.

No sarcastic remarks. And you'll have to focus your energy on what Sam wants or you'll ruin this whole thing."

"Gee. Way to make a guy feel welcome," Landon grumbles, and I squeeze his knee under the table in apology.

I try to steer the conversation forward. "So we'll meet at midnight at Saint Catherine's?"

Meg nods and just then the warning bell rings, and our fellow classmates get up to throw their trash away like good little Pavlovian dogs. We stay seated.

"I'll bring some candles and a few other things we'll need. You bring the list and your spell. I'll also need a lock of your hair and a vial of your blood."

Landon and I both freeze.

"Blood?" I ask, voice climbing up an octave in alarm.

She grins a positively evil grin. "Just kidding about the blood. Gonna need your hair though. Just a couple strands should suffice." She glances at Landon, who still has a horrified look on his face. "What? I can't make voodoo jokes like you?"

Landon says nothing but squeezes his eyes shut, like he can't believe that this is the world he's living in. Meg gives him a playful punch on the shoulder and says, "See you at midnight," before walking off, her whole witchy being vibrating with expectation and "positive energy."

Landon opens his eyes. "If this works, she won't let either of us forget it, you know."

"Nope," I say. "So we'll just have to join her coven and learn how to read tarot cards."

"At least if there's a virgin sacrifice, we're both safe."

I burst out laughing, then get up to face the rest of the school day. "See you at midnight."

....

"It's freaking freezing out here," Landon complains through chattering teeth.

"Yeah. I told you to bundle up. This is Ohio. In October. Remember?" I shake my head at him even as I'm removing my jacket and helping him into it. Doesn't matter to me. I wore a thick sweatshirt and a thermal under that, so the cold night air can't touch me.

He zips my jacket, an Adidas and thrift-store find, and rubs his arms for warmth. "Thanks. So where's Meg?"

"Right here."

We turn and Meg's walking up the narrow drive of the cemetery straight toward us. We agreed to meet at a small mausoleum at the top of one of the hills because (a) it's very secluded up here, and (b) we all know exactly where this mausoleum is. Even though Meg's Wiccan now, and Landon and I are as atheist as they come, the stained-glass window in the back of it is nothing short of gorgeous. It's got Jesus in bright crimson robes, hands lifted upward in prayer, a halo of yellow and orange encircling his head.

So, I guess we're going to be doing a little magical—excuse me, magickal—ritual right in front of that.

"Got the blood?" Meg asks as she reaches us.

"Ha-ha. You're so funny," Landon says, then mumbles, "White magic my ass . . ."

Meg rolls her eyes and throws the backpack she's wearing to the ground. Something inside it clinks. "We need to set up candles in a circle, using the big one to point north. Sam, pluck out three pieces of hair and fold them into the list, in thirds, then thirds again. We have to invite the Goddess into our circle first, then you can start your spell."

I take the list out of my back pocket. I copied it on a fresh sheet of paper for the occasion, using my best handwriting. I give it one last glance, then pluck my hair and fold it into my list as she requests, wincing only a little. Meg kneels and starts removing things from her pack. A book of matches, four glass-encased red column candles, a black leather-bound journal, a paperback book entitled *The White Arts*, and a ball of red twine.

"Why all the red?" I ask, surveying the items with distrust.

"Duh, Sam. Red is the color of love."

"Right," I mumble, because obviously I'm a moron, and Landon covers his mouth to keep from laughing.

"You," Meg says, looking up at Landon and jabbing something pointy in her hand at him. "Since you insist on being here, you need to purify yourself."

"Me? Why me?"

"Because we all have to. I did before I came here and Sam will during the ritual, but you're the one that needs it most. Your connection with Sam's past could seriously screw up the whole intent of this spell." Meg jabs the pointy thing at him again. "I mean it. Light this and wave the smoke all over you."

Landon casts me a wary glance before taking the little cone of incense from Meg's hand. He's got a lighter in his pocket, so he waves away Meg's offer of matches and flicks the lighter until he gets a flame.

As the smoke dances out from the point of the cone, Landon makes like he's rubbing it all over his body. It kind of wraps around him like he's the caterpillar in *Alice in Wonderland.* The smoke itself smells like roses and sandalwood, which I figure must be on purpose. Roses equal love, right?

"You too, Sam."

Landon doesn't meet my eye as he passes me the cone, knowing that if we make eye contact we'll both collapse into a fit of laughter that Meg won't find humorous in the slightest. I do a funny little dance trying to get the smoke all over me too, then Meg takes it from me and sets it in the circle of red candles she set up next to the mausoleum. The larger one is indeed pointing north, and it just so happens to also be the highest candle on the hill.

"Don't touch each other anymore, okay?" Meg instructs us, then looks sharply at me. "You don't want his essence on you, Sam."

Landon opens his mouth to make what I'm sure is a wisecrack about putting his "essence" on me, but I shoot him a murderous look before he can form the words.

Meg continues on, oblivious. She hands me the leather-bound journal, opened to a page written in her own handwriting; the ink, of course, is red. "Read this to invoke the Goddess, and then once we get a sign that She's present, you'll step inside the circle and that's when you'll read your spell. You'll read it three times then dip the list into the northern flame and let it burn in the wind. Got it?"

I've got it. Also, I must be out of my freaking mind.

I nod to Meg. "Sure. When should I start?"

"Do you feel ready?"

I think this is when I'm supposed to contemplate my inner readiness or examine my conscience or something, but I'm positive my conscience can handle a Wiccan ritual. "Yes," I say very seriously to satisfy Meg's concern.

"Okay then," she says, pausing to build anticipation, "let's begin."

I look down at her journal, realizing for the first time that these aren't words from one of her many instructional manuals, but something Meg's written herself. I'm a little humbled by that, strange as it is, and that changes something for me, shifts the tone of the whole ritual. I begin to read as sincerely as I can, concentrating on what I'm saying and trying to absorb the meaning of each word.

When I'm done with what Meg wrote, I feel strangely calm. Around me, the cemetery is still and silent, as if holding its breath. Then, as I turn to ask Meg exactly what kind of sign we should be looking for, a sudden gust of wind tears over the hillside, so strong that it rattles the chains locking the mausoleum doors together and makes the heavy branches above our heads groan as if in pain. The tiny hairs on my arms rise up and a chill works its way from the back of my neck down to the base of my spine.

I'm no coward, but suddenly this whole voodoo-ritual-at-midnight-in-a-graveyard thing seems like it might be a stupid idea.

"Shit," Landon hisses behind me as the wind continues. I glance over my shoulder at him. His eyes are wide and darting all around us. His unease doesn't make me feel any better about the situation.

Meg, too, is looking around us, but she has a hand held out, signaling us to stay put and be quiet. Then, as if it had never happened, the wind stops. My hair settles back down against my scalp and Meg lowers her hand.

"She's here. Oh my god, Sam, that was amazing! Did you feel that?"

"Yeah," I answer but look to Landon as if he can provide confirmation that I'm not crazy, that really just happened. All he can give me in return is a dazed nod of his head.

"Go. Read your spell!" Meg shoves me toward the circle, but she's too full of adrenaline from the Goddess's sign and I'm too stunned, and I end up stumbling. Landon catches my hand and pulls me upright before I completely lose my balance. We both glance over at Meg, afraid she'll yell at us for touching, but luckily she's too busy watching the trees, looking for another sign.

"Thanks," I whisper to him, and our eyes meet for a second. His irises are mostly gray in the moonlight, and I see a healthy dose of apprehension in them before he lets go of my hand.

I step inside the circle and, to my relief, there's no wind and no other strange sign. I half expected lightning or a hooting owl or something.

Unfolding the Latin spell, I take a deep breath and begin to read. Somehow, seeming sincere isn't much of a challenge now. My voice is loud and strong and echoes off the side of the mausoleum. Meg can't understand my words, but I'm sure Landon catches most of my meaning as I read:

"Venus—
Find for me a perfect fit,
A boy of beauty, talent, and wit,
Someone to love, and to love me,
As you will it, so mote it be."

(The rhyming, as you might have guessed, was even more impressive in perfectly conjugated Latin, but that's the English version. Brilliant, right? Move over, Shakespeare.)

I read it two more times to complete Meg's incantation, and then kneel in the middle of the circle, stretching the list containing three strands of my hair over the flame of the northernmost candle.

Almost instantly, the notebook paper catches fire. I watch it burn until the flame crawls up to my fingertips, and then I let it drop. It disintegrates into ashes before it hits the ground and a quick, singular burst of wind carries them away.

I look over at Meg, who is staring at me with an expression of wonder that makes me feel horribly self-conscious. "What do I do now?"

Meg jerks as if I've just woken her. "What? Oh. Um, you have to close the circle. Thank the Goddess and then blow out the candles one by one. East, south, west, then north."

"Okay." I turn back, saying awkwardly to the night air, "Um, thanks for listening, Goddess." Then I blow out the candles in order and turn to my friends. "Well. That was interesting."

"Sam," Meg says, strawberry-blonde brows coming together in a V. She closes the distance between us and puts a hand on my elbow. "This is going to work. Didn't you feel Her? She's got plans for you, baby. *Big* plans. I can't even believe what I just saw. You're a natural witch, Sam! Who knew? The Goddess loves you!"

Meg then proceeds to dance around the ritual circle like a drunken ballerina and Landon's immediately at my side.

"You okay?" he says to me, his voice low so Meg can't hear.

"Yeah," I answer, watching Meg pirouette, then dip down to pick up a candle. She is humming something that sounds like a carnival tune, happier than I've ever seen her. "That was weird, right?"

"Yeah, really weird," Landon answers. His eyes follow Meg too, and we let her distract us. It's much easier than admitting that we're a little spooked, and that the whole thing has us thinking that Meg could be right about her religion.

Which is just freaking ridiculous.

The ridiculousness of it doesn't stop me from taking a step closer to Landon when another gust of wind whips through the graveyard, though.

"Ready to go home?"

I smile at Landon because I know that (a) he's offering to go home because I want to get the hell out of here, and (b) he's offering to go home because *he* wants to get the hell out of here.

"Please."

On my word, Landon turns and calls out to Meg, who has stopped dancing and is zipping the last of the ritual supplies into her bag. "Hey, Meg, let's go."

Meg stands up and salutes Landon, giggling. "Yes, Sergeant Gray." She runs to us, planting herself between me and Landon as we walk down the hill and follow the winding path out of the cemetery. She babbles on and on about the Goddess and the details of the spell, and speculates as to what kind of boy the Goddess will bring me. She keeps it up until we pull in front of her house to drop her off, and when she leaves, the silence between me and Landon feels especially quiet.

"You swear you're okay?" Landon finally asks as he takes the last turn onto my sleepy street.

I shrug and stare out the window at the houses. Besides the general spookiness of the spell, there's something off about what I'm feeling. It's almost empty.

"Sam . . ." Landon says, and it's a warning not to try to get out of talking about it. And he's right. I don't know why I'm hesitating. Landon's always been my least judgmental friend. The only thing I can't talk to Landon about is Landon, which is what makes this so hard.

"It's just . . ." I begin, searching for the words. I turn to look at him as he pulls up to my house. "How did you meet him? The guy that you . . . you know."

Landon pulls over in front of my house, but doesn't take his eyes off the road ahead. "It was a weird string of coincidences. Believe me, it wasn't exactly easy to meet someone else. He didn't just fall into my lap, so to speak."

"So . . ." I look down at my knotted fingers, trying to muster the courage to ask what I want to ask. "It's not just me? This is hard for other people? For you?"

"God, Sam. Of course it's not you. It's this stupid little town. If we were somewhere else—New York, or L.A., even—you'd have a million guys following you around, begging for a chance. And all of them would be Perfect Tens, like you want. You'd have to narrow them down and choose. Like *The Bachelor* or something."

I chuckle at that. "You're a liar, but you're a good friend to say so."

Landon's lips make a thin line. "Not lying. Really, Sam. It's not you, okay? It's not you. Any guy who meets you will want to be with you, trust me. As long as he's not straight, anyway."

I snort and shrug him away, but there's a hot flush creeping up my neck.

Another reason why I fell for Landon? Silver-tongued. He always says the right thing.

"Thanks." I squeeze his hand. "I guess if this spell

doesn't work, I'll just have to move to L.A."

"What a terrible fate," Landon says, then winks. "Night, Sam."

"Night."

As he drives off and I turn myself toward the back door, another powerful surge of wind gushes all around me, rattling the shutters of my house and whistling through the trees. Perhaps the Goddess *is* with me, like Meg thinks.

I roll my eyes and walk toward the house.

If that's true, the boy She brings had better be *gorgeous.*

Four

I don't see Meg or Landon again until Monday at school, which is just as well. Between the report I had to write on *Crime and Punishment*, working on my writing samples for college applications, and calculus problems out the wazoo, I didn't have time for much socializing.

It's fourth period, right before lunch, and I look up from my psychology book to see Meg waving her arms at me like an idiot in the hallway. Before Mr. Henshaw can see her, I spring from my desk and approach his, asking for the hall pass.

"Are you having some kind of fit or something?" I hiss as soon as I'm in the hallway.

Meg's expression is rapturous. "She answered you, Sam. She *answered you.*"

I know immediately what she's talking about and my heart gives a loud *ka-thunk* in my chest. "Where?" I ask.

"Music room." Meg does a little ballet twirl, then freezes, eyes wide and full of drama. "Hurry."

We take off jogging (well, I jog; Meg sort of skips and leaps) toward the music wing of the school, which is way on the other side of the building, past the cafeteria.

Before we get to the double doors that lead into the band room, the sound of a saxophone and a brushed drum surrounds me like a night breeze, chill and bluesy. I stop, letting the sound carry me away, and Meg has to grab my hand and pull me the rest of the way to the doors.

"Look," she whispers, pointing to the tiny square of glass in one door that is our only view of the jazz ensemble within.

I draw in a deep breath, casting an apprehensive glance to Meg before looking through the smudged pane.

The jazz band sits in a semicircle, save for a drum set and keyboard off to one side. No one's playing, though, except for the drummer and a saxophone player, whose face is obstructed by a tall music stand.

I scan the rest of the ensemble's faces as they watch the sax player with slack-jawed awe. There are a few kids I know from my days in the middle school band, back when I used to pretend to play trumpet in the back row. Landon also plays trumpet, and like schoolwork, is decent at it without any practicing. Meg still plays violin in the orchestra, and she'll slap you if you give her any shit about it. At any rate, I'm no stranger to the way instruments and bands work, which is what makes this sight so weird. I'm pretty sure they're all supposed to be playing.

"Which . . ." I start to ask Meg, but right then the sax player steps out from behind the music stand and I stop breathing.

He's gorgeous. Okay, that's an understatement. The

sax player is *stunning*. He's tall and slender, with thick, wavy hair the color of the midnight sky that falls nearly to his chin, and large, dark brown eyes that complement features like a strong jaw and patrician nose.

"Meg," I say, snapping to get her attention. "The list. What was on my list?"

"Um, let's see . . ." She pauses to think, eyes all squinty, lips pursed. "Thick hair, nice eyes . . ."

"Yes, yes," I say, motioning to go on as my gaze travels back to the sax player. The rest of the band has started to join in, reluctantly tearing their admiring stares away from him. "Sexy, right? Attractive. Talented. He's all of those things."

"And you can bet he's got the rest, Sam. Taste? Style? Ambition? Just look at him." Contrary to her words, her hand is on my shoulder, pulling me away from the door. She's laughing a little, like she can barely contain herself. "Foreign exchange student. He was in Madame Vinson's class this morning. Sam, he's from Paris."

Oh my god. A sexy French exchange student. Who plays jazz. I turn back to look at him more through the window, saying to Meg, "Your goddess doesn't half-ass anything, does She?"

Meg giggles. "Of course not."

"What's his name?"

"Gus," Meg says, popping up to look through the window with me.

Gus. It's not quite as romantic as I'd pictured it, but it's kind of cute.

"I mean, that's his nickname. His real name is Augustin Chevalier. And Chevalier means—"

"Knight," I finish for her, a dreamy smile forming on my lips. "My knight in shining armor?"

Meg bumps me with her shoulder, laughing. "Perhaps. We'll see. Class is ending soon. You can ask him out and decide for yourself."

"Ask him out?" My voice rises up with alarm, loud enough to be heard over the jazz ensemble playing. For as much work as I'd put into this list, I guess I kind of figured the boy would at least do the asking. Was I going to have to do everything? "But," I say, starting into what might be a litany of excuses, "do you know for sure I'm . . . you know . . . his type?"

"He's gay, if that's what you're asking. He said so when he introduced himself to the class this morning." Meg turns away from the window to study me, her lips making a flat line across her face. "Don't chicken out on me. The Goddess has answered you. You can't blow Her off."

"She's not my goddess," I argue.

"Oh, now She's not your goddess, even though just a few minutes ago She had answered your prayers." Meg sighs and puts a hand on my upper arm, squeezing slightly. "Look, Sam. I know. This is hard, and it's been since Landon, but . . . it's also *been since Landon*, if you catch my drift here. You need to go for it."

I glance one more time into the band room. Gus's saxophone emits a plaintive melody, floating around the band's supporting chord progression. It's beautiful, and so is he, and Meg's right. I'm so tired of being lonely and he seems so wonderful. I need to go for this.

Just then the bell rings, and the jazz students start toward the doors. Panicked, I grab Meg by the wrist and drag her, squealing, into the main hallway outside the music wing.

"Where are you going?"

"We can't be right outside those doors!" I explain, exasperated. "He'll think we're stalking him."

"Relax," she says, and takes off back toward the band room. "I told him to wait for us. He wants to meet you."

"Oh my god, Meg. No," I say, mortified. I can actually feel the blush forming on my skin, but I run to follow her anyway.

As soon as I'm back in the music wing I hear a deep, silky voice say, "Ah, Meg. Eet ees so nice to see you again. But where ees zis boy you 'ave told me about?"

I am totally unprepared as I turn the corner and Gus's eyes meet mine. I halt so suddenly that my sneakers squeak on the floor and it feels like my thundering heart slams into my rib cage from the inertia. It seems to right itself, only to get stuck in my throat so that I can't speak and all I can hear is its stuttering beat in my ears.

"Meg!" the silky voice says again, but this time that lovely voice is attached to eyes that are so rich and dark, I have to wonder how they're real. Then he turns them on Meg. "You 'ave lied to me. Your Sam ees not 'andsome, as you said." My stupid, spazzoid heart plummets into my stomach at that. Then, with a smirk so sexy it should be outlawed, Gus turns back to me and says, "*Il est magnifique!*"

"That means—"

"I know what it means," I cut Meg off and take a step closer to Gus, now wishing that she'd just go away and let me have a moment alone with a sexy Frenchman. A sexy Frenchman who thinks I'm gorgeous. "I'm Sam," I say, extending my hand.

"Samuel?" Gus asks. The vowels take their time on his tongue, and the *el* is accented. It's got a delicious, exotic feel to it, so it's a shame that's not really my name. He takes my hand in his, not shaking it but using it to draw me closer.

"Samson, actually."

"Samson," Gus repeats, and screw Samuel. Samson sounds much better from that mouth. "I am Augustin René Chevalier. But everyone calls me Gus."

It sounds a little like *goose* to be honest, but it's adorable. I let him fold my hand into his. The jazz band is piling out of the instrument closet, headed to their next classes, and I can see them but I can't really hear them. It's like Gus and I have our own little private bubble.

"Welcome to Athens High School," I say, cheesy as it is. "In the middle of a semester, even. Odd how that happened . . ."

Gus only smiles and starts to walk toward the classrooms. I don't know where his saxophone is. I don't know where his book bag is. Maybe sexy French students don't use books. And he hasn't dropped my hand so, good heavens, I'm holding hands with a boy in the hallway.

"*Oui.* I should not 'ave arrived until January, but my

school sent me early on uh . . . Meg, what ees zat word?"

"Scholarship," Meg says from behind us, and I'd completely forgotten that she was there. I turn my head to look at her, and she glances pointedly at my hand joined with Gus's before wiggling her eyebrows.

"*Merci.* Scholarship. But perhaps eet was perfect timing, no?" Gus squeezes my hand and my gaze is drawn back to his amazing eyes.

"*Oui*," I answer (and how embarrassing, I sound breathless even to myself), and squeeze back. "If you would like someone to show you around Athens—"

"Ah, zat would be *très bon*! I 'ave not seen any of zis town since I 'ave arrived." As we near the cafeteria, I can't help but notice a few students staring, and even more whispering. I fight to keep a triumphant smile from forming on my lips. Yep, that's me, Sam Raines, holding hands with a gorgeous French guy. Eat your hearts out.

"I, um, I have lunch now," I stammer out, and Gus pouts.

"I do not eat until after ze next class. May I see you after school, Samson?" His eyes sparkle with the most flattering hopefulness.

I shiver at the sound of my name. "Yes. Please. Can I meet you . . . ?"

"In ze band room. I will 'ave to take my instrument 'ome wiz me."

I wince. "I walk home. I mean, I don't have a car."

"And I cannot drive in zis country, but I walk too. Walk togezer, zen?"

I have to lift my chin a little to see into his eyes, as he's just enough taller than me to merit it. "Sounds great," I say, even though I have no clue where he lives and even if we'd be walking in the same direction. Whatever. I'll walk a hundred miles in the wrong direction if he wants, as long as he keeps looking at me and talking like that.

"I will see you after school, Samson. I will be counting ze minutes."

"Me too," I say, and he squeezes my hand again and disappears into a crowd of students all headed toward the science wing.

When I turn around to find Meg, I'm sure I look dumbfounded. I can feel my mouth hanging open in utter shock-induced stupidity. Sort of like how the cheerleaders look when you ask them a question with a big word in it.

My words come out in a rasp. "He just . . ."

"I know."

"He held my hand."

"He did."

"He wants to see me after school."

"I heard."

"Meg," I say, poking her forearm repeatedly, "did that really just happen?"

"I believe that, yes, an incredibly hot foreign exchange student wants you to be his lover, which is, I must say, *très romantique*. So, uh . . . you can thank me with a dinner at Seven Sauces whenever. Maybe after your wildly successful first date." Meg's grinning as she studies a hangnail with too much concentration.

I sigh. Dinner at Seven Sauces, the best restaurant in town, is going to eat a huge hole in my wallet, but hey, the list was Meg's idea. I suppose she deserves it, but I can't let her be right that easily. "Let's not get ahead of ourselves. Maybe he's got horrible taste in movies or something. He may not be a Perfect Ten."

Meg narrows her eyes at me. "Please. He's practically an eleven. Just so you know, I'm going to have the filet mignon and the lobster. And maybe some of that delicious scallop dish. Bring your credit card."

She leaves me alone to walk back to get my things, and by the time I sit down at the lunch table with her, she has a list of possible desserts she wants as well. As I listen to her ramble on about chocolate torte, my mind wanders back to the feel of Gus's hand in mine, and the rest of the lunch period passes in a blur of jazz music and blissful daydreams.

....

As I gather my things from my locker at the end of the day, there's a riot of butterflies in my stomach that won't stop fluttering no matter what I do. By the time I'm passing the cafeteria, it's not just a handful of butterflies but an entire freaking *flock*, and they're all flapping their wings in mismatched staccato rhythms.

"Sam."

Landon's familiar voice causes the flapping to stutter.

I turn to my right, where Landon is standing with a group of guys I recognize from the baseball team. He breaks away from the group and jogs to me.

"Baseball players now?" I ask, brow arching.

"Hey, they're in the state championship this Saturday. Just wishing them luck." He smiles lazily, glancing back at them to wave as we walk away. Because he's sly, I'm sure I'm the only one in the hallway who notices when his eyes drift down to check out the third baseman's ass. "Where are you off to?"

"Meg didn't tell you?" I ask, surprised. I was sure Meg would run to tell Landon first thing, followed shortly by the whole school. "I'm walking the new foreign exchange student home."

"The French guy?" I nod. Landon is sufficiently impressed. "Wow. That was . . . fast. How did you manage to—"

"Are you doubting my skills?" I say, smirking at him, but my stomach does a somersault when I turn and see the band room door up ahead. He's not the only one doubting.

"Baby, I know your moves. I know your lines. So yeah, you could say I'm doubting a little." Landon laughs as I plow my shoulder into his arm and send him stumbling. When he rights himself he looks at me with those big eyes of his, and although they're still alight with humor, they've softened considerably. "Is he as gorgeous as everyone says?"

"Sexy. Attractive. Nice eyes. Thick hair. Talented," I rattle off, counting on my fingers.

"Sounds familiar," Landon says, then his eyes go wide. "You don't actually think . . ."

I snort. "Of course not. A mere coincidence, that's my theory. But still, it's pretty weird, you have to admit. And he showed up *today*. Some fluky mix-up about a scholarship. I mean, what are the odds?"

"Yeah," Landon mumbles, and gets that look on his face that he gets when his brain has moved on to a subject different from what the rest of us are discussing. I'm probably boring the hell out of him.

"Okay, well, I need to go to the band room," I say when we get to the door. It's a welcome excuse to part ways since the conversation has obviously run its course.

"Samson. Zere you are. I zought maybe I would 'ave to walk 'ome alone." Gus walks through the door, slipping his hand easily into mine, as if it belongs there, as if we've done this for years—as if he owns me. And he just might. "But you 'ave brought anozer boy?"

"Um," I stammer. Just then I realize that Gus's irises are so dark I can barely see the pupils in them. They're gorgeous, and it's distracting, to say the least. "Sorry, Gus. This is Landon."

Gus shrugs the strap of his saxophone case higher on his shoulder (still no books; is he just smart enough to go without?) and extends his free hand to Landon. "I am Augustin René Chevalier. You are Samson's friend?"

"Yeah," Landon says, shaking Gus's proffered hand. His face is pinched into a weird smile, like it's horribly difficult to conjure something more for the sexiest

Frenchman this side of the Atlantic. I shoot him a death glare and the smile becomes wider, if not stretched a little too thin. "You know, I could just give you guys a ride."

"Eet ees so kind of you to offer, Landon, but I want as much time as I can wiz Samson. You understand, of course?"

I don't really catch Landon's answer because all the butterflies in my stomach swoop up to my ears and all I can hear is the thundering beat of my pulse. Gus wants as much time as possible. *With me.*

He must have said something else because he squeezes my hand gently to get my attention and leans down to my eye level. "Should we go?"

I nod, unable to trust my voice, and give Landon a sheepish wave as I walk hand in hand with Gus out the doors. Once we're in the fresh air, with the sun shining down as warm as it can in October, my heartbeat returns to steady, and my ears become unclogged. All around us, Athens High School's student body is talking, getting into secondhand cars, and scattering in every direction. The hubbub seems even more full of excitement than usual, and I grin like an idiot.

"Zis Landon," Gus begins, once we're out of earshot of other students. Gus is, luckily, headed west in the direction of my house, not that it matters. He's the Pied Piper and I'm a rat. "Ees 'e a lover?"

"What? No," I say quickly. But Gus's perfect face is wearing an expression that tells me he's both doubtful of my words and amused by them. "He was," I amend.

"Ah. And 'e ees not anymore?"

"Not anymore," I answer, keeping my gaze locked on his to discourage any doubt. "Not for years."

"And zere 'as been no one else?"

"For me or for him?"

Gus laughs. "For you, Samson. I am curious about you."

"No. No one else." I feel my face color, but Gus pulls me closer to him so that our shoulders are touching as we walk. We start up a hill and I silently thank my lucky stars (or the Goddess?) that I've been walking these hills since I was five. Wheezing is so unsexy.

"You were in love wiz 'im."

"I . . ." I want to protest, or change the subject—anything that will steer us away from the topic of Landon and toward more important things. Things like trips abroad or the Eiffel Tower or why, exactly, it's called *French* kissing. But Gus is looking at me so sweetly, so intently, like he has a genuine interest in every detail of my life, that I give in. "Yes. You could tell?"

His smile is almost pitying. "*Oui.* Zere was a certain . . . feeling zere, yes. But eet ees old, just a glimmer."

"And you? Have you ever been in love?"

The question seems to delight Gus and his steps quicken, though they're still graceful. It reminds me of Meg. "Of course! To love ees divine, yes? Eet ees essential to ze soul. Wizout love we would not 'ave poetry, or paintings, or songs."

I have often heard people say they were swooning, but until the moment Gus began to talk of love, I hadn't really understood the meaning of the word. Suddenly I'm light-headed, almost dizzy, and the edges of everything around us feather and blur. It is as though I'm viewing everything through a translucent film of bliss.

Then, as he talks, the butterflies calm themselves into a soothing stir, and I listen. He tells me about his home, a little village just outside of Paris, about his music, about his family. The cadence of his voice rises and falls like a familiar melody, and pretty soon I'm telling him about myself in the same patterns. I learn that he dreams of working for a politician one day, that he's no good at sports, that he digs the American indie rock scene, and he passes the time with his friends at home dancing in clubs and lounging in parks. All of this, of course, while cracking a self-deprecating joke every now and then.

I can only smile as I think of all the desserts Meg is going to order at Seven Sauces. She was right. Gus is the Perfect Ten, and she is never going to let me forget it.

We come to a stop in front of a small but beautiful house on a street several blocks away from mine. It's covered in ivy and has a stone walkway and a few trellises, like a little cottage in an enchanted wood.

"Zis ees ze Ewings' 'ouse. Zey are my parents 'ere in America."

I pull my eyes away from the house and look into Gus's eyes. "Are they nice?"

"Wonderful, Samson. Zey are very kind." His lips curl into an apologetic smile. "I would invite you in, but I am not sure of zeir rules. Zey will not be 'ome until zis evening."

Although one part of me wants to say, "Who cares about their rules? Let's go make out," another part of me, a bigger part, is swooning again over the fact that this boy has manners and behaves like a gentleman. It makes me wonder if he'll open doors for me or stand when I leave the dinner table.

"I understand. Can I . . . can I call you?"

Gus looks flattered by my request, which in turn flatters me. He hands me his phone so that I can put my number into it. "Of course! 'Ere. You must take my number. And . . . would it be too forward to ask you to 'ave dinner wiz me zis Friday evening?"

"If it is, that's okay with me." I laugh breathlessly. (Geez, Sam.) "I could give you a tour of Athens too. Show you around."

As we exchange phones, I'm already making a list of places I've got to take him—places where we can dance, listen to music, have a good meal, and get to know each other. Places where I can shine and show him I could be his Perfect Ten too.

"I'd be honored to show you around town," I say, and sure, it sounds like a cheesy line from an old movie, but right now I kind of feel like I'm stuck in one. "I'll call you tonight and we'll make plans."

"I will be waiting by ze phone." Gus smiles, slow and dangerous, and then he lifts a hand and settles his palm on my cheek. Before I can tell myself to be cool, I'm leaning into his touch like some lovesick teenager. Which isn't exactly off base.

Then Gus leans down and presses his lips to mine. It's a short kiss, a chaste kiss, but that hardly matters. I'm Molly Ringwald, my wish has come true, and we're kissing over a cake on my sixteenth birthday. His lips are soft, gentle, and mine feel tingly against them, as if they're waking up after being asleep for so long. They've missed this. *I've* missed this.

A disloyal little whimper of protest breaks through my lips as he pulls away, and those brown eyes of his are dancing with amusement.

"I zink I am going to love America very much," Gus says, or rather purrs, to me, and I hum my agreement.

"American hospitality cannot be rivaled," I say back in what I think is a sexy manner. But it's hard to grade myself on sexiness fairly when the guy who just kissed me blows the curve out of the water.

Gus's eyes get even darker then, a look so intense and concentrated on me that it has that chorus of butterflies in a tizzy again. For a second I think he's going to kiss me again, but favored by a goddess or not, I'm not that lucky. Instead, he leans close to me and whispers in that silky voice of his, "Perhaps you will show me more of zat American 'ospitality Friday, Samson? But for now, I must say *au revoir*."

"Bye," I say to him, and fight my lips from forming a pout as he walks toward his house. I watch until he disappears through the door and then turn in the direction of home.

Late that night, after two hours of calculus and Latin

and after an hour on the phone with Gus talking about everything and nothing, I call Meg.

"Did he kiss you?" she says before I can even offer a greeting.

"Yeah," I reply, feeling myself blush, but to stop her from asking the details, I add, "I'm going to take him to dinner Friday. Maybe to see the jazz trio from the university play. I don't know, I can't decide, what do you think?"

In her excitement to offer opinions, she forgets to ask more about my walk home with Gus, which is fine with me for some reason. Usually I tell Meg just about everything, but this I want to keep for myself. Gus is too wonderful, too perfect, and I can't share him just yet.

I think about calling Landon after I hang up with Meg, but that doesn't feel right either. I've lamented my lack of a boyfriend to him, but somehow discussing the perfection of Augustin René Chevalier seems a little cruel. I know we haven't been anything but friends for years and he'll be happy for me, but still, he's an ex, and this is unexplored territory for us. I'm not looking forward to telling him.

With a sigh, I roll over on top of my psychology book and dial the number of Seven Sauces. I make a reservation for me and Meg for Saturday night, absently running a finger over my lips as I do, as if I can still feel the warmth of Gus's kiss from hours ago. With a kiss like that, it wouldn't be surprising. And with a kiss like that, I really owe Meg a chocolate torte at the very least.

Five

The week crawls by. Even with walking Gus home every day and talking to him for hours on the phone every night, it's just not the same as a date. Since that cuts into our after-school Donkey trips, I nearly drive Meg crazy with my ramblings about Gus at lunch. She pays me back by rambling about Michael, who, unfortunately, skips out on his class a few times to sit with Meg at our table. I'm a complete third wheel while she chatters with him, so I scribble notes for stories in my notebook and try not to throw up chicken salad when they kiss.

It's Wednesday before I talk to Landon again. I see him on my way to the band room, talking to the hippie kids this time, and he gives me a half smile before falling into step beside me.

"Things must be going well."

"I definitely owe Meg Seven Sauces."

Landon chuckles but it peters out quickly. "So, is it, like, official now?"

There's no chance of stopping a smile from spreading across my face so I don't fight it. It's too strong, even for

Landon's sake. "I don't know. I mean, we haven't even had our first date yet, but we talk all the time. I've walked him home twice now. He um . . . well, he kissed me."

Landon kind of jerks his head back, as if that surprises him, then he gives me a wide smile and shrugs. "Sounds like it's official to me. So when's the first date?"

"Friday," I say. We've arrived at the music wing and I stop in front of the doors. It's a little silly because Landon's one of my best friends, but I kind of don't want Gus to see me talking to him again. On the other hand, it's nice to be able to tell Landon about Gus. I add, "Going to hear some jazz, and I need to figure out a restaurant."

"I've always been a little partial to Casa Nueva myself," Landon says, as if I don't remember that. Landon and I had our first (and third and sixth) date at Casa.

"The jazz trio is playing there, though. I mean, is it weird to eat there and then stick around for the band?"

Landon squints as he thinks. "I don't know. You might want a change of venue. If nothing else, you'd be able to show him more of the town if you eat somewhere else."

"Good thinking," I say. Landon was always good at planning stuff. "Thanks."

"No problem." Landon grins, then his eyes flick up to something over my shoulder. "Well, have fun. I'll see you around."

"Landon. Eet ees good to see you again. Will you be joining us?" Gus appears from behind me, his hand closing over mine, and he pulls me toward him slightly so that our sides are touching. It's like tiny little flames break out where his body meets mine and all I want to do is kiss him right there in the hallway, detentions be damned.

"No, thank you," Landon says, voice polite. "Have a nice time. I'll see you later, Sam."

As he walks away from us, Gus bends down and gives me my wish, kissing me deeply. Since we're in school still, he keeps it short, but not before sliding his tongue over mine in a way that's probably illegal in the red states.

When he pulls away I lean toward him, not ready to give up the closeness, even if we have to knock off the kissing. "Hmnn," I hum. "So is that just regular kissing in France?"

"Pardon?" Gus asks, and a burst of triumph warms my chest when I see that he's leaning toward me too, eyes cloudy as if I've cast a spell on him.

Ha, maybe I have.

"Oh, ze French kiss. I understand." He laughs, a sound almost as melodic as his saxophone playing. "You are funny, Samson."

"I try," I say, pulling him by the hand through the doors to the outside world, where freedom awaits—and we can kiss all we want. "No fair kissing me like that, by the way."

"Eet ees more zan fair, Samson. I am no match for ze way you kiss."

Honestly. Who says stuff like that?

I'll tell you who. The perfect guy, who magic brought to me.

"Do you really want to go home?" I ask.

"Why? What did you 'ave in mind?"

I shrug. I don't have anything in mind, besides wanting to prolong our good-bye.

"We could get coffee at the Donkey," I suggest. "Or go to the College Green and watch the crazy guy preach about the apocalypse, or get something to eat from one of the vendors and sit on the graffiti wall."

"Zere ees a man 'oo preaches about ze apocalypse?" Gus asks, and it's as if I've just offered him the secret to life.

"Yeah," I say, nodding my head with enthusiasm. "Apparently we're abominations, and if we don't repent, God is going to smite us."

Gus's lips form a wicked, mischievous smile at that. And that's how we end up on the College Green, kissing and laughing on a patch of soft grass while a crazy man rants about hellfire and end times in the background.

....

It's not often that people clap when I enter a room, and it's more than a little strange. Nevertheless, after I emerge from the bathroom in my outfit, I do my little turn on the catwalk while Meg and my mother, Gina, whoop and whistle.

It's Friday, Date Night, so of course I called Meg in a panic because I have nothing to wear.

Which isn't true. I have a lot. Like the vintage Guns N' Roses concert tee I'm wearing, which I found in a thrift store, my dad's old corduroy blazer over that, my favorite pair of Chucks (houndstooth, thank you very much), and jeans that Meg tells me will "bring all the boys to the yard." (Her words. Not mine. I wouldn't be caught dead using that expression.) But this is more about moral support than it is finding the right thing to wear.

Obviously, the outfit works. Both women are beaming at me. Meg's sitting cross-legged on my bed, eating my mom's chicken and noodles from a gigantic bowl.

"Gus won't stand a chance," she says, smiling around a mouthful.

My mom nods. With her rounded face and orangey-blonde hair, she looks more likely to be Meg's mother than mine. "You look just like your father in that jacket, Sam. I think he bought that when we were grad students at Denison. Meg, he was so handsome. Like a young Richard Gere." My mother sighs nostalgically and Meg indulges her with a wink as she sucks up a noodle.

I grimace at the comparison, even though it's a compliment. Dad is kind of handsome. But I don't need my mom daydreaming about him when I'm trying to get ready to meet the hottest boy I've ever seen. That's just weird.

I ignore it and try to tame my overgrown curls into something presentable with a metric ton of product.

"No, no," Meg says, finally setting aside her bowl and rushing to my (unsolicited) assistance. She bats my hands away from my hair. "Leave it messy. Trust me."

"But . . ." I start to protest, but Mom joins Meg, both

of them fussing over my hair until it's messy again, this time purposefully and casually chic. I look at myself in the mirror, then at the two of them, and sigh. They're right. I don't know why, but I look better when my hair is crazy. It defies all logic.

Mom giggles. "Ooh la la. Ze Frenchman will swoon."

I see Meg grinning at me in the mirror and smile back. She leans her head on Mom's shoulder. "*Oui.* Wait until you see him, Gina. Gus is *très merveilleux*, and he just might be perfect for Sam."

"Good. It's about time. He's been moping around the house far too much lately."

"When, exactly, have I been moping around the house?" I ask, turning to face my mother. "I've been out every weekend since school started."

My mother blinks at me. "Yes. With Meg. And as much as I love her, she's not exactly boyfriend material."

Meg bats her eyelashes at me and I snort. "Point taken. It's not my fault, though. I ran out of options."

"Until now," Meg says.

"Until now," I agree, and turn to look at myself in the mirror again. To my relief and surprise, I don't look half bad. "So . . . dinner at Toscanos and then seeing the university's jazz trio at Casa. Good plan?"

"Oh, Toscanos. Their breadsticks, and the ravioli . . ." Meg breathes, and I can almost hear her mouth watering. Mom will probably feed her cookies after I leave (Meg is avoiding home again because she was out past curfew the night I cast the spell, and she's in the proverbial doghouse), but still. Meg's first love is not Michael, it's food, and Toscanos ranks up there with Seven Sauces for her. "Great choice. And you can't beat the candlelight."

I flush a bit. "Exactly what I was thinking."

My mother's right eyebrow shoots up. "Uh-huh. Well. A gorgeous French boy and candlelight? You should probably be home by eleven."

"Mom . . ."

She laughs. "One. Like usual. And call if you'll be later. But be careful, Samson. With your heart and otherwise."

I catch her drift. Though she's never said as much, I wouldn't doubt that she knows what happened between me and Landon. She's got superhuman powers of detection, not that she would have needed them with the way Landon and I acted. It was probably more than a little obvious. "Don't worry, Mom. I'll be careful."

"Good." She stands and kisses my temple before making her way out of my room, leaving me with Meg. Meg stands too, gathering her empty bowl.

"I should go too. Michael's taking me to a movie tonight."

"The one about the bachelorette party?"

"Hell no. But not one where everything blows up either. We compromised on a horror flick." She grins. "Something about an old spell gone awry on ancient Indian burial ground."

I feel the blood drain from my face. "Do spells go awry often?"

Meg steps close to me, a sinister smile on her lips.

"All the time. Some people just can't handle the power." She cackles as my eyes widen, giving me a slight shove. "Kidding. Geez, Sam. You did a love spell. It's not like you're conjuring up the soul of a serial killer."

"Well, how should I know? It's not like I've done this before."

"Relax, grasshopper. You'll learn." Meg wrinkles her nose at me. "I agree with your mom, just so you know."

"About moping around the house?"

"About being careful," Meg clarifies. "I'm really happy Gus is here for you, but just . . . go slow, okay? And if he's truly the Perfect Ten, he'll want to be careful too."

"You do sound like my mother."

"I sound like *my* mother," Meg says, snorting. "Seriously. I don't want this to be Landon two-point-oh."

"Me either." I pull Meg in for a hug, planting a small kiss on her forehead. "I just really like him, Meg."

"I know you do. Which is exactly why I'm worried." She squeezes me hard.

"Well, that's exactly why I'm not. I don't want to screw this up, literally and figuratively. I'll go slow, heart and otherwise," I promise, though I know it will be easier said than done. Gus is tempting, to say the very least. "Have fun tonight. Make him pay for once."

Meg's rolling her eyes as I let go of her. "He's saving for college, you know."

"Yeah, well, so are you."

Meg glares. "Go on. Go to your French boy before I get even more annoyed with you."

"You love me."

"Unfortunately, yes. Go." She literally shoves me until I'm out the front door, and stands there waving at me and grinning like a goon until I've driven halfway down the street.

I wonder if there's some kind of hex I can put on Michael to make him see how lucky he is, something where he gets a stabbing pain every time he takes her for granted. That delicious thought keeps me smiling all the way to Gus's house.

....

Dinner is perfect. Beyond perfect. Gus loves the food, and it stirs up memories of a trip he took to Tuscany only a year ago, so I spend most of dinner laughing as he regales me with tales of getting lost in the countryside with his friends and having far too much to drink on several occasions. I somehow manage not to spill anything or say anything stupid. A pianist plays a baby grand in the corner of the restaurant, and Meg was totally right about Toscanos' candlelight. Gus's handsome face glows, warm and fluttering, making him appear even more like something out of a fairy tale than before.

It's a short walk to Casa Nueva to see the jazz trio next, but I haven't told him about that yet. We just take our time, enjoying the weather, the sights and sounds of the campus and surrounding town, and each other. Gus holds my hand as we walk, and I point out various buildings to him, either from Athens's history or mine.

"That's Ellis Hall," I say, waving toward a large brick building dating back to when the college was first founded. "College of English. That's where my dad works, though he doesn't teach much anymore."

"Ah, yes. I am told 'e ees a famous man."

I shrug, suddenly self-conscious. "I don't know if he's famous. Not like Stephen King or something. But his work seems to impress people."

Gus is quiet for a moment, and then he says, "And does 'is work impress you, Samson?"

"Of course," I say quickly. "My father is a fantastic writer."

"But . . . ?" Gus prods, and I feel his eyes on me as we walk, studying me.

"But," I start. "I guess everyone expects me to write like him, you know? I'm applying for creative writing schools and I'm afraid of putting my name on my college applications, like they'll expect the great Allen Raines's son to be so much more than I actually am."

Gus considers that, then squeezes my hand. "You 'ave a way wiz words, Samson, even when you speak. I 'ave no doubt zat you are a great writer."

"I'm good. I'm just not my dad. I don't write like him. Hell, I don't even write the same kind of fiction."

"No?" Gus asks me, and I shake my head.

"My dad writes these beautiful, meaningful stories," I say. "Things that students will study a hundred years from now. Me, on the other hand . . . I write science fiction. Sometimes even fantasy. I like stuff like aliens and magic and worlds that don't actually exist." I feel my face burn, and look back to Gus bravely. He's smiling at me.

"I see. And Star Wars? 'Arry Potter? Lord of ze Rings? Are zey not meaningful?" He squeezes my hand again. "Zey are art, Samson. All art 'as meaning. Especially stories zat are in ozer worlds. I am sure your writing ees beautiful."

That makes me lose my breath, and all I can do is gaze into Gus's eyes as my lungs refuse to work and my heart goes *thumpity-thump* inside my chest. The sun has just dipped below the horizon and now the sky is a masterpiece of neons and pastels, all mirrored in the dark brown of Gus's eyes.

"Thank you," I manage to squeak out, then clear my throat. "Speaking of art . . . A jazz trio from the university is playing at a little brewery tonight—the saxophone professor and two grad students. I thought you might be interested. If not, we can find something else to do."

My qualifier is moot, though, because now we're close enough to the restaurant that the strains of fusion are leaking out every time the front door opens, and Gus's face has relaxed into that same, nearly ecstatic look I saw when he was playing his saxophone. I squeeze his hand and laugh. "Okay. Jazz trio it is!"

Gus holds open the door for me, and we enter the restaurant. The place is packed with college students and older people alike, all bobbing their heads or tapping their feet in time with the plucking and slapping of the string bass. A bar made out of rich walnut curves around a half dozen giant copper tanks where, I assume, their hand-crafted beers ferment. The tables, the floor, the shelves, and even parts of the ceiling are made of the same walnut, all whimsically carved in abstract shapes. Gus stares openly, taking it all in, clearly impressed.

I speak to him, and he leans his ear close to my mouth to hear me over the music. "When my parents brought me here when I was little, I used to pretend I was a hobbit and this was my house in the Shire. Is it any wonder I write fantasy?"

Gus laughs a deep, melodious laugh, and suddenly the place seems even more magical (magickal?) than when I was a kid. I lead him to a small table at the side of the room, one with a perfect view of the small stage, and order us each a Diet Coke. Gus is already gone, lost in a musical reverie, eyes glazed over as he watches the trio perform. I push his drink toward him and let him enjoy, taking in the sax's reedy melody.

We sit like that for nearly an hour, Gus watching the players, me watching Gus. He's different when he listens to the musicians. Enraptured, for sure, but also observant. It's like he's studying the sax player's every riff and improvisation, memorizing it, logging it away for later. Maybe just to remember, maybe to try to play himself. It's fascinating, and I feel a little drunk watching him, as if his passion for music is going straight to my head.

I rub my foot against his under the table and his gaze snaps to mine, a smile curling up his lips almost guiltily, like he's been caught doing something forbidden.

“Is this what you want to do?” I ask him, and he tilts his head, straining to hear me over the jazz.

“No,” he says, frowning just a touch. “I mean, yes, zis ees what I want to do. Zis ees my passion, but eet ees ’ard to make a living playing jazz. Which I am sure you understand if you want to write.”

I smile. “Yeah, but who needs food?”

Gus laughs. “We will ’ave to be . . . eh, what ees ze word?”

“Skinny?” I guess.

He laughs again. “Not ze word I was looking for, but *oui.* We will be like skeletons. I was zinking somezing different . . . maybe about commitment?”

I give it a try. “Dedicated?”

“*Oui!*” Gus proclaims. “*Profondément engagé.* Eet ees like marriage to our passion. We must be dedicated. We must dream and create all ze time, ozerwise eet ees not art.”

I understand what he’s saying, completely, and I see it then: the two of us in some dump of a flat in Paris, me with my words and him with his music, struggling to make ends meet but in love and in love with life all the same. It’s wonderful, it’s perfect, and I’m lost in the fantasy when Gus jumps in his seat. He reaches behind him, pulls a vibrating cell phone from his back pocket, and glances at the screen.

“I am sorry, Samson. Eet ees a call from ’ome. I must take eet.”

I shrug it off as he starts toward the exit, headed toward the peace and quiet outside. "I'll be here. Go talk."

Just then the bassist announces into a microphone that the trio's going to take a short break to get more beer, which causes a rousing chorus of shouts from around the bar. Most people get out of their seats to do exactly that, and as the crowd migrates, I notice a familiar face on the other side of the room.

As I raise a brow, Landon gives me a sheepish look and heads in my direction.

"Where's Frenchie?"

"Call from home," I say, waving toward the outside. "Didn't know you'd be here."

"Yeah, sorry, kind of a last-minute thing." Landon shoves his hands into his pockets, staring in the direction of the group he was with. "A friend called and asked me to meet him. Jeff. You remember Jeff?"

I vaguely remember Jeff, or at least the mention of his name. He'd been in the all-state band two summers in a row with Landon. Of course, I'd mostly been annoyed at the time because Landon in Dayton for a week meant that I wouldn't get laid for a week.

"Yeah, kind of." I flick a glance across the room, where a boy watches us with unease. Must be Jeff. "All-state band?"

Landon nods. "That and the debate finals last summer. Remember when I had to go to Cleveland? Jeff's on the debate team at his school too, so he was there. And he takes lessons with Professor Benson and was coming down to watch him play, and called me to meet him. He wants to major in music, I guess. You know, trying to get his foot in the door and stuff like that."

Landon's rambling, which isn't normal for him. At all. And then it all comes together, slamming inside my brain like two freight trains coming head to head in a tunnel. Jeff is the reason why Landon hasn't been lonely for the last two years. Jeff, this weird kid from the northern part of the state, who plays in the all-state band and qualified for the debate finals—an obvious geek—is the reason why Landon doesn't feel the need to do stupid voodoo spells at midnight.

"Gus is here to see Professor Benson too," I say, and Landon nods. I think maybe he was still talking and I cut him off, but I'm not sure. I keep talking because I can't seem to be able to stop. "He's perfect, you know?"

"Professor Benson?" Landon guesses, confused.

"No. Gus. He just talked about my writing like he really understood. He's as passionate as I am, just about music. He really gets me, Landon."

Landon's gaze travels back over to Jeff across the room, who hasn't stopped watching us. "I'm glad." His eyes then come back to mine, big and soft, and he laughs uneasily. "Just don't become a Wiccan, okay? Meg's the only one allowed to be that batshit."

I chuckle because that's what's expected of me. Landon clears his throat. The musicians are gathering on the little stage.

"I guess I should get back," Landon says, nodding his head in the direction of Jeff the Debate Geek and his all-state friends.

"Yeah. I need to find Gus. See you later?"

"Sure," Landon answers, gives me a half smile, then leaves me. For just a second I stand there awkwardly while everyone else is talking and laughing all around me. It's a strange feeling, being alone while not being alone. I nearly bolt out the door but force myself to walk. The night breeze lifts my hair at the roots as I step out; the temperature has fallen but it feels good against my skin. Oddly calming.

Gus is leaning against the glass window of an antique store next door to Casa. He has his phone against his ear, a finger plugging his other to block out the noise of passing cars and drunk college students, and he's talking fast and excited in French. When he sees me, the wide smile on his face gets even wider and he stands up straight.

He says something low into the phone, something that I can tell is apologetic even if I don't understand the words.

"Oui. Je t'aime. A la prochaine . . ."

Gus takes his phone away from his ear and tucks it into his pocket. "I apologize, Samson. I am yours for ze rest of ze night, I promise."

"Mine, huh? That's a dangerous promise." I wiggle my eyebrows at him and Gus laughs. "Want to listen to more jazz?"

Gus turns his head in the direction of Casa's entrance. The door opens and a couple tumbles out, along with the strains of a saxophone. When he turns back, his cheeks are pink. "I don't zink I want to listen to jazz anymore."

"No?" I ask, and he shakes his head, then closes the distance between us with one step, wrapping his arms around me. The press of his warm body against mine makes my brain go all unfocused and scrambled, until he says, "Know a place a little more . . . private, *mon ami*?"

"I know a place," I say, and Gus makes a noise that is a mixture of a sigh and a groan, and I take his hand and lead him out of uptown Athens, toward a secret place where we can be totally and completely alone.

Six

I watch from across the table as Meg's eyes move back and forth over the menu, like she's watching a Ping-Pong match instead of deciding what to eat.

"Order both."

"Oh my god, Sam. I'd gain twenty pounds."

"I'll help you eat them."

Meg slams the menu shut with a crack and lays it on top of her bread plate. "Scallops. I cannot resist their scallops."

I grin at her. My menu sits on the table, unopened. I always know what I want at Seven Sauces. Their lamb might just be my favorite meal of all time. "And dessert?"

"There's no way I can choose between desserts. I'll have to order both. It's a sacrifice I must make." She looks at me, eyes twinkling with delight. She looks gorgeous tonight, and if I were straight I'd feel like the luckiest man in the world to be sitting across from her. Hell, I kind of do anyway. She's curled her hair and it's held back with barrettes behind her ears, and even though she's wearing black, it's more Victorian than goth. "How did the date go? Or should I just assume that since you didn't cancel our reservation, it was perfect?"

"It was. He's got it all. Everything I wanted."

Meg's gives me an I-told-you-so smile. She takes a drink from her water glass before saying, "The Goddess knows what she's doing."

I lean back in my chair and turn my glass by the stem, watching it leave a ring of sweat on the white tablecloth. "She might." I laugh. "Landon made me swear not to become Wiccan, though."

Meg rolls her eyes. "He's such a doubting Thomas."

"Isn't that a Christian thing?"

She tries to kick me under the table. "You know what I mean. I'm just saying it wouldn't hurt either of you to believe in something bigger than yourselves."

"I believe in stuff," I argue.

"Like what?" Meg leans up on her elbows, waiting for an answer.

I turn my glass some more. "I believe in human connections, I guess."

"Sex."

"No, definitely not that," I say, laughing with embarrassment. "But love. Friendship. Trust. Loyalty."

Meg says nothing but studies me, eyes narrowed, like she's trying to find a flaw in anything I've said. Fortunately, our waiter appears at the table and spares me her scrutiny as we place our orders.

"Do you ever get anything besides lamb?"

"I know what I like," I say, and wink at her.

"Adorable animals, bloody on your plate."

"It was an ugly lamb, I'm sure."

Meg laughs, and her voice softens until she's quiet. Then she leans forward and asks, "So I take it that you and Gus didn't . . . ?"

The question is blunt but not unexpected. Meg can be just plain nosy sometimes. But I take my time answering, teasing her. I even wiggle my eyebrows suggestively as I take a long drink of water. Her mouth falls open in shock.

"You did!"

"No!" I shake my head. "Geez, I'm just messing with you. Like you said yesterday, I don't want him to be Landon two-point-oh. I plan on taking things slow." I raise a brow haughtily. "Of course, that doesn't mean we can't make out on the College Green for an hour . . ."

"You slut," she says, totally pulling a face in feigned shock, but I can tell she's relieved. "Well, I'm proud of you for resisting the foreign charms of Augustin René Chevalier. I wasn't sure that you had, after Landon said—"

"What would Landon know about it?"

Meg closes her mouth and looks at me, taken aback. "He just said you left pretty early with Gus and he was concerned."

"I don't need his concern," I snap. "Besides, he doesn't get to be concerned about me if he won't let me be concerned about him."

"What are you talking about?"

"He didn't tell me about Jeff, did he? Not a word. I had to figure that out myself."

"Well, no, he didn't," Meg says, and although I figured Landon had told her about it, it still kind of bums me out to know that she's privy to the info, and they've obviously discussed Landon's fling without me. "But he didn't know how to talk to you about it. Are you mad?"

"What on earth would I be mad about?"

Meg reaches across the table and holds my hand, and it takes all of my willpower not to snatch it away. She lowers her voice. "Well, not telling you, for one. But I get the feeling that maybe you're just mad that Landon had someone else."

"Landon is free to do whatever he wants. I broke up with *him*, remember?"

She shrugs me off and offers, "That doesn't mean you can't be hurt, still."

"I'm not hurt," I say, and honestly, I'm not sure if it's the truth or not. "It's just . . . you and Michael are obviously doing so well you've got your whole hotel plan, everyone at school seems like they've paired off, even Archie, and I guess I feel a little betrayed that Landon's not in the same situation as me." I draw in a breath. "I'm happy for him. Really. I'm just sad for me."

"But now . . ." she begins, patting my hand in a way that would be patronizing for anyone but Meg. "Now you have Gus."

"Now I have Gus." I smile. "So I think we need a toast, don't you?"

Meg picks up her glass, and I pick up mine.

"To the Goddess?"

"Sure, why not?" I say, feeling generous. "And to the Perfect Ten."

"Hear, hear!" Meg says, and we clink on it. After we sip our water as if it's expensive champagne, she finds another topic. "So Michael wants to wear a leisure suit for prom . . ."

I let her ramble about her stupid boyfriend until dinner comes. It's not our waiter who brings it; it never is in this place. Waiters at Seven Sauces seem to be there to make suggestions and entertain, but not to actually do the dirty work of carrying food out. Instead, it's a boy who looks to be about thirteen. He sets our food in front of us shyly, head down, and I have to wonder if he's been trained that way or if he's really just that afraid of other human beings.

"Thank you," I say to him, and he raises his face just a little, I assume to say you're welcome, but instead he opens his mouth and freezes.

I'm not sure, but I think I might freeze a little too. The kid is beautiful, and even though he's obviously younger than me, I'd misjudged his age because of his demeanor. He's at least fifteen and has the kind of face that the Dutch artists would have loved to paint. High cheekbones, deliciously pouted lips, eyelashes a mile long, and a little upturned nose. His eyes are pale, liquid blue, and his blond hair is just long enough to tuck behind his ears and has the faintest wave to it.

"Uh, Sam, right?" he asks. His voice has a breathy quality to it, and it reminds me of torch songs and black-and-white movies.

"Yes. I'm sorry, do we know each other?"

"No. Not really," he says. His pouty lips form a smile that manages to be both shy and sexy somehow. "I know you, but you probably don't know me. You're a senior, right?"

"Yeah," I answer, and try to hold his gaze, but it's almost too much for either of us. He looks down, and I fidget with my napkin.

"I, um . . . I see you around school," he says, then extends a hand. I take it. His skin is smooth against mine. Smooth and really warm. "I'm Jamie Fisher. Sophomore."

"Right. I think I've seen you around," I say. It's a lie, but it's the right one, and Jamie is instantly flattered. He beams and straightens and (because I'm a seventeen-year-old boy and not blind, okay?) I can't help but notice that he's got a body artists would love to paint too. Preferably undressed.

I risk a glance at Meg and she has her fist to her mouth, trying to stifle laughter.

"Is there anything else I can get you? More water? Dessert?"

"I think we're fine for now. Thanks, Jamie."

"Sure. Anytime, Sam," he says, and something about the way he says it makes me think he's not talking about just food. He walks away and maybe, just maybe, I watch him all the way back to the kitchens.

"Oh my *god*." Meg bites on her finger to stifle her laughter. "When it rains, it pours."

I raise a brow. "What are you talking about?"

"What am I talking about? The cute sophomore with the massive crush on you, that's what I'm talking about!"

"What? No." I wave her away and take a drink of water.

"Please. I'm surprised he didn't offer himself up as dessert," Meg says, giggling again. "He didn't even talk to me, but he certainly couldn't take his eyes off you. Great Goddess, Sam. You should get his number."

I shake my head at her. "Are you out of your mind? I have Gus now, remember? The sexy French guy that may or may not have been sent from above?"

"Just in case, that's all I'm saying."

"In case of what?"

"Well," Meg starts, and I know she's choosing her words carefully. "What if Gus isn't quite as perfect as you think? Or what if Jamie's actually even more perfect?"

"He's, like, fifteen."

"And adorable."

She's right. He's so cute it's nearly unbearable. But I shake my head. "No. Come on, I feel bad even talking about this. I can't do that to Gus."

"Sam, maybe the Goddess is giving you choices. Ever think of that?"

"Or I'm looking a gift horse in the mouth."

Meg leans back in her chair, relenting. "Fine. But if you ask me, it wouldn't hurt to get his number. I mean, when has it ever hurt anything to have a cute blond worshipping at your feet?"

I laugh, and Meg lets the subject drop as we both dig into our amazing entrees. Halfway through my lamb, I get a phone call. I shoot Meg an apologetic look, which she waves away upon hearing that it's Gus.

"Talk to the gorgeous Frenchman," she commands.

"I miss you," Gus says before I can even say hello.

"I miss you."

"Last night was . . ." Gus hums while he searches for a way to describe the indescribable. "Perfection."

"Just the word I was going to use." I close my eyes and remember the way his lips felt on mine, and I know that if I open them and look at Meg, she'll be snickering at my red face.

"Am I interrupting somezing?"

"I'm out to dinner with Meg, but she's too busy gorging herself on scallops to talk to me anyways."

Gus chuckles in that deep, sexy voice of his. "So I should not be jealous zat you are out wiz someone else?"

"Not at all." I sigh. "Are you busy tomorrow? I have to finish up a paper for English, but maybe you can help."

"*Oui.* Zose Russian writers. Zey are so complicated. I will do all I can to 'elp you, Samson. I do not want you to get a bad grade. But maybe I shouldn't come? I might be a distraction, no?"

"I want to be distracted."

Sexy chuckling again. "Zen I will do my best to distract you."

"My place? Two-ish?"

"Of course. I will—"

Gus's voice cuts out for a second, then comes back in.

"Sorry. I am getting a call from 'ome zat I must take. See you tomorrow?"

"See you then."

I hang up and risk opening my eyes. Meg's sticking her finger in her mouth and making gagging noises. Then she dips her voice down low in what I assume is an attempt to mimic me. "Oh, Gus. Come distract me. Save me from my English homework, you handsome devil. *Je te veux tellement!*"

In spite of the fact that we're in the nicest restaurant in Athens, I toss a piece of bread at her face. She just laughs.

"You didn't have to hang up. I could have endured that sickening conversation a little while longer."

I shrug and bite down on a piece of lamb, chewing before I answer. "He had a phone call from home he had to take anyway. It's fine."

Her face scrunches. "From home? It's, like, two in the morning there."

"Is it?" I do the math and realize she's right. "Huh. I don't know. He got a phone call about this time last night too. Maybe his parents are night owls."

"You sure it's his parents?"

"He said it was a call from home. I just assumed—"

"Yeah, but are you sure?"

I suddenly feel uneasy, because I'm not sure. I'm not sure at all. I mean, what kind of parents stay up until two a.m.? Even if they're crazy European parents, it's a little strange. And he never said it was his mother, or father, or even one of his many sisters.

"What are you trying to say?" I growl at Meg, angry that she's making me even give this a second thought.

"Nothing. It's just a little fishy, though, isn't it? He hasn't mentioned, like, a boyfriend or something back home?"

"No!" I shake my head vehemently. "I mean, he told me he was in love once, but he definitely talked about it in the past tense."

Meg blows out a breath and picks up her fork, stabbing at a scallop. "Okay, if you're sure."

I'm not sure, I'm not at all sure now, and my chest is tight and there's a weird pain on the left side. And I hate Meg just a little bit for that. I push my plate away. My appetite's disappeared.

"Don't you like it? I can get you something else."

I look up and Jamie's at our table, smiling sweetly at me and ignoring Meg's entire existence. Not that it matters. Meg's basically burying her head in the sand. She's staring at her plate and not looking at either of us.

Gus, having another boyfriend in Paris. What a load of crap. The mere insinuation is so infuriating that something within me snaps, gives way, and breaks, and I look up into Jamie's eyes and give him my best smile.

"How about your number?"

Jamie takes a moment to recover from the shock, then finally whispers, "Mine?"

"Yeah. Unless there's a cuter blond boy working back in the kitchen or something. In which case, you can bring me his number. But I doubt it."

Jamie smiles that combination shy-but-sexy smile again. Such a neat trick. "I can get you that. If you're sure."

I'm not. "I am."

"Then I'll be right back." Jamie walks away, I can only assume to find a pen, but this time I don't watch him go. I'm too busy fuming. When he's out of earshot, Meg kicks me underneath the table.

"What are you doing?"

"Just in case," I say, throwing her words right back at her.

"I'm sure Gus is just talking to friends. I really didn't mean to make you paranoid."

"Too late for that," I snap, and Meg quiets. Then she looks up at me, wincing.

"Ignore what I said, okay? Just forget about it."

"Maybe you're right, though. And I like him so much, but what do I know about him really?" I wonder out loud.

Meg looks stricken. "I'm so sorry. You want to just call it a night? We can forget dessert."

"No," I say, relenting. I let out a breath. "It's okay. You're a good friend. You get me involved with witchcraft to help my love life and then get all worried about if the guy your deity sends is good enough for me. It's actually kind of sweet, in this weird, twisted way. You deserve some chocolate torte. Even if Gus turns out to be a jerk, the way he kisses alone is worth that."

Meg laughs sadly and then nods. "Okay. I do love you, Sam."

"Love you too. Get the torte. Jamie's coming back, anyways."

Jamie slides up to the table and hands me his number, which is printed neatly on the back of an old receipt. I look up at him and say, "Wow, you are just . . ."

I have no idea how to even describe what Jamie is, but he gets what I'm trying to say. "You too. Call me?"

"I will," I promise, even though I don't know how much I really mean it. I tuck his number into my pocket and say, "And I think we're going to have dessert."

Seven

I can't believe it. Gus is sitting at the counter in my kitchen, eating one of my mother's chocolate-chip-and-walnut cookies with a mug of milk, and they're chattering away in French. They haven't said a word to me for fifteen minutes, but they've laughed plenty, and if it wasn't so darn cute I'd feel terribly left out.

Finally I make my plea. "Gus, I need to get to work or this essay will never get written."

"Yes, Samson. Eet ees time to work, I suppose." Gus heaves a sigh and pushes the plate of cookies away from him.

"Oh no you don't. Take these with you," my mother says, beaming at Gus. "You need sustenance when exploring the parallels of Russian symbolism."

"Gina, you are *très belle*."

My mother—so embarrassing—winks at Gus, and as Gus takes the plate from her offering hands, she leans to whisper in my ear, "He's utterly charming. So I want that bedroom door of yours open at all times, understand me, young man?"

I snort. "Yes, ma'am."

My mother rolls her eyes and pushes me off after Gus, and soon Gus and I are sitting on my bedroom floor, my books scattered around us, my laptop open to my essay. He looks over my work, gives me a suggestion to link Dostoyevsky to . . . something, I don't even know because Gus chooses that moment to touch my lips with his fingers, then draw me in for a slow, tantalizing kiss. I sink into him, and it's only when I start to feel blood pounding in my ears that I put my hand on his chest and gently push us apart.

Gus sits back, clearly disappointed but amused nonetheless. "I 'ave 'eard zat Americans can be, 'ow do you say . . . conservative?"

I blink. "What are you talking about?"

He shrugs, a move that seems out of place for his level of sophistication. "You stop," he says, placing a hand on my chest as if to illustrate, "when we get too close. Are you religious, Samson?"

"No," I say. I feel my whole face darkening. "It's not that."

Gus nods as if he understands. "Landon," he guesses, and I don't disagree. He moves his hand, fingers trailing up and down my chest in hypnotic waves. "Sometimes you need somezing new to erase the old."

I close my eyes and let myself enjoy his touch, the sensation of his fingers lingering over my skin. It would be nice to give in to it, let Gus keep touching, keep going. Let him make new memories for me.

Is that what I want to do? Erase Landon, or, at least,

the painful stuff involving him? On one hand it seems like a good idea. On the other, I might wind up in the exact same place I'm in now. Then I would need someone to erase Gus, then someone to replace him, and so on.

I open my mouth to question Gus's methods, but his phone dings and he stops to fish for it in the pocket of the hoodie he's wearing. He takes it out, glances at the screen, and grins.

"Friend from home?"

His head snaps up as if he's surprised I'm still in the room with him. "What? Oh, *oui*. I zink zey miss me," he says, and winks.

"I'm sure they do." I watch him type something back and lean over a little to see the screen, but the words are meaningless to me. For all I know he could be typing back nursery rhymes. "Do you miss them?"

Gus's face falls a bit, just enough to be noticeable. "Yes. Eet ees 'ard to be away, zough I 'ave found very good company 'ere."

Yesterday I would have gone all light-headed at the compliment, but today I'm not quite mollified. There's something nagging at me, in the back of my head. Lots of what-ifs and unanswered questions, and they're all pestering me in a voice that sounds remarkably like Meg's.

"Is this the same friend that called you last night? And the night before?"

Gus's face goes blank and I can't tell what he's thinking. He nods slowly. *"Oui."*

"And she . . . or he . . ."

"'E," Gus says, voice muted so that I barely hear him.

"He," I correct, "is just a friend?"

"Just a friend." Then Gus gives me a strange smile, a pitying smile. "Samson, you 'ave nozing to worry about. I am 'ere. Wiz you."

I stare at him for a moment, searching for any signs of lying in his eyes, but I don't see any. Then he leans in and kisses me. It's sweet, deep, and reassuring, making my insides go all mushy, and suddenly I don't give a damn who was on the phone.

Gus is right. He's here, with me. He's really and truly mine. And Meg can take all her insinuations and distrust and shove it.

....

The week passes so fast that it barely registers as a blip on my radar. Gus and I walk home together every day and we talk on the phone every night, but it's the weekend that means we can spend hours at a time together, and I live for that. That's when he feels most like my boyfriend; like this is real and not one of my daydreams.

Milo Jenkins is having a party at his house on Friday because his parents left him home alone while they went to Hawaii, which is a really stupid idea, but I'm not going to complain. Athens High hasn't had a good house party since the summer, and we're all a little itchy to get out of control and start another fresh batch of rumors.

Gus and I head there (so that he can see how Americans party, I tell him. It's all educational, right?) and I know Meg and Landon are going to put in appearances too, hopefully sans Michael, but I doubt I'll get that lucky.

Milo's house is on the good side of town, close to Landon's, so I borrow my dad's car. It's a five-year-old Toyota Camry but it does the job. Gus holds my hand on the middle console, and I smile all the way there.

Cars are practically parked on top of each other in the old narrow street, and as soon as we get out of the car we can hear the bass line of music thumping in the distance.

"Eet ees almost like 'ome," Gus says, a mischievous grin on his face.

"Loud music and teenagers drinking?" I chide.

"Somezing like zat," he says, laughing.

We don't knock because the front door is standing wide open. The inside of the house is packed. Just one cursory glance around the bottom floor tells me that most of the senior class is here, as well as a healthy smattering of juniors and sophomores. Gus waves to a couple of people he knows from the jazz ensemble, and I tell him to go talk while I grab a few drinks. The smell of cheap beer leads me to the back of the house where a keg is sitting in the center of a sunroom behind the kitchen. It's quieter here, and surprisingly empty considering it's where the beer is.

"Should have known this is where I'd find my friends," I say. Meg's sitting on Michael's lap in a little wicker chair, plastic cups in their hands, looking about two seconds away from tearing each other's clothes off, and Landon's leaning up against a long window, somehow managing to look both appalled and bored.

"Oh thank god," Landon murmurs and makes his way to me, keeping his voice pitched low so only I can hear. "Save me. They've been making out all night."

"Disgusting," I whisper back, and grab two plastic cups before pumping foamy beer for both me and Gus. "Come back inside. I'm giving Gus the full American teenager experience tonight."

"Oh?" Landon asks, and we wave at Meg and Michael as we head deeper into the house, as if they even notice us. "You two doing okay?"

We shoulder our way through, passing classmates who are dancing or laughing, and the music is so loud I have to shout. "Of course. Why wouldn't we be?"

"No reason," Landon says, and even with his voice at a yell, I can hear he's lying.

"Ugh, not you too!" I snap, whirling around to face him. Beer spills on the floor. "Between you and Meg, I don't need a mother."

"What? Am I not allowed to be worried about you now that you have a boyfriend?"

I ignore his question and ask one of my own. "Did she tell you about the phone calls?"

Landon winces, sheepish, and that's all the answer I need.

"It's nothing. Okay? I talked to him about it and he explained. It's just friends from home, nothing more. Stop your worrying and stop making me so freaking paranoid. Everything's fine."

That shuts Landon up, even though I can tell he's literally biting his tongue so that he can't say more. I roll my eyes and continue toward Gus, who I left somewhere in the front room of the house. Landon follows, a few steps behind, as if he's scared that any minute I could round on him again.

When I see Gus, I have to smile. He's on one of Milo's horrid floral-print couches with his back to me, surrounded by his fellow jazz players, and it's like he's holding court—a king among peasants. He's in the middle of telling a story that has people laughing, hanging on his every word, and I don't interrupt. I lean over his shoulder and dangle the beer in front of his face, and he stops talking to thank me with a peck on the lips.

"*Mon amour*, do you know my friends?" Gus tugs on my arm, and I let him tug until my free arm is wrapped around him. I shoot a glance back to Landon, whose eyes dart away from me, and he takes a big swig of his beer. Gus introduces me to the jazz ensemble, even though I went to elementary school with most of them, and I don't bother introducing Landon because I know all of them are at least friendly acquaintances of his. Then Gus goes back to his story and lets go of me. I settle in an overstuffed armchair across from him and make myself a peasant too, listening to his musical voice as he spins a tale about a night involving sneaking into an underground club in Paris. Landon follows because I guess the risk of me yelling at him again isn't nearly as bad as watching Michael eat Meg's face, and perches on the arm of my chair.

It doesn't take long. Maybe fifteen minutes of happiness where I forget about Meg's suspicions and Landon's concerns, where all I do is watch my gorgeous French boyfriend work the crowd like a freaking pro, and then his phone rings.

Before his ringtone stops I hear him apologize to his friends for the interruption. I look up, and his brown eyes catch mine, so I stand and walk to him.

"Friends?" He nods, his eyes wide and sad-looking. "Go upstairs and talk. I'm sure there are a few bedrooms that haven't been claimed yet."

"I am sorry, Samson."

I shake my head at him and do my best to smile. "Go. Just don't miss too much of the party, okay?"

I watch him climb the stairs, his phone pressed to his ear, then I sit back down next to Landon. The music seems even louder than before; the *thump-tha-thump* of the bass is drilling into my brain. I close my eyes and rub my temples. When I open them again, the jazz kids have all moved on to more entertaining things and I feel alone with Landon, even though we're surrounded by our classmates.

"You okay?"

"Yeah, I think," I answer him, rubbing harder at my temples. "When he left, did he look . . . I don't know . . ."

"Guilty?" Landon suggests, using the word I was thinking even though it's the last word I want to hear. "Yeah, he did."

Landon's hand is on my back, comforting and warm, and I lean into his touch. "I like him so much, Landon.

He's charming and he's smart and he's wonderful."

"He is all that," Landon agrees. "But that doesn't mean he's not a liar."

He leans down, resting his head on mine. I feel his unruly hair against my curls. "Tell me what to do."

"I can't do that."

I nod slowly, understanding. This isn't Landon's battle. I sit with him a few minutes longer, stalling. Someone needs to turn down the music. My brain is pounding in time to some rapper I don't even recognize and every beat thrums against my nerves and makes me want to jump or scream.

Then suddenly I'm standing. "I'm going to go find him," I hear myself say.

"I'll be here," Landon promises, and I know it's more than a mere promise to stay in one place.

Meg and Michael emerge from the kitchen as I'm heading up the stairs, and even though I can tell she's a little tipsy by the way she's clutching Michael, her face flashes concern up at mine.

The stairs seem too steep, as if my muscles are having trouble putting one foot in front of the other and pulling my body upward. When I reach the top, my chest is tight and my lungs are burning. There's only one direction to go. Milo's second floor is just a long hallway with a lot of doors, and though a few are closed (and goodness knows I don't want to interrupt what's going on in *those* rooms), some are ajar.

I don't want to look. I don't want to find Gus, and yet my feet are moving me forward anyway.

As I tread with careful, soft steps down the hall, the familiar, velvety tones of Gus's voice rise up over the rap music and my own haggard breathing.

He's laughing.

I follow the sound until I reach one of the ajar doors, and somehow I bring myself to peer through the small opening. Gus is lying on a bed, head supported by a few frilly pillows. I can only assume the bedroom belongs to Milo's little sister, as everything is purple and covered in lace, but Gus looks completely unaware of his surroundings. He continues to laugh, then babbles a little in French, words moving so quickly I can't catch even a vague meaning. But it's not the words I'm concerned about, it's the way Gus's voice dips down low and buttery, a whisper that borders on sultry and is, without a doubt, intimate. It's the kind of voice that, if used on me, would make me blush; it's the kind of voice Landon and I would use with each other when we would catch each other in the hallway between classes and make promises about what, exactly, we could do in our time alone after school. It's a voice I want Gus to use with me. Only me.

I watch him for another minute, noting not just his voice but his dreamy smile and the way he runs his fingers across his chest, as if mimicking someone else's touch. Then I push the door open and step inside.

Gus's face freezes when he sees me. Slowly, he pulls his phone away from his ear and ends the call, then he sits up and holds a hand out to me, which I don't take.

"Sorry, a friend calling to say—"

"Don't lie," I say, and my voice is quiet but also threatening, my words carrying a warning. "Who is he?"

Gus folds his hands into his lap, over his phone. He stares at it, tracing the edge of it with his index finger.

"A boyfriend?"

"Yes," Gus answers levelly, raising his head to look me in the eye.

"Are you in love with him?"

"Yes."

All the fears, all the suspicion, all the dread I've been feeling since Meg got me thinking about it combine and form a heavy, bruising knot in my stomach. Part of me wants to scream at him, call him names, kick him, but another part, a bigger part, wants to sink to the floor and cry in a little ball.

"Why didn't you tell me?"

"Samson," Gus says, a bit of laughter trickling from his throat, and I want to wipe the little smirk he has off his face, "eet ees not important. When I left, 'e and I agreed zat we would see ozer people while I was 'ere."

"See other people? Even though you're in love with him?" I ask, my voice rising with disbelief.

"*Oui.* Neizer of us like to be alone, so it was for ze best."

"So I'm just the American guy you're leading on and keeping around for company so that after a few months you can go back to . . . Jean-Luc or Pierre or whoever the hell—"

"Gabriel," Gus says, and despite the fact that his voice is soft, it halts me midsentence. "'Is name ees Gabriel."

"I don't give a shit what his name is!" I bellow.

"Zere ees no reason to be upset."

"No, no reason at all," I spit. "Just that you lied, and you're in love with someone else, and you're going to go home to him when this is all over and you'll be fine and it won't matter how much I like you because you already have someone."

Gus sits up on his knees and reaches for my hand, and this time I let him take it. I turn away from him, embarrassed at my outburst. "I am sorry," he says gently. "I did not realize zat you felt so strongly."

I want to ask how he could have missed that, but I can't. My voice is bone dry. I hate this. I hate the knot twisting in my stomach, I hate the feeling that I'm just a replacement, a second best; I hate that I thought he was perfect and he thought of me as something to pass the time. And more than anything I hate that I'm sure he can read all of that on my face and I just want to get out of here before I make a bigger ass of myself.

"I like you too. You 'ave been ze best zing about America. We can still be togezer."

"No, we can't, Gus."

Gus makes a tsking sound and tries to pull me closer to him, but I won't budge. "Don't be unreasonable. We could 'ave a lot of fun."

"I don't want to just have fun with you. Why don't you get that?" I snatch my hand away from his. "I don't want to be with a liar, and I don't want to be with someone who's in love with someone else."

"Why does zat matter?"

"Why *doesn't* it matter to you?" I ask, and my voice breaks a little. "I want a guy who's in love with me. And you can't be, so this is over."

"Reconsider." He says the one simple word so adorably in his accent that I almost do.

I can't pull myself together enough to speak the word *no*, so I shake my head and leave him there in Milo's sister's room, sad among the lace and purple.

Landon's sitting at the top of the stairs, waiting on me. He must be able to gather the entire story from the look on my face because he scrambles to his feet and pulls me into a hug before I can say a word.

"Want to punch something?" he whispers into my ear, and I nod against his shoulder.

"Get me out of here, Landon."

"Come on. I'll drive. We can pick up your car tomorrow. Want Meg too?"

I nod again and walk with him downstairs. He's leading me like a child, his hand in mine, and I couldn't care less that practically all of Athens High turns to watch the spectacle. I'm sure it must be more than a little confusing, my ex holding my hand after I'd just snuck away to see Gus, and me so close to tears I can taste the snot in the back of my throat. Sam Raines will once again be front-page news in the high school gossip column, I can count on that.

I don't see Landon signal to Meg, but I see her push away from Michael and say something dismissive to him, and the three of us step out of the front door at the same time. Meg's hand slips into my free one.

"You were right," I say to her. "He has a boyfriend in France named Gabriel."

"That's a stupid name," I hear Landon mutter, and his anger on my behalf nearly makes me smile.

"I'm sorry I was right. I didn't want to be right," Meg says, squeezing my hand.

We pile into Landon's car and he makes the short drive to his house. We don't bother being quiet on the way to Landon's room—his parents are out, or away for the weekend or whatever, and Landon's on his own as usual. We settle on his bed, and Meg and Landon sandwich me, hugging me between them. I tuck my head in the valley between Meg's chin and shoulder and put up a valiant fight against tears. We sit like that, in silence, breathing each other in, for what feels like half the night. I feel like I'm soaking in their strength; I feel like it's already beginning to repair me.

"He was so perfect," I finally say.

"Perfect wouldn't have lied to you," Meg corrects me.

"Or hurt you," Landon adds.

"Well, I thought he was." I sniff against Meg's shoulder, trying to keep those persistent tears back. "He seemed so wonderful. I think . . . I think I could have fallen in love with him."

"Lucky you didn't, I guess," Meg says, and I feel her lift her head, probably exchanging a look with Landon, and they're probably both as relieved as I am that it didn't get to that point.

"Sure," I mumble. "Lucky."

Then Landon's hands are warm on my back. "You can cry in front of us, you know. We won't tell."

I lift my head up. "I'm okay."

"No, you're not. You're hurt."

"I'm seventeen. I'm not—"

"Not supposed to cry?" Landon finishes for me. He arches a brow. "Is that like how we're not supposed to want a boyfriend who actually cares or freak out when sex actually means something? Come on. You know that shit's not true either."

It's the first time Landon has even come close to talking about what happened between us, and the pain already present in my heart from Gus coils around older, deeper pain for a moment.

"I don't want to cry over him."

"Then don't. But if you feel like you should, you can."

Landon says the words but I know they're meant to be from Meg as well, because she squeezes me tight in her thin little arms. I'm not sure how much time passes, but it's long enough that my mother calls my cell phone to check on me, and Landon reluctantly offers to drive me home.

I dream about Gus that night, and the list. In the dream, we're in the cemetery and a burst of wind yanks the list out of my hands, and it flies into Gus's. Then all I can do is watch hopelessly, struggling not to cry, as he rips the list to shreds.

Eight

A Cheez-It hits the tip of my nose.

"Earth to Sam."

It's the Tenth Circle of Hell, otherwise known as lunch period on Monday, and I would rather be anywhere, *anywhere* on earth, than Athens High School. Usually I say that jokingly, because I'm nerdy enough to actually enjoy the learning part of school. Nothing's more satisfying than a philosophical talk about *Animal Farm* or a challenging set of calculus problems. But today rumors are swirling all around me; I hear my name and Gus's paired in hushed tones in the hallways, and it serves as a reminder that I won't be walking him home anymore, or sneaking a quick kiss before eighth period.

Over Meg's voice, I catch a nasal, female voice behind me saying, ". . . but then he left with Landon. Do you think . . . ?"

"I'm sure, Marie," another unfamiliar voice answers. "You know, gay guys can be sluts too."

I close my eyes and wish I could be invisible. And deaf. And perhaps comatose too, just for good measure.

"Sam."

I grunt and open my eyes. Meg's staring at me, face looming in front of mine as she leans over the cafeteria table. "Come on. You've got to eat."

I pick a cucumber off my wilted sandwich and stuff it in my mouth, smacking my lips as I chew with my mouth open. "I'm eating," I say through cucumber bits, then swallow.

The table shakes and I turn to my right as Landon plops down beside me. His lunch period isn't for another twenty minutes—Gus's lunch period, I remind myself with a groan—so he's skipping out on something.

"Okay, so I've done rumor control on the baseball team, the basketball team, the lacrosse team, the AV Club, Latin Club, Honor Society, the cheerleaders, the 4-H kids, and most of the orchestra, but there's no way in hell I can catch all of the band. I'm sure most of them have heard the story from Gus. At least his version of it anyway, whatever he's saying."

"What is Gus saying?" I ask, hating the hopeful notes I hear in my own voice.

Landon gives me a sad smile. "Just that he wants you back."

"Good," I grumble. "He can just keep on wanting."

"Good for you!" Meg coos, patting my hand on my can of Diet Coke. "Besides, you want to be single when the Goddess brings you the *real* Perfect Ten."

"If your goddess had anything to do with Gus, I think I'll pass on the next one too," I say.

Meg sticks out her bottom lip and I think she'd probably argue with me or call me a blasphemer if this were a different day, and I didn't look like I'd been flattened by a Zamboni machine.

"Thanks, Landon," I say, turning back to him.

"No problem." He leans on the table, elbowing my disgusting sandwich out of the way. "I've had a lot of people congratulate me, actually."

"Congratulate you?" I ask. "About what?"

His eyes are dancing with humor. "About us getting back together."

I laugh—a weird, shocked kind of laugh that's a little clipped. Landon chuckles too.

"Of course, then I had to explain that we weren't back together or anything, which kind of took the fun out of it. But . . ." He smiles at me, all warm and kind of wonderful, almost like he used to. "Seems like we had a few fans."

"Who knew?" I laugh for real this time. "Anyway, thanks. Hopefully in a few days I'll stop hearing the words 'Sam' and 'filthy whore' in the same sentence. And, you know, people won't think we're together again."

"Yeah. Hopefully." Landon's eyes drift to Meg's before he takes a determined interest in his fingernails. "Anyway, better get back to band . . ."

"Donkey after school?" Meg asks him, and I jerk my head in her direction. I'm surprised at the offer. It's usually me who does the inviting where Landon is concerned.

Landon's whole face brightens. "Sure! See you guys then!"

When he's gone I raise an eyebrow at her, but she just shrugs and shoves a fistful of Cheez-Its in her mouth, saying around a glob of orange, "Eat, Sam. Or I'll make you."

And because Meg has, on occasion, actually followed through with a few of her threats, I take a bite of my sandwich and swallow it down.

....

By some miracle (or maybe that whole Goddess thing is trying to work for me still), I don't see Gus until Wednesday. I'm walking through the hallway just after the dismissal bell, ready to grab my coat and get something warm and filled with caffeine from the Donkey, when I hear Gus's deep voice coming from around the next corner. In a panic, I dart into the first open door I see.

Unfamiliar smells assault my senses. It's kind of like sweet dried grass in the summertime, and sawdust, and something like plastic with a bit of a chemical zing. At first I wonder if I'm in the shop room, since I've never seen it and honestly have no idea where it is in the school. I stay as far away from things that could lop off an appendage as I can.

But then my eyes catch up to my nose. All around me are canvases, hung on walls, situated on tables, posed on easels. It's the canvas frames I'm smelling, and the paint. I'm in the art room.

And holy Moses, don't artists ever clean up after themselves? The place is a mess. Everything's covered with splatters of paint, making it look deserving of the modern art section of every museum I've ever visited.

Brushes are everywhere, jars with mysterious liquids inside them, scissors, random scraps of paper, tubes of paint, and even what looks to be a human head, although on further inspection I can tell it's just a model.

I take a few steps toward one of the tables and pick up a sheet of paper on it. It's a sketch of a bird, but it's unlike any bird I've ever seen. It's *prettier* than any bird I've ever seen. It's sleek, with long feathers and a long neck, and a needle-nose beak that curves slightly downward.

"It's a Jubjub bird," a voice says somewhere off to my right, and I jump five feet in the air. It's Jamie, from Seven Sauces, and he's smiling shyly, though he's clearly pleased with himself that he was able to scare me.

I clutch at my chest. "Are you trying to kill me?"

"Not really." He steps close to me and takes one side of the sketch, turning it so we can both see it. I study the drawing, now realizing that it must be his.

"The Jubjub bird from *Through the Looking Glass*?" Jamie nods. I look again at the beautiful bird, impressed. "It's good. Really good."

Jamie takes the drawing from me and lays it on the table again before wiping his hands off on his cargo pants, which I can see are stained with all colors of paint. "Lewis Carroll says it lives alone but also in a perpetual state of passion."

The Jubjub's plight sounds all too familiar, and I have to wonder what made Jamie want to draw it. "It must be very lonely," I say, feeling a tug at my heart.

He doesn't answer. "Are you lost?" he asks instead.

"What? No."

He studies me, and I have the feeling that he can see things I'd rather keep secret. "Hiding, then?"

I wince. "Yeah, I guess."

"From Gus?"

So he knows about Gus. I immediately feel awful about asking for Jamie's number. I nod slowly.

"Oh. He's really gorgeous, Sam."

Guilt bubbles in my stomach, gurgling and uncomfortable like bad gas. "Thanks, but we're not exactly together anymore."

Jamie sniffs. "I know. I was at Milo's."

"You were?" I ask, and immediately regret it because Jamie's pretty face falls. "I'm sorry. I didn't see you."

"You had other things going on." Jamie shrugs it off. "Anyway. I'm sorry about Gus. Did you really like him?"

When he asks, the whole thing seems to come back at me all at once, and before I can get a grip, tears prickle in my eyes. "Yeah. I guess I did."

"I can see why. I mean, I certainly can't hold it against you for not calling."

Ouch.

"Hey." I reach out and touch him, and although he raises a brow at it, he also moves closer so that my hand can make more contact over his bare skin. "I shouldn't have asked for your number when I did. Gus and I, well, I guess we were already having some trouble then. But I meant what I said."

"About?" Jamie asks, hopeful.

"About you being cute." I watch his porcelain skin turn soft pink. "But I'm sorry. I shouldn't have done that. At least not then."

"Well, you can still call," Jamie says, then smiles shyly, adding, "If you want."

My stomach flutters. He's just so pretty, with his golden-blond hair and those big eyes and pouty lips, and I can't help but think of what Meg said. Maybe Gus wasn't the one I was waiting for. Maybe, just maybe, the boy of my dreams isn't going to come in on horseback, wearing a suit of armor, ready to save me from this loneliness. Maybe he won't even be terribly charismatic and have an adorable accent. I didn't ask for those things, after all. Perhaps the boy of my dreams will sneak into my heart quietly, and his shy charm will hook me better than any alluring Frenchman could.

"I'd like that." We smile at each other, and a beat passes before I can gather my wits enough to make conversation. "So why are you here so late? Working on the Jubjub?"

"No," Jamie says with a slight shake of his head. "I'm working on a painting. A . . . well, a watercolor, I guess. It's over here, if you want to see it."

"I'd love to see it."

Jamie crooks his finger, silently beckoning me to follow as he heads back into a little nook in the room, small enough for just one person to work in. He bites his lip as he points to his current project, which is on an easel in front of a stool.

I step in front of it, and I am *stunned.*

The canvas looks like it might be on fire. Bold reds mix with vibrant orange and sunny yellows, contrasted with sweeping lines of black. The curves create a feather here, a wing there, a beak at the top corner. It's another bird, even prettier than the Jubjub, and this one is flying, wings outstretched, reaching toward the sun.

"It's a phoenix," he whispers as I'm admiring his work. "I kind of wanted to capture the moment when it burst into flames, right before the rebirth from ashes."

"Jamie, this is beautiful." I turn to him in awe. "I mean, I know nothing about art, but this looks like it should be in a museum, not . . . well, *here.*"

Jamie laughs, and again I'm taken aback by the airy quality of his voice, like how the wind whistles through tree branches. I find myself wanting to close my eyes and just listen. "Thanks. It's not done yet. I still don't have the flames quite right. But most of the others aren't done either. I like to wait for inspiration to hit, and you just never know when it will strike."

"Others?" I ask, then answer myself as I look around his small workspace. There are painted birds everywhere—a peacock of blues and golds and greens, a hawk in reddish browns, a dodo in purple and pink, swans, seagulls, and creatures that look like they're straight out of Middle-earth or some other fantastical universe. "Wow."

Jamie just smiles. "I love watercolors. Some people don't because they don't give you a precise line, but that's why I like them. They're the opposite of precise. They're chaotic and surprising and imperfect."

"You like imperfection?" I ask.

Jamie nods, eyes sparkling with humor. "There's a lot of beauty in imperfection."

I look at his phoenix. There is certainly a lot of beauty there, but I can't say I see any imperfections. "Can I watch?"

Jamie turns to me sharply, incredulous. "You . . . you want to watch me paint?"

"Yeah, unless it's too personal. I get that. I don't like anyone standing over my shoulder while I write." He squints at me. "I like to write," I explain.

"I know," he says. "I read your articles in the school paper."

"I'm glad someone does, though they're not very good. I'm really more into fiction."

"Like your father?"

"No," I say, a bit too quickly, and although it shouldn't be a surprise that he knows my father is a writer, it still catches me off guard. "Not really like my father at all. Dad and I are . . . very different."

"Different styles?" Jamie asks.

I nod. "I'm the Douglas Adams to his Shakespeare."

Jamie ducks down, catching my lowered gaze and bringing it back up. "The world needs both Douglas Adamses and Shakespeares. Otherwise we'd have the same stories, over and over again."

"Thanks," I say. "So, anyway, would I make you nervous if I sat here while you painted?"

"No," Jamie says. He wrinkles his button nose. "But I do have to warn you. I get into the zone while I work. I may not be much of a conversationalist."

I laugh at that because I can totally understand "the zone." "I hear you. I'll keep my chattering to a minimum. Wouldn't want to disturb the *artiste*."

"Chatter away, Sam. Sometimes I listen to music while I paint, but mostly it's just silence. Some conversation would do me good."

"You sure?"

"Yeah," he says, his soft voice floating. "Stay."

So I stay for an hour, watching him as he works on his phoenix. Even though he clearly doesn't mind my company and we chat a bit, getting to know each other, I do try to stay quiet as he works, and I watch, enraptured. From my vantage point, it's hard to tell what's more beautiful—the phoenix like a bright flame on his canvas, or the way his pretty face relaxes in ecstatic bliss as he strokes his brush over the canvas, again and again.

....

"You missed lunch today."

It's Friday afternoon. Meg couldn't go to the Donkey because her older sister is in town and they're all going out to eat tonight and she's expected to be a willing participant. So Landon and I are at his house, and his parents still aren't home, which means we don't even bother opening the windows since it's colder than a witch's you-know-what outside. No offense to Meg, of course.

Landon blows out smoke and then hands me the joint, which I take and lean back against the pile of pillows as I take a hit.

"And apparently you missed band."

Landon snorts. "Your lunch period is way better than Sousa's ten millionth march. No one should be forced to endure hearing three piccolos playing at the same time."

"I went to watch Jamie work." Landon raises a brow at me, so I explain. "He's a sophomore. Jamie Fisher? Blond? He's into art and stuff."

"Oh, so the whole 'watching Jamie work' thing wasn't a euphemism?"

I kick lazily at Landon, who's sitting cross-legged by my feet. He reaches up and steals the joint back. "No, I like watching him paint. He's, like, serene or something when he does it. I have this theory that we both go to the same place—when we're working, I mean. He's in this creative, peaceful headspace. It's exactly where I am when I write. I keep thinking that if I was writing at the same time he was painting, maybe we'd meet up, and he'd start painting me, and I'd write him into my story."

Landon blinks. "Wow, this pot is stronger than I thought."

"Shut up."

Landon laughs and slides down on his stomach, stretching out beside me. "I think I know him. Hangs out with Sean Houser and Kit MacDonald?"

I try to think. "I don't know. Maybe? We don't talk all that much."

"Too busy 'watching him work'?"

I glare at him. "It's not like that."

Landon nods, a know-it-all smirk spreading his lips wide. "Sure. You and the pretty boy just talk. But not about his friends."

"There's nothing going on with us. Really."

"But you want there to be?"

I take the joint and breathe in, turning the thought over in my mind. "I don't know. I like him, but I don't want to jump in like I did with Gus. I think he might fit my list better than Gus, when it comes down to it. He's really shy but that doesn't stop him from being fun. Or ambitious. You know, he works as a busboy at Seven Sauces to pay for art school when he graduates. And there's something so charming about how quiet he is. But I'm kind of scared I'll spook him, you know? Like if I'm too forward, he'll just run away."

"Is he out?"

"We've never really talked about that either," I answer. Landon shoots me a dubious look. "I really do just watch him paint most of the time."

Landon sits up suddenly, shaking the bed and disturbing my comfort. "Gus asked me about you today, by the way."

"About me?"

Landon nods. "Must have been desperate. He wanted advice on how to get you back."

I sit up too, and I feel my heart like a jackhammer in my chest, which is just ridiculous because I'm over Gus and I couldn't care less if he wants me back. "What did you say?"

"Basically, I told him you're a stubborn bastard and it's an exercise in futility."

I let that digest for a minute, then sit back, nodding in agreement. "Damn straight," I say.

He chuckles at that, then sobers before asking, "Gonna ask Jamie out?"

"Should I?"

Landon looks out the window, and for a minute I don't think he's going to answer me. He seems to have gotten lost in a daydream. Then he turns his face back to me, trying to smile, but his eyes are tired and dull, so it doesn't quite achieve the desired effect. "If you like him, Sam, go for it. Who knows? Maybe he really is the one the Goddess sent."

I nod, because maybe that's true, and I'm beginning to hope it is. But that's not what I'm concerned about right now. I don't like the way Landon looks so *weary.*

"We don't have to do anything tonight if you don't want," I offer, trying to let him off the hook. "I'm tired too."

Landon groans in frustration. "It's Friday. Shouldn't we be ready to stay out all night doing God knows what? We're seventeen, damn it."

I laugh and pat his knee. "It's been a weird week, what with the whole Gus thing and you running rumor control."

"We could watch bad movies and make fun of them."

"Or we could watch *The Breakfast Club* again."

"Sam, I love you, but if I have to see Molly Ringwald's face anytime in the near future, my head is going to explode."

I pout. "But it's John Hughes."

"Head." He points to his temple. "Explode."

"Fine. Bad movies."

Landon gets up to dispose of what's left of our joint, which is about nothing by this point. He steps into his tiny bathroom and I hear a toilet flush, then he reappears in the doorway. I roll over on my stomach and look at him.

"What's up with you and Jeff?"

He leans against the door frame and runs a hand through his hair, making it even messier than normal. "Nothing now, really. Everything happened over the summer."

"So the night at Casa . . . ?"

Landon smiles. "That really was about seeing the jazz professor."

"Didn't work out?"

"Nah." Landon shoves his hands into his pockets. "Like I said, it wasn't a big deal."

I nod, understanding. I don't ask anything else, as much as I want to. If Landon says it wasn't a big deal, then there's nothing more to talk about.

"What bad movies do you have? Should we raid your dad's collection?"

Landon laughs and pushes off the door frame, offering his hand to me to help me up. He pulls me to my feet and then I'm standing so close to him we could almost Eskimo kiss. This close, the dark circles under his eyes look nearly black.

"You sure about the movie? I can get out of here and let you sleep."

Landon shakes his head. "No, stay. Keep me company for a while."

I pause. He's so tired, but he's been all alone in this huge old house for a week. Goddess knows I'm not one to feel unsympathetic to loneliness, and so I stay.

Nine

There's no avoiding Gus at school the following Tuesday. I can almost feel it before it happens too, like an itch just under my skin that makes me nervous and twitchy. And since my intuition is seldom wrong, I'm on edge all day, suspicious of every corner, waiting for something to surprise me.

He finally catches me after school. By that time I've braced myself and I'm ready.

"Samson, please talk to me."

I'm sitting on the steps that lead out the back doors of the school to the student parking lot, waiting on Landon and Meg so we can do our Donkey routine. I stand, hoisting my bag up over my shoulder. "What is there to say, exactly? You have a boyfriend. And it's not me."

Gus looks appropriately sheepish, and it's so cute I almost want to pull him into my arms.

Almost.

"I do not like ze way zings ended. I zink if we go somewhere and talk—"

"Again, there's nothing to talk about."

"But if I can explain more about Gabriel—"

"Are you still in love with him?"

Gus blinks, then his face falls. *"Oui."*

"Then there's nothing to discuss."

"If you would just listen to reason—"

"What reason?" I snap.

"Samson, please—"

"Is there a problem?" I feel a small hand slip into my own, and a warm shoulder pressing against mine. I turn my head and Jamie's smiling up at me. It's a beautiful, life-saving smile. I squeeze his hand and he turns to Gus, canting his head to the side. "My boyfriend and I need to get going, so unless this is important, perhaps you should move along."

The look Jamie gives Gus is equal parts guts and pure will, and Gus is clearly as surprised as I am. He moves backward a bit, nearly losing his footing on the stairs.

"Boyfriend?" Gus asks, and for a second I actually pity him. He looks genuinely hurt.

"*Oui,*" Jamie says in a mocking tone. "He's told you it's over. Take the hint, Frenchie."

Gus looks at me as if I can provide some sort of confirmation, so I jerk my head in the direction of the parking lot, telling him exactly where he can go. With a slight pout of his lips, he finally leaves, glancing behind himself at me once as he's walking away.

As soon as he's out of earshot, Jamie takes my face in his hands. "Are you okay?"

"Are you?" I ask incredulously. Somehow, the quiet

artist saved my whole day by risking his own neck. "I can't believe you did that. You're my hero."

Jamie strokes his thumbs across my cheeks and releases me. "I didn't like how uncomfortable you looked."

"He could have punched you or something."

"Nah, look at me. I'm huge." He makes a show of flexing nonexistent muscles in his skinny arms and I chuckle. "Besides, it would have been worth it."

I can't help myself. I melt a little at that. Okay, a lot. I feel like I could drip onto the sidewalk like a candle that's been burning too long, warm and gooey.

Jamie studies me thoughtfully. "You didn't come during lunch today."

"Sorry," I say, regretting skipping out on him even more than I did at lunch, when Meg was falling apart over finding flirty texts between Michael and another girl on his phone, and I was doing massive tear/snot cleanup in the girls' restroom. "Meg had a crisis. Her boyfriend's an asshole."

Jamie gives me a small smile. "I understand that. I mean, Kit's boyfriend is a major jerk and she's always upset for one reason or another."

I squint at him. "Kit's a girl?"

"I've never told you about Kit?" Jamie asks, who looks as bewildered by that as I feel.

"No." I reach out and take his hand, and he lets me. I can feel dried paint on his palm as our hands mold together. "You know, as much as I love watching you paint, maybe we should do something that requires an actual conversation."

"What do you mean? Like—like a date or something?" Jamie asks, adorably hopeful.

"Exactly like a date."

"Oh."

"Well, if you're not interested—"

"I'm interested!" he interjects, and I have to chuckle a little.

"How about Saturday?" I ask, and just as I do, Landon and Meg step out of the school, chattering their heads off at each other. They stop cold when they see me with Jamie, hands entwined. "I'll pick you up at seven and we can, I don't know, find something to do?"

Light laughter flutters from Jamie's throat. "Sounds great."

"Perfect." I squeeze his hand one more time before dropping it. Over his shoulder, Landon and Meg are making faces at me, trying to get me to laugh. I shoot them a dirty look. "I'll see you Saturday. Or tomorrow, I guess. If you don't mind me bugging you in the art room during lunch."

"Tomorrow," Jamie agrees, and begins to walk away, but I hate to see him go. I call out after him.

"Hey, can I walk you home?"

Jamie turns. He points in the exact opposite direction of my house: the east end. It's down the hill and literally on the other side of the town's train tracks. "My house is that way."

I point west. "I'm over there."

Jamie ponders that. "Then why don't I walk you? I

don't mind. And there's somewhere I'd like to go, anyway."

"Great idea, Jamie," Meg says, insinuating herself into the conversation. "Sam can drive you home."

I shoot her a look because I was doing just fine on my own, thank you very much. She covers her mouth with her hand and whisper-shouts at me, "We'll see if this is the one the Goddess truly sent."

I look at Landon, who shrugs as if to say, *Maybe she's not crazy. Go for it,* and I turn back to Jamie.

"Okay, fair knight, lead the way."

....

There's something different about the way Jamie and I talk to each other now that we're out of the school, the art room; now that we both aren't distracted by watercolors and bird wings. Maybe it's the fresh air, or the new light, or maybe it's just the freedom, but we move from polite small talk to genuine conversation. Jamie, unlike I had first pegged him, doesn't suffer from a lack of confidence even if he is quiet and reserved. He knows what he's about. He's got opinions and he's not afraid of sharing them; he just doesn't argue them aggressively like Landon, but he doesn't make jokes to distract away from real conversation like Gus either.

Luckily, there's not much we disagree about. Our biggest sticking point is that he says the Back to the Future series is better than Indiana Jones. I can't let that slide.

"Come on," I say. "Harrison Ford and Sean Connery

in the same frame. Archaeology. Nazis. You can't beat it."

"Christopher Lloyd and Michael J. Fox," Jamie counters. "Time travel. Punching the school bully in the face."

He's got a point there, but I sigh dramatically as if he's completely hopeless. We've walked as far as the cemetery, and I'm about to ask him if it would be weird for him to cut through it when he points at the gate.

"Mind if we go through there?"

"You read my mind."

But instead of going straight through the middle, like Meg and I usually do, Jamie veers off to the left, on a narrower and twisting path. He obviously knows where he's going, so I just follow his lead. Then suddenly Jamie stops, looking down at one of the gravestones with an expression on his face that I can't read. In front of him, a nearly perfect rectangle of grass is slightly greener and prettier than the grass surrounding it, and there is a plastic bird on each side, staked into the ground. They're the kind with the wings that spin like propellers with the wind, like you see in some people's yards. Several pots of silk flower arrangements are placed around the headstone. I read the name.

"James Fisher," I say out loud.

Jamie nods. "My dad."

I read the dates. The last number tells me that Jamie's dad passed away only two years ago, and if I'm doing the math right, he was only forty-six.

"I'm so sorry. I didn't know."

"I didn't tell you," Jamie says.

"What happened?"

"Early-onset ALS," Jamie said. I shake my head, unfamiliar. "It's what Stephen Hawking has. However, Hawking's developed rather slowly. My dad's progressed quickly, far too quickly for treatments to do much good. No one knows why he got it; there's no family history. No one knows why it happened so early and so quickly either. All we really know is that it was a lucky thing that my mom happens to be a nurse. Dad was able to live at home, and Mom made his last years as comfortable as she could for him."

"That had to have been so hard," I say dumbly, unsure of what else to say.

Jamie acknowledges that with a hum. "It was. But there's a small bit of comfort in knowing that he's not miserable and in pain anymore."

"I'm sure," I say. I look away from the stone and to Jamie. "You miss him."

"Every day," Jamie answers. "I miss having a dad, you know? Mom's great, but there's so much stuff that I wish my dad could be there for. Stupid stuff like making the honor roll, or finishing a difficult painting."

"It's not stupid stuff," I say. "I understand. You want him to see what you've accomplished and be proud."

"Yes," Jamie agrees.

"I get it. My dad misses a lot in my life and I always wish he was there," I say, then my words echo back to me and I cringe. "I'm sorry. That must have sounded really ungrateful and insensitive."

"It didn't," Jamie says. His pale eyes study me, gaze gentle as can be. "Your dad is gone a lot then?"

"Yeah. It started when I was in eighth grade. That's when he got famous." I use air quotes around the word *famous* because Dad isn't exactly someone who gets recognized on the street. He's literary famous. I continue. "It was always something. Book tours. Meetings with agents and editors and publishers and awards ceremonies. Seems like he's always got a few of those to attend."

"Seems like he is deserving," Jamie says. "My private art teacher made me read a few of his books. She said he was like a painter with words. She was right. He's a genius. I actually painted a piece based on *Backyards of the City*."

"Really? You didn't tell me you'd read any of his stuff."

"I didn't want to seem like a stalker."

I laugh. "Thanks, then."

Jamie is thoughtful. "Eighth grade. I was in eighth grade when Dad died. Seems like that's when everything's changing and you figure so much out. It's like the worst time to be without a father, however you're without one."

I nod, a lump in my throat making it nearly impossible to speak.

Jamie bends down and straightens the petals of a silk tulip. "I never got to tell my dad that I'm gay. I figure he had to know anyway, but I could never get the words out. He was so sick. It never seemed right to bring it up when he had so much else to worry about."

"Would he have been upset?"

Jamie shakes his head. "Not at all."

I reach down and take his hand into mine. Both our hands are bare and his fingers are like ice cubes. "You're freezing."

As if just now realizing it, Jamie shivers. "I guess I am. Are you sure you can drive me home?"

"Yeah, Mom will let me use the car," I say. I squeeze his hand. "Thanks for taking me here, Jamie."

Jamie looks into my eyes. "It's weird, Sam, but I had a feeling you'd get it. Maybe even more than my friends do." He looks away. "This will probably make me sound like a creeper, but there's always been something about you. Kit would joke about how I should ask you out, probably because you're one of, like, the only three gay people she knows. But I could never fight the feeling that she might be right. Every time I saw you I felt this strange pull. Like I just had to get to know you. Of course, I probably never would have had the guts to ask you out. If you hadn't been seated at my table at Seven Sauces, I probably wouldn't even have ever spoken to you."

For a moment, I consider telling him about the spell, about how perhaps this isn't all just coincidental that we finally spoke when we did. How I didn't even know he existed, then I do this spell and suddenly he's there at my table, and cute and talented and most likely all of the ten things I asked the Goddess for.

"Maybe it's fate," I say instead, smirking.

"Maybe," he says with a laugh. "Well, whatever it

was—fate or coincidence or gods conspiring—I'm thankful I finally got the chance to talk to you."

I get chills when he says that, and it has nothing to do with the cold. "Me too."

I thank him again when I drop him off at his house, a little two-story saltbox that could use a fresh coat of paint.

"So Saturday?" he asks.

"Saturday," I say, and I'm already counting down the minutes. I almost kiss him before he gets out of the car, but I hold back for some reason. I guess because I feel like our first kiss should be a moment entirely unto itself. He gives my hand a good squeeze before he leaves, though, and I drive away happy, not thinking about Gus, not thinking about Landon, and not thinking about loneliness.

....

Landon desperately needs help with his Latin so we stay far longer than usual at the Donkey the next day. That's just fine by me, and great for Meg, who had too much of her family over the weekend and is still moping about Michael. She fills Landon in, and all either of us can do is tell her it'll be okay, even though with Michael nothing's ever really going to be okay. But we're tired of that argument. I just hope it makes her reconsider her hotel plans.

I'm on my third chai, feeling a little wired, and the sun is well on its way to setting when I hear a scratchy voice say to Ted, "Hey, Teddy. Wanna hit me up with something strong?"

I turn my head and catch a whiff of leather and some kind of cologne, which is far spicier than anything I'd wear myself but that doesn't stop me from wanting to wrap myself around it and breathe it in. The bearer of that scent—and the scratchy voice—leans against the counter space next to me, and he turns and gives me a wink before yelling again at Ted.

"Espresso, Ted, or I'm gonna die!"

"Give me a minute, Travis. Geez. You're not actually going to die from lack of caffeine."

"Not willing to take the gamble," the guy named Travis shoots back at him, and then does the weirdest thing. He sticks his tongue out, revealing a shiny bar through the middle of it, and clicks it against his top teeth. Then he turns back to me and clicks in my direction.

I look at Landon to see if he's seeing this too, and he is. In fact, he's staring at this dude like I've never seen Landon stare before. He looks well and truly stunned, but it's in this completely worshipful way, and Landon is not the worshipping type.

Can't say I blame him. Tongue-Ring Travis is like Billy Idol's younger, hotter brother. The side of his head is shaved and long platinum-blond hair flops over it in this careless, deflated manner. He's got about ten earrings in each ear, big hoops and gauges, and one of his high-arching eyebrows is scarred like he once had a ring there too but it got pulled out.

Judging from the looks of him, a bar brawl seems like it could be a common occurrence in his life. He's part rock 'n' roll, part greaser, and all trouble. And the craziest thing is, regardless of the piercings and the leather jacket and the chains he's sporting, his face is . . . delicate. Blond scruff covers his jaw, but it's no match for the fragile features of his face, or the big whiskey-colored eyes that radiate warmth even while he's barking at Ted.

I theorize in that second that he was called "pretty" one too many times in his life, and the rebel-wear is his mode of overcompensation.

"Like tongue rings?"

Shit. While I've been psychoanalyzing, I've also been staring.

"Y-yes," I manage to stammer out.

"I bet you do," Travis purrs out in that scratchy voice, and scoots himself closer to me at the bar. Then his face is looming a mere centimeter from mine and he's clicking said tongue ring at me again. "Take a picture, it'll last longer."

"All right, Ponyboy, here's your coffee. Now stop harassing teenagers and find yourself another rumble." Ted sets down a paper cup of espresso in front of Travis and holds out his hand, expecting payment.

"Very clever, Teddy. I'd almost be willing to bet that you read or something."

To my utter shock, Ted's face blossoms into a warm smile and he swipes the bill Travis holds out for him. "Not since high school."

"You and me both, Sodapop. Later."

Then Travis is gone and I can't help but imagine a

tornado of cologne and anarchy swirling in his wake, like a good-smelling, gorgeous Tasmanian Devil. I swivel around to Landon to ask what, exactly, just went down, but he's already beaten me to the punch.

"Ted, that guy just now, was that . . . ?"

"Travis Blake," Ted says, barely looking up as he wipes down the bar with a coffee-stained cloth. "Lead guitarist for Liquid."

"I thought so. He's . . ." Landon doesn't finish his sentence, like he's too overwhelmed by Travis Blake's mere presence to think. Which is understandable.

"Yeah, he's a force," Ted replies. "Know his band?"

Landon nods. "Saw them at the Blue Gator last summer. They were amazing."

Landon's musical snobbery is even more deep-seated than mine, so if he's complimenting this band, they must be good. And that explains why Landon looked at Travis like he was a celebrity, not just some hot dude in a leather jacket.

"Yeah. He's in talks with a few labels, I think," Ted says but annoyingly doesn't elaborate, and then he's off to refill sugar canisters or something equally lame.

"Metal?" I ask, assuming from Travis's look that he's into the hard stuff.

"No. It's rock and it's edgy, but more electronic. Like . . ." Landon pauses, struggling to put it into words. "Like if you took Muse's guitar riffs and vocals, the Cure's darkness, and Depeche Mode's beats and put them all together in this glorious superband."

"That sounds amazing."

"It really is. We should go see them."

We look at Meg.

"No. No way," she says before I can even ask. "I'm not sneaking into some bar so that you guys can see that guy in his metal-whatever band. Besides, he was clearly straight. Gorgeous in that James Dean kind of way, but totally and completely straight."

"Chill out," I say. "Who said we're even interested?"

"Please. There are puddles of drool on the floor," Meg says, wrinkling her nose. "And you need to concentrate on Jamie, not some straight guy that's probably nearing thirty."

"Wow, don't jump to any conclusions there, Meg. Besides, we don't even know when they're playing next."

"Friday," Landon says, and Meg and I whip our heads in his direction. He shrugs, sheepish. "They're playing Friday at the Smiling Skull. I saw a flyer."

"There's no way we can get into the Smiling Skull," I say, deflated. It's a biker bar at worst and a total dive at best. And no matter what kind of fancy fake IDs Landon's friends might be able to swing, there's no way any of us could pull off looking twenty-one among that kind of crowd.

"No," Landon sighs out, "there's no way. Besides, Meg's right. You have a date with Jamie this weekend, and he could be your Perfect Ten, so concentrate on that."

I kind of pout and look to Meg for pity. "Landon just wants to keep the pretty rocker to himself," I whine.

"Doesn't make me any less right," Meg says, her nose pointing in the air.

"Exactly, so just enjoy a cute sophomore and stop being so fickle," Landon says, and finally closes his Latin book.

"I'm not being fickle. Travis was just . . . interesting, that's all," I say in defense. Then I picture Jamie, adorable Jamie, and *poof*! Travis is nothing but a distant memory. See? Totally not fickle. "Besides, it's not exactly a hardship to concentrate on Jamie."

"Or to, um, 'watch him work,'" Landon says, air-quoting.

I roll my eyes and shove Landon so hard that he has to grab on to the counter to keep from falling off his stool.

Ten

As it turns out, my good intentions were bested by fate, or the Goddess, or at the very least something completely beyond my control.

The following day, with only the purest thoughts about Jamie in my head (okay, maybe not *pure*, but nice thoughts nonetheless), I step out of the Donkey with a tall chai in hand and—*bam!*—someone barrels into me so hard that I wind up flat on my back on the sidewalk, wearing every drop of my chai, my books and papers scattered around me like the chalk outline at a murder scene.

"Shit," I hear a gravelly voice say, and I know that voice. My response is nearly Pavlovian, even though I've only heard it once before. I can't help it. His voice is droolworthy. "Sorry, dude."

Travis hunches over me, his blond hair falling all around his face. From this angle he looks like he walked off the cover of a Harlequin paperback. I imagine the title would be something lame like *Rebel with a Cause*, and that the heroine would slowly turn him from a bad boy to a suitable gentleman she could bring home to Mother. As long as he kept that wild streak in the bedroom, of course.

Which isn't too far off from the fantasies I'm sure I'll have about him later. But at the moment, with chai all over me, that's neither here nor there.

"Caffeine really isn't that life or death," I say, trying to temper my annoyance with humor.

He merely quirks a smile down at me. "I suppose not. Not if I'm gonna take out innocent bystanders in my quest for espresso."

He leans back and offers me a hand. I take it, shoving my humiliation aside as he helps me to my feet. Before he lets go and starts to help me gather my things, I notice his hands are rough, calloused—the sure sign of a practiced guitar player.

When I have all my possessions back in my arms he stands back, hands shoved in the pockets of his black skinny jeans, looking at the ground. "Shoulda looked where I was going."

"It's okay."

"You're wearing your coffee, man."

"Chai."

He looks up, rolling his eyes. "Whatever. Let me buy you some more."

"You don't have to do that."

"If I don't, I'll feel guilty for weeks. Let me get you another."

I cock my head, studying him. Those amber eyes are

soft, not hard, and apologetic. "You've quite the conscience for a badass."

"Who says I'm a badass?"

"Isn't that the look you're going for?" I gesture vaguely at him. "The leather jacket, the boots, the half-shaved head, the smudged eyeliner that's probably left over from last night."

Travis takes his hands out of his pockets and holds them up in the universal sign of surrender. "Okay, Mr. Observant. What are you, a psychiatrist or something?"

"A writer," I say back, and Travis actually looks impressed by that. "And if it'll quiet your conscience, buy me a cup of chai."

"What the hell is that stuff, anyway? You smell like cinnamon."

"You're not generally supposed to wear it," I say, glaring at him. "And it's tea."

"Smells like fruity hippie shit."

"It is, which is why I like it."

His face snaps up, his eyes meeting mine. We stare at each other for a minute, at some sort of stalemate over our difference in beverage choices as if it signifies an insurmountable difference in our personalities, and then he shrugs it off with a snort. I am, apparently, forgiven for being a hipster.

"Wait here," he says, lips parting into the sexiest, most promising smile I've seen. Ever. "I'll bring you more fruity hippie shit."

Two minutes later he's back and I'm holding a new

cup of chai and the old chai on my clothes is starting to get really cold. Which kind of sucks in early November. Travis takes one look at my shivering self and shakes his head, his hair flopping over his eyes.

"Come on, my apartment's right across the street," he says, stepping out into the street without even a glance of concern toward oncoming traffic. "You're freezing. You can borrow one of my badass jackets."

I follow him, sprinting into the street to catch up—not without looking both ways first, mind you. Travis isn't lying. His apartment is literally across the street, and he's fitting his key into the lock as I reach him. He kicks at the bottom of the door a couple of times and it swings open, revealing a flight of stairs.

Travis gestures for me to go in first, but I hesitate. He rolls his eyes. "I'm not going to harvest your organs or something."

I know that. Or at least I think I can sense that about him, but still. It hasn't occurred to me until now that I just followed a guy I don't even know to his house. Alone. But I can't really voice those fears out loud, that would be insulting to both of us, so I just stand there like an idiot.

"How old are you, exactly?"

"I'll be eighteen in a month," I say.

He nods, flicking his tongue ring against his top lip. "So when do kids these days outgrow that whole stranger danger thing?"

"I'm not scared—"

"Tell you what," Travis says, and he takes a step

closer to me so that our chests almost meet. The chai is cold against my skin but I feel his warmth beyond that, and my body aches to get closer. And it's such a *good* ache. "Come in, and I promise I'll put my kitchen knives away. Maybe I'll even keep my hands to myself."

I make a noise that may or may not be a small moan. "Okay."

He leads me up his stairs and into a small apartment at the top, which looks to be about three rooms in total. The staircase comes up to the living room. There's a kitchen next to it, and a little hallway where his bedroom must be.

Not that I'm even thinking about that.

I stand at the top of the stairs, watching as he digs through a pile of clothes on a futon against the wall. The whole place is kind of a mess, the way I figure college students live, with posters of bands and women with huge boobs on the wall. Then he whips a T-shirt at my face that I catch before it hits me. It's black, and on the front, in a deep turquoise color, the name Liquid is printed. The letters themselves look like they're dripping.

"Your band?" I ask, and he doesn't seem the slightest bit surprised that I know this information. He continues rummaging in the mess of clothing.

"Yeah. They sell like shit. Want another?"

I look at the shirt and smile. "No thanks. I'd like to hear your band, though."

He straightens and looks at me. "You're seventeen?"

I feel myself blush, suddenly embarrassed by my age. "Yeah. How old are you?"

"Twenty-one." I sink at that answer. Almost out of college. Almost into a different stage of life altogether. For some reason, age feels like a bigger stumbling block between us than his penchant for posters of women in leather bathing suits. "But I'm asking because you could hear us, if you went to the Smiling Skull tomorrow night."

He goes back to searching and pulls out a jacket that, surprisingly, isn't leather, but is black all the same.

I take the jacket from his hands with a nod of thanks. "I can't sneak in there. No way."

"No, but I could leave your name at the door. If I want you there, they won't ask questions."

My mouth falls open. "And you want me there?"

He jerks his shoulder. "It's the least I can do, after soaking you in chai. Don't expect too much, though. Vanessa's been playing like shit lately and Brendon's voice is still screwed from his cold."

"Landon says you guys are really good."

Travis blinks at me. "Well, if *Landon* says so . . ."

I close my eyes, embarrassed again. "He's my best friend. Kind of a self-proclaimed music critic. If he says you're good, you are."

He shrugs. "We've got a few possibilities. Indie labels, maybe something bigger."

"Wow," I say lamely. "So you're what, going to drop out of school?"

"Already did." I blink, and Travis rolls his eyes with an impatience that tells me he's already been over this with multiple people. "College isn't for everybody, man. Don't start."

I shake my head. "I'm not. If I had your talent I wouldn't go to college either."

"You don't know anything about my talent. Yet." He clicks his tongue ring against his teeth. "But you will if you come see us. Invite Landon too. Whoever. If they're with you, they're in."

"Okay, thanks."

"Whatever. You gonna put that stuff on or just stand there freezing?"

"What? Oh." I look down at the clothes he's given me and realize he wants me to change. Now. In front of him. I am rarely self-conscious about my body, but for the first time in years, maybe since Landon undressed me the first time, I feel bashful.

Then I square my shoulders and tug my shirt over my head, because damn it, this is why I do sit-ups.

Before I have the Liquid shirt pulled down over my skin, Travis's hands are on me. On the skin of my stomach. I let out a yelp, startled, and he just chuckles, his breath coming out in hot bursts against my neck as he pulls me against him.

"Sorry, I know I promised to keep my hands to myself . . ."

"No, it's just . . ." Wow, he's close and he smells *so good* and his hands are like fire on me. I struggle to pull myself together and nod to the posters over his shoulder. "You seemed like maybe boys weren't your thing."

"Boys are just one of my many things," he growls out, and pulls me closer so that his hands fan out across the skin of my back and our mouths are close enough to kiss.

And Great Goddess I hope we're going to.

"Oh," I whisper. "Good."

"Yeah, it's good." Then he does kiss me. Kind of. He licks at my lips, sliding that metal knob in his tongue between them to part them, and *then* he kisses me. He tastes like he smells—spicy and dark, and I swear for a second that this must be what danger itself tastes like. The good kind of danger. When your heart is racing and blood is pulsing in your veins and you know something's coming. Something amazing.

When he pulls away all I can do is hold on to his shirt, steadying my swaying body, like how the drunk college kids hold on to the lamp posts uptown on Friday nights. He chuckles again.

"What name should I leave at the door?"

"I'm, um . . ." Shit. What *is* my name? Travis laughs, wicked and mocking, and it clears my head just enough to remember. "I'm Sam. Sam Raines."

Travis takes the black jacket from my hands and helps me into it, clearly amused. I'm moving slowly, still like a drunk, and I think I might actually be in shock. Kissing Travis Blake was definitely the last thing I imagined I'd do today.

"Get home safe, Sam. I'll see you tomorrow." He takes my chin in his hands, forcing me to look at him, his skin as rough as his manhandling of me. Part of me feels insulted by that; part of me hopes he'll do it again. "Bring my jacket back. And tell your mom you won't be home until morning. We've got plans after the show."

I suck in a breath, thrilled and terrified at what he means, but I nod to him and say as casually as I can, "See ya," before heading down his stairs without a backward glance.

....

The note I pass to Landon through Rachel Gliesner the next day at school simply reads, *Tonight. The Smiling Skull. Pick me up at 9.*

Of course I get a note back in big capital letters saying, *WHAT???* that I don't answer. At least not until after Latin, when Landon corners me in the hallway.

"How?" he says.

"Travis is going to leave my name at the door," I answer, trying not to look overly pleased with myself. That only leads to more questions from Landon, which I shrug off by saying I just bumped into Travis at the Donkey yesterday—literally, ha—and he promised to get me in. I leave out the whole thing about borrowing his jacket and the spilled chai in general, and I most certainly leave out the part where Travis kissed me dirtier than I've ever been kissed in my life.

Not that it matters. I was only up all night thinking (er, fantasizing) about it.

"Tell Meg if you see her before I do," I say, knowing that sending her a text will be useless. Having a cell phone out during school hours means instant detention at Athens High, and Meg is one of those strange people who prides herself on going her entire high school career without receiving a detention.

At lunchtime, I head to the art room. Jamie's whole being lights up when he sees me, and my stomach clenches with guilt about Travis. But that wasn't my fault, I reason. Travis kissed me without provocation. Hell, he practically jumped me. There was nothing I could do. Besides, it's not like me and Jamie are a couple. We haven't even gone on a date yet.

"Hey," he says, coming over to me and plastering himself against my side. He's gotten a little bolder with me since I asked him out, and I'm really beginning to love that he doesn't hesitate to touch me anymore.

I wrap an arm around his waist and hold him close. "Hey. What are you working on today?"

His smile is proud, but of the shy variety. "I finished the Jubjub earlier, so I was just going to clean up."

"Can I see?"

He nods at me and lifts a paint-stained finger in the direction of an easel in his corner. I leave him to wipe off his hands and make my way to the canvas. The finished Jubjub is electric magenta and purple, soaring among stormy, silvery clouds. It's beautiful as it struggles against the thunder, its eyes focused on something below, its expression almost human and full of desire.

"It's amazing, Jamie. How do you do this?"

Jamie comes to stand by my side, looking at his painted bird with a critical eye. "You like it?"

"I love it."

"Then it's yours."

"What?" I turn to him, startled. "You can't . . . you should sell this or something."

Jamie shakes his head and looks me in the eye, determined. "I want you to have it. Unless you'd rather have another. Like the phoenix or something. It's not done yet, but you can have it when I'm finished. Or any of them. Whichever you want. Or if you don't want them I can paint something else."

I pull Jamie into my arms, nearly crushing him to me. "Are you sure?" I ask him. It's unbelievable that he would want to give me the painting, but then, if he's the real Perfect Ten, that seems about par for the course.

He pushes me back, just enough so he can look into my eyes. "Yeah. But only if we're still on for tomorrow."

"Tomorrow, yes," I say even as my mind drifts off to tonight, when I'll be listening to Travis's band play and who knows what else afterward. The guilt punches me in the gut again.

"So what should I wear?"

I give him a sheepish smile. "I don't know what we're doing yet. Been trying to wrack my brain for an idea since I asked, but nothing around here seems suitable."

Jamie gives me one of his smiles, his special brand of coy. "I don't care what we do, Sam. I'm still just kind of in shock that you're interested."

I can't help but chuckle a little. "Why is it shocking that I'd be interested in a gorgeous, talented artist?"

Jamie grins. "Gorgeous, huh? If you say so."

"Jamie, if I could paint, you'd be my first subject." He laughs and it's like a summer breeze flowing through the room. Just then, an idea blindsides me. A brilliant idea that might really impress the gorgeous artist. "Hey, would you be willing to wake up early and travel a little tomorrow?"

He narrows his eyes, suspicious. "How early?"

"Like, nine-ish? I want to take you somewhere."

"If you must," he says, feigning irritation. His eyes are laughing. But then he gets a horrified look on his face. "Wait . . . I don't have to wear a suit, do I?"

I laugh and wrap my arms around him, and his body fits so well into the folds of mine that I almost sigh. "No. Jeans are fine. But look good, Fisher. I don't want to be able to take my eyes off you all day long."

"Color me intrigued," he says, slow and sly. "I'll definitely look my best."

His best, I realize with a slight groan, could actually kill me.

I spend the rest of the lunch period helping him wash out his brushes, our soapy hands touching often under the water in the sink, accidentally on purpose, my stomach in a nervous knot over our date the next day, Travis almost—but not quite—forgotten.

....

The bouncer at the Smiling Skull looks as though he could pick me up with one finger and snap my neck with two. Which is why I sort of stutter out my name as he looks over the lists on his clipboard. He finds my name but gives me a suspicious look, flashing a menacing yellow-toothed smile at me before saying, "You give anyone any trouble and your ass is brass."

If he were anything but a four-hundred-pound biker I would have criticized his use of a rhyming cliché, but the mental image of being pulverized by his huge hands makes me think better of it.

I grab both Landon and Meg and step inside the bar. It's just as rough as I always pictured it. Everything looks a little beat up, including the people. The floor is covered with something sticky, my guess is residue from about forty years' worth of beer spilling from frosted mugs. And it's green inside. I don't know whose bright idea it was to paint the walls kelly green, but for a townie bar, it's almost comical the way everything's lit up like Kermit the Frog. Makes the huge skull and crossbones painted above the bar look a little less threatening.

"I still would like to know how you did this," Landon says, and Meg nods vigorously in agreement. They both did their best to look the part tonight, dressing in nearly all black, tight clothes, hair messy, and Meg's even wearing a metric ton of black eye makeup. It would have looked good on Landon too. Would have made his pretty eyes stand out against his pale skin, but I don't comment on that.

"The powers of persuasion," I say as an answer, which doesn't convince either of them in the slightest.

"With Travis Blake? Yeah, right," Landon snorts, and then, as if I'd planned it, Travis appears behind me, one arm snaking around my waist possessively.

"You're here," he says, and nowhere in his voice is there a note of surprise.

"Had to return your jacket, didn't I?" I say back, touching the collar of his jacket, which I'm wearing.

"Looks good on you," he says, then leans in, mouth on the shell of my ear, my back pressed tightly against his front. "Going to look good on my floor tonight."

I hiss out a curse. I've never met anyone like him before, never known anyone who could say such filthy things with such powerful confidence, never known someone whose voice alone could make my knees buckle. And I've certainly never met anyone who could make me enjoy feeling like I'm nothing but a possession. I can't make sense of it or of him. My brain is a mushy mess of rights and wrongs, contradictory feelings, and in the end, all I can do is agree with him.

"See you after, then?" he asks, already knowing my answer. "Enjoy the show."

He nips at my neck before leaving, disappearing through a door next to the makeshift stage by the bar. I turn to Landon and Meg, barely seeing them because I can't think and I'm pretty sure my body is full of aching, burning fire.

It's Meg who speaks first. "What was that?"

"What?" I ask her.

"What do you mean what?" She's staring at me with a weird expression on her face that just might be awe. "Are you some sort of groupie now?"

"No," I say, defensive. "He invited me to the show yesterday and we talked a bit. That's all."

"And what about Jamie?"

"I'm seeing Jamie tomorrow."

"And having sex with Travis tonight, apparently."

"I never said—"

"Please, you all but promised him just now." Now Meg is angry. But it's like she's not just angry, there's something underneath. Worry, maybe. Or worse, disappointment. I feel my cheeks flush with a bit of shame and try to explain myself.

"I like Jamie. A lot, okay? But it's not like it's serious yet. I barely know him. And Travis . . . he does something to me, you know?"

"Yeah, I bet I know what he does to you," Meg says, disgusted.

"Yeah? So? I'm not allowed to flirt or have fun? Just because you think Jamie's the one your precious goddess sent—"

"He might be!" Meg exclaims, then she lowers her voice so only me and Landon can hear. "But you know Travis isn't. Just look at him."

My anger flares. "Being a little judgmental, aren't we?"

"Please. Do you honestly think you're the first name he's put on a special list? You're probably not even the only one tonight." Meg nods to the front of the stage, where quite a few beautiful human beings, boys and girls, have gathered, vying for the front row. "Is that what you want to be? Just one in a crowd?"

"Maybe that's the way it would be, but maybe not," I say.

Meg's eyes widen. "Good Goddess, Sam. Please do not be one of those people who think they can change someone else. Especially someone like Travis Blake. He probably doesn't even know what the word *monogamous* means."

I snort. "I can't believe you, of all people, have the nerve to say that to me."

"Don't you dare make this about Michael."

I grab my hair in frustration. "I know. I can never make anything about Michael, can I?"

Meg ignores me and turns to Landon instead. "You talk some sense into him. I need some fresh air."

Meg stalks toward the door and I turn toward the stage, which means I don't have to look at Landon. I feel him next to me, watching me. He shifts uncomfortably, then says, "Low blow, man."

"Whatever. It's true."

"Still," Landon says. Onstage, someone is testing microphones. "You know she's right about Travis."

I want to scream or kick something, but instead I only grit my teeth. "Maybe."

"Don't be mad. I'm just confused, that's all." Landon's voice is so calm it makes me feel completely out of control. "I mean, I know you. You're way too smart to have to be told all the stuff Meg just said. So I guess I just don't know what you're doing here."

"I don't know how to explain."

"Try."

Because he's Landon, and I can always be honest with Landon, I finally look at him and say, "I got a little freaked out. With Gus."

Landon says nothing, but makes a circular motion with his hand, signaling for me to go on.

"I stopped him. When we were kissing and it was clear he wanted to keep going, I stopped him. And he called me out about it."

Landon waves my words away. "Then it was instinct. You knew he wasn't as into you as you wanted him to be. Which is why I'm so confused that you're going home with Travis tonight. I mean, you said you didn't want a hookup."

"I know," I admit, somewhat ungraciously. I glance over at the stage. No sign yet that the band is ready, and Travis has disappeared. "But . . . about Gus . . . I don't know that it was instinct, Landon. I think I was just scared. It was a little overwhelming with you and me."

I pause while Landon chuckles. "Everything about us was overwhelming, Sam."

"I know. But . . ." I shrug and Landon nods, and I know he's picking up what I'm laying down. "I don't have that kind of fear with Travis, like I did with Gus."

"Fear that you might get hurt. Fear that it's all going to get screwed up."

"Yes."

"Because you're not invested with Travis. So it's easy."

"Yes, exactly!" I proclaim, relieved. "It's easy. There's nothing riding on it. Nothing holding me back. In a way, he feels . . ."

"Safer?" Landon ventures.

I look at him. Over the last few years his face has lost some of the boyishness I liked so much about him when we first met. His round features have sharpened a little, and maybe it's not that his face has hardened, but it's not as soft either. He's more handsome than cute. It fits, because at this moment, he seems light-years more mature than me.

"Safer," I agree.

Landon crosses his arms over his chest, thinking hard. I can practically see the gears up there turning. "I can see that. By your logic, it would be a lot easier to go home with Travis, as opposed to Gus or even Jamie, have some fun, not worry about what it means in the morning because you already know. But . . ."

"I should have known there was a 'but.'"

"I think you might miss out on the best part that way."

There is far more truth and emotion in that statement than I can handle at the moment.

It's then that the lights suddenly go down and Travis and his band, Liquid, walk out onstage. There's screaming, even before the first chord, and Travis looks out over the crowd. His eyes lock on mine, holding me hostage until he finally breaks the gaze and looks down at his guitar. After a few beats from a kick drum, his hands go flying, and music spills from his guitar like it had been trapped within, dying to get out.

Their lead singer has a hell of a voice, their bassist is incredible, and their drummer is most likely a prodigy. But I keep my eyes on Travis. He's the real star. Even though the others put up a valiant fight for attention, there's something about Travis that pulls. His hair hangs down in his face, obscuring eyes rimmed with liner, a focus so intense on his guitar that I'm actually jealous of the instrument.

I turn to Landon and see that I'm not the only one who feels a pull toward Travis Blake.

"Would you go home with him?" I ask, a delicate question shouted over the noise.

Landon's eyes never leave Travis, but his mouth forms a smirk. "There's a lot to be said for *safety*, sometimes."

I laugh and go back to watching the band.

Meg returns a few minutes later, arms crossed over her chest and cheeks flushed. Although I'd like to assume it's from the cold outside, she focuses a lethal stare in my direction, and I know she's still angry as hell.

"Hey," I shout to her. "I'm sorry. I was a jerk. You were just being a concerned friend again. Which is awesome."

She nods. "I'm going to stop it if I keep getting my head bit off."

Point taken, I nod back and I think and hope that argument is over. For now. She's staring at Travis now too, and although I can tell she's trying not to, her body's moving a bit to the music, her old ballet instincts taking over with graceful swaying even with a guitar wailing and synthesizers throwing down a heavy beat.

"So what did you decide?" she asks.

As soon as the question is out of her mouth, a bleach-blonde waitress saunters up to us in a pair of ripped jeans and a leather vest. Only a leather vest. She looks like she walked out of one of the posters on Travis's wall. And even though none of us are particularly interested in the female gender, all three of us stare.

"From Travis," the blonde says with a wink, and leaves a drink with each of us. I look at Meg, who is trying her best not to look scandalized, and then take a sip. I almost choke. It's like battery acid. I'm not a big drinker but I know enough to recognize that whatever it is, it packs a hell of a punch. But then the crowd erupts and I turn to watch the band again. Travis is on his knees, ripping into a guitar solo that sends electricity through my body. Then he looks up at me through the fringe of his bangs and licks his lips.

My body lights up again. I could swear the whole room senses something between us, and I can't help but smile triumphantly.

That gorgeous rocker on the stage is mine. At least for tonight. And maybe that's not a bad thing.

"I don't really have to decide anything right this minute, do I?" I ask my friends. Meg shoots me a look, but Landon's eyes twinkle with mischief.

"Not right this minute," he says, then he taps on my glass. "I'm not sure this will help, though. At least not in a good way."

I look into the clouded purple contents of the drink Travis sent to me like it's a crystal ball with all the answers. I see nothing about my future in its depths. I wave it in front of Meg's face. "Can you read vodka swirls? Or is it only tea leaves?"

Meg gives me a slight knock on the side of my head. "Think with your brain, Sam. Think about Jamie and your list. You don't need tea leaves to hear what the Goddess is saying to you."

"Maybe. Or maybe She's telling me to go for it."

I give Meg and Landon a wicked smile, down my drink, and signal to the waitress for another.

....

I've had three of those purple drinks by the time Liquid is done with their set, and I wouldn't call myself *trashed*, per se, not in the strictest sense of the word. More like euphorically intoxicated.

Landon and I dance nonstop, and Meg joins in when she's not taking our cups away or chasing waitresses off. Apparently Travis told them to keep the drinks coming, and Meg has taken it upon herself to ration the alcohol. I'm assuming so we don't embarrass ourselves. Or more importantly, her.

When the show's over, the place goes dark for a full minute and the crowd begs and screams for more. But in the blackness, I feel strong, lean arms around me and I know the audience isn't going to get an encore. Travis has saved the encore for me.

He's kissing me as the lights come back up, and when he pulls away, Landon and Meg are staring, jaws dropped.

"Thanks for the drink. Or drinks," I sort of slur out. I sway a little to the music still humming in my brain.

"It's called a Black Widow," he says, eyeing me. "They're pretty but lethal. How many did you have?"

"Three," Meg answers for me at the exact moment I hiccup through the words, "Just one, I swear."

Travis chuckles, and Good Goddess is he sexy when he chuckles. I lay my head on his shoulder. His whole shirt is soaked with sweat. He smells like someone who has been doing cardio for a few hours, but yet, somehow, he doesn't smell bad at all. Just sort of manly. Rocker godly. I giggle into his wet shirt.

"Feeling okay?" Travis whispers to me, and I pull back so I can look into his face. It's like he's said some magic spell and now we're the only two people in the room.

Heh. Magick.

"I feel awesome," I hear myself answer. And then, with all the finesse I can muster (which isn't much after three Black Widows), I cram my tongue down Travis's throat. He apparently isn't too surprised, or maybe he's just used to people sticking their tongues in his mouth, because he kisses back without the slightest flinch. When we pull away, we're both panting, and my ego balloons at that.

I go to kiss him again and he stops me, his hand cupping my jaw. "We should get out of here," he murmurs, glancing around us pointedly. I follow his gaze. Most of the young crowd that came here to see his band have left, and what remains are older men who look like they're ready to round up a posse and be a little less tolerant of the boy in eyeliner kissing another boy.

"Huh. Yeah. Where should we go?" I ask, doing my best to act innocent. I fail and giggle, and there goes the last of my dignity.

"I think he needs to go home," I hear Meg say somewhere off to my right, and damn, the spell is broken.

Travis's hand is on my chin again, turning my gaze to meet his. "You really had three?"

"Just three," I say, to clear up the confusion.

"Right. A mere three Black Widows." Travis is amused. "I forget how to play guitar after three."

"But you're so good at guitar," I say, and it's all whiny. Landon snorts and I reach behind myself to give him a playful punch. I miss.

Travis breathes a very creative curse. "I told Melanie to go easy on you."

"I can handle liquor," I say with a pout. Then I sort of sway into him and bump my nose on his shoulder.

"Obviously," Travis says, but he's not upset. He's still just amused, perhaps even entertained. Ha, now he's the one getting the show.

"You need to go home, Sam," Meg says again.

Travis doesn't take his eyes off me. "You want to go home?"

"With you," I say. Finally, the answer to the question that he never really even asked, the question I've been debating all night. And now? There's not a doubt in my mind. Even after all the discussion and arguments with my friends. And maybe it's the Black Widow (nope, Widows, plural) talking, but I feel like I can trust him. Like maybe he has no intention of seeing me again after tonight, but he has no intention of hurting me either.

Travis grins at my friends. "I guess he's decided."

That's when Landon straightens to his full height, which is just about the same as Travis's, and shakes his head. "I don't think so, man. He's wasted."

"He needs to sleep it off. And probably take some aspirin," Meg says.

"You think I don't know how to handle a drunk friend?" Travis asks, and I think we all know that out of the four of us, Travis most likely has substantially more experience helping drunk friends than we do. I mean, he's a *rock star*.

I giggle uncontrollably again and Travis shrugs my arm over his shoulder so that he can support my weight.

"It's the handling him I'm worried about," Landon says. It registers somewhere in my hazy brain that he says it with more anger than is really necessary.

Travis just stares at him. "Really? Who are you? His mother? His boyfriend?"

"I'm just a friend."

"A friend who doesn't think Sam is capable of making his own decisions."

"You call this being fully capable of making his own decisions?" I sense Landon is gesturing at me, and I'm pissed at his implications, and all that manifests as giggles. Again.

But then I'm being transferred to Meg for support, and Travis and Landon step away to the side of the bar. I can't hear what they're saying over the other voices in the room and the classic rock coming from the jukebox that I hadn't noticed before, but I can see that whatever is being said is not pretty. Then Travis leans in to Landon.

For a second I think Travis is going to kiss him. I mean, as far as strategies go, it wouldn't be a bad idea. Kiss Landon as stupid as he kissed me the other day, then we can sneak out the door. But Travis says something directly in Landon's ear. Landon stiffens, but then something changes. He blows out a breath and nods to Travis. Then Travis is back, his arms around me.

"I promise, I'll get him home in one piece," he says to Meg, and I nod.

"Trust me, it will be okay," I say to her.

She looks like she'd like to fight about it, but Landon shakes his head, and she relents. "I'll tell your mom you're staying with me. Goddess, Sam, be safe. Text me. Continually, okay? Like every five minutes."

I can't promise her that, but I tell her again that everything will be okay. With one last glance at Landon, Travis turns us toward the door. He leads me outside to a bright orange Mustang that looks like it's on the verge of death. He helps me into the passenger seat and squats down next to the car. His shirt is still soaked with sweat, and his hair, I notice now too, is damp as well. He has to be freezing in this night air. I can't help myself. I reach out and touch his hair. He smiles at me, warmer than he ever has before, and gives my hand a squeeze before reaching under my seat and rummaging around for something.

He finds what he was looking for and hands it to me. It's a plastic bag from a local pharmacy, with the receipt still in it. I pull it out and read. He bought three things: Mountain Dew, 16 oz., Haribo Gummi Bears, 1lb., and *Rolling Stone*, September issue. I feel like this receipt sums up Travis in a way anything I'd write could not.

I look at Travis in question. "A plastic bag?"

He jerks a shoulder. "In the words of the great Garth Algar, if you're gonna spew, spew into this."

I don't ask him who Garth Algar is. I'll Google it when I'm sober. And luckily, I don't need to use the bag as Travis drives.

Travis's apartment is entirely too bright when we enter, but I like that it's a little familiar, as if that somehow makes all of this strange night not so out of the ordinary. I wobble slightly at the top of the stairs, and Travis catches my elbow, steadying me.

"Good?"

"Good," I reply. Then start off down his short hallway, toward his bedroom.

"Hey, Hemingway, where you going?"

"Bedroom," I say, although the echo in my ears sounds more like "bwedvoom." Way to go, Sam. Then I get it. I turn and point at Travis. "Ha, you're funny. And smart."

"Nah, I'm just using all my writer material on you. I

mean, who else am I going to use it on?" Travis takes my hand. "Water. Ibuprofen. Then bed for you."

"But, I thought—"

"I know what you thought. I spent the better part of the night thinking it too. But you, Mr. Self-Control, had to go and have three Black Widows."

I open my mouth to protest but Travis has fully adopted the role of the responsible designated driver for the evening. "Nope," he says, wagging a finger at me. Then he sighs when I pout. "Okay, maybe a little kissing. But then sleep. And if you still want to be in my bed when you wake up sober, we'll see about something more."

He gives me a bottle of water, a couple of pills, and crawls into bed with me. There are several more protests, which are silenced each time by Travis kissing me, and after a while I do fall asleep, visions of a sexy rock god dancing in my head.

....

My skull is splitting open when I wake up. I check to make sure it's still in one piece, and that's when I remember I'm not in my own room, but in Travis's, covered in his dark gray comforter. I sit up so fast I could swear my brain sloshes against my skull, and I grab my aching head and moan.

"You okay?" a scratchy voice says in the dark. Travis. Although my eyes haven't adjusted well enough to see him, I can feel the heat of his slim body against mine. "Need to throw up?"

I shake my head, which hurts, and say, "No. But I need to pee."

He gestures to a door across the hall, and I get up, carefully. I pee (how can I pee for five minutes straight when I'm this dehydrated?), flush, and fall with graceless apathy back into his bed.

"Here, drink this," I hear him say, and I open an eye. Travis is sitting up, offering me a bottle of blue Gatorade. "It'll help, I promise."

"What time is it?" I ask, my voice weak and whispery.

"Almost three a.m. Now drink."

I stare at him, confused, so he waves the bottle in front of my face. I take it and weakly unscrew the cap before downing half of it. I look around myself. Travis's room is how I pictured it: messy, masculine, and all shades of gray and black. His bed is hard, a little lumpy, and none of the sheets are tucked in at the sides. There are more posters of scantily clad women covering his walls, but also posters of the Cure and Depeche Mode. On the shelf next to the bed, there's even an autographed picture of Travis with someone, and I have to squint to make out the writing.

"David Bowie?"

"Yeah," Travis says, not taking his eyes off my face. "He was a great dude. Positive vibes all over the place."

I drink more of the Gatorade and his hand wanders

over the comforter, coming to rest on my knee.

"My head hurts," I say dumbly, because I don't know what else to say and all I really want to do is curl up under the covers and die.

Travis nods and motions for me to drink more Gatorade, which I do. I screw the cap back on the bottle and hand it back to him. It's then that I notice for the first time that he's placed a bucket next to my side of the bed.

"You thought of everything."

He shrugs. "Brendon has a tendency to drink too much. So does Vanessa. I'm a seasoned caretaker of drunkards." He squeezes my knee. "You all right? Remember everything?"

I try to think, but my thoughts are muddy. "You guys sounded awesome. The waitress wasn't wearing much. Meg and I fought, but Landon seemed okay until you came along. Then we came back here and . . ."

Travis looks down. "And we made out more than we probably should have. You were pretty trashed."

"But that was it."

Travis nods.

I close my eyes. So many what-ifs and should-haves and could-haves crowd my thoughts, so many possibilities that could have turned into regret, and he took all of those possibilities away and made me safe instead.

I swallow. Hard. "Thank you, Travis."

He understands what I'm saying to him. "Of course." He grins, wide and entirely too proud of himself. "I'm a gentleman and a scholar."

I laugh, which makes my head throb in ways I didn't know it could. I must make a noise at the pain because Travis reaches out and runs a hand through my hair. The gentle lift makes my scalp tingle and numbs some of my headache.

His gold eyes are fixed on mine, and his voice is gentle. "Any particular reason why you drank so much tonight?"

"I don't know," I whine, and hate how pathetic I sound. "The Black Widows were good and . . . I was a little confused, I guess. So I just kept drinking them."

"Hell of a way to search for clarity." Travis shrugs. "Whatever your method, dude. I'm just sorry I didn't have Melanie cut you off after the first one. At least Meg was there for you. And you should have warned me you were bringing a boyfriend along. I mean, shit. I thought he was going to kill me for a second."

"What?" I ask, my still-drunk brain futilely trying to catch up. "Jamie?"

"Jamie? I meant Landon. There's a Jamie too?" Travis snorts at me. "And here I thought I was the one being a player."

"Landon's not my boyfriend."

"But Jamie is?"

"No, he's not either. Why would you think Landon's my boyfriend?"

Travis lies down on his side, stretched out next to me. He's changed out of what he was wearing onstage, and now he's in a pair of green flannel pajama pants and a wife-beater, revealing artistic tattoos on his arms that I'd ask about if I wasn't in so much pain. "Oh, just his totally over-the-top 'hurt him and I'll kill you' act."

"He's just protective."

Travis's lips twitch. "Sure. Dude hated me."

I force a laugh, which makes my head feel like it might burst. "He wants you for himself. He was probably just jealous."

Travis eyes me. "I don't think it's me he wants."

If I had any fight in me, I would argue with that and explain that Landon and I are just friends. An especially close type of friends, I suppose, but still, just friends. "I'm sorry if he was rude," I say instead.

"Nah. He was fine. There was some yelling involved. Bared teeth, that sort of thing. Nothing I can't handle."

I remember now. How Landon acted, how Travis took him aside, out of earshot. I roll over on my side and look at Travis.

"What did you say to him that made him change his mind?"

"I told him he could punch me in the face if I laid a finger on you while you were drunk."

"You didn't."

"Why do you doubt me?"

I stare at him, then chuckle. Gingerly. "Well, I'm not sure he'll be happy that he doesn't get to punch you, even if I get to keep my virtue."

"Your virtue? Please. I'd guess Landon took your *virtue* long before last night."

"Shuddup." My cheeks grow hot, and Travis laughs a gravelly laugh. I choose that moment to move closer to him (hey, I'm an opportunist), and he follows my lead, pulling me until we're facing each other, our legs wrapped around each other's backs.

"Feeling sober?" he asks.

"All too sober," I say, and the joke lands with a thud.

"Clear head, though?" he asks, and as he does, he nips at my bottom lip.

"Um, well, not when you do that," I say as his lips trail lower, straight down my chin to my neck.

His laugh now is low, sexier. Dangerous. "Trust me, at least?"

"I think so. It's me I don't trust," I say. "I haven't acted like myself since I first saw you. You do something to me."

"I have that effect on men." I feel the curve of his smile against my neck. "And women."

I hum. "I bet you do."

"But you can trust me, Sam. Badass jackets and eyeliner aside, I'm not a bad guy."

Then Travis shifts us, expertly, and suddenly I'm flat on my back and his weight is on me, all one hundred and fifty-five pounds (rough estimate) of pure James Dean swagger. And I can't say I mind.

"And it's a good thing I'm not a bad guy. 'Cause I wanted you. Real bad. Still want you." He leans down and kisses me, just as dirty as the first time, all messy tongues and teeth and spit. His hair falls into my face, and I reach up and take it into my hands, surprised at how soft it is, and at the groan that comes from his mouth as I tug it a little. "You're hot. This geeky, smart kind of hot."

I lean my head back so that he can nip at my neck. "You're into geeks, huh?"

"That's top-secret information. I'd only admit it under severe torture," he answers between bites, and although I'm hardly the sadistic type, I have to admit that kissing like this is the best kind of torture there is. I'm about to crack some stupid joke about the UN approving making out as a torture technique when his hand wanders down. Too far down.

I freeze up, suddenly all too aware of the direction his hand is going, of the direction *we're* headed.

Travis notices the change immediately and draws back, sitting back on his heels. "Sorry, I forgot how old you are."

"It's not my age," I say, although the petulant manner in which I say it does nothing to prove that. "I'm not a virgin."

"Nah," Travis says, a smirk playing at his lips. "But you haven't since Landon, have you?"

I don't like the implications behind that statement, and I most certainly don't like how he knows that so confidently.

"I want you," I say to him, because that's the biggest truth of all the truths wandering through my hazy head right now.

"I know," Travis agrees, but somehow manages not to sound cocky. "And it's okay to be scared of that."

I don't argue with him. What's the point? He sees right through me. Instead, I reach up and brush his hair back from his eyes. "I'm sorry."

"Don't be," he replies, then he stands up, stretching. "Look, I'm not one of those relationship guys. I mean, I may be a good guy, but I'm also a musician, ya know? So I'm not promising anything, but . . . I would like to see you again. Maybe someplace that doesn't serve Black Widows."

"Really?" I ask, unable to believe it. He wants to give me a second chance.

"Yeah. I mean, nothing serious, okay? I don't do the whole romance thing. I just want a shot with you when you aren't drunk. Or hungover."

I laugh, but I have to look away from him because it is seriously regrettable that I got too drunk to really enjoy him tonight. I sit up and start looking for my phone, but Travis is a step ahead of me. My phone is resting on top of my clothes, neatly folded, and when I investigate my messages I can see Travis has already added himself in my contacts, and Landon and Meg have texted me a million times checking up.

"I'll drive you home. You could stay but I'm not sure how long I can keep up this good guy act with you in my bed," Travis says while I tug on my clothes. His eyes watch me carefully, greedily, and I feel more than flattered when he runs his tongue ring around the rim of his lips, licking his chops like I'm the most appetizing dessert he's ever laid eyes on.

It's almost three thirty when Travis pulls his beat-up old Mustang up to my curb. I tell him thanks, which covers all manner of sins, and he leans over, kissing me again. This time it's soft, teasing, neat—all of which he negates by nipping at my bottom lip before pulling away.

"Call me," he says. "Or I'll call you. Whatever. I don't really wait by the phone, ya know? But God help us when you're ready. I'm going to eat you alive."

Hours ago I would have seen that as a threat, but now I just smile in return and hope he doesn't make promises that he doesn't intend to keep.

"Later," I say as I step out onto the sidewalk. The Mustang is gone before I reach my door. I let myself inside, swallow five aspirin, and lie down. I have to meet Jamie in six hours, and I refuse to look hungover when I pick him up because, Goddess knows, that boy will look *gorgeous*.

Eleven

The November air is cool but there's not a cloud in the sky, and the bright morning sun makes me reach for my sunglasses as I drive down State Street. I've got at least a ten-minute drive ahead of me before I reach Jamie's house on the east side, knowing Athens's screwed-up stoplight system. Just enough time to call Landon.

I ignore the uneasiness in my stomach and hit his number on my speed dial.

"Hello?"

"Before you ask, yes, I'm all right, I have all of my organs still, and no, I didn't have sex with him. He didn't even try. Well, not until I was sober, anyway."

There's some clanging on the other end of the line and I would put money on it that Landon's doing his weekly room cleaning. Not that he's a neat freak. No, he's way too cool for that.

"Good. Glad to hear he didn't make a dress out of your skin or something," Landon says, and although I hear some relief in his voice, he's also strangely detached.

"Hey," I say, and the clattering in the background

stops. "Thank you for looking out for me. Travis said you were pretty upset."

"I was kind of a jerk to him, honestly."

"Well, he may have mentioned that too."

"I would have understood if he'd beaten the shit out of me. I think I accused him of being a sexual predator at one point."

I press the phone closer to my ear, maneuvering my car with only one hand. I can barely hear Landon. His voice is weaker than normal, almost fragile sounding.

"You were worried about me. He understood that." I pause, thinking of what Travis said last night. "That's all it was, right? Worry?"

Landon pauses too. I hear more rustling on his end of the line. "Yeah. Of course." Another pause, then, "I guess I didn't need to be. I mean, he's not exactly the type of guy who's going to stick around forever, but he seems decent. He wanted to take care of you."

I pull up to a stoplight, grateful for a slight reprieve from engine noise. "Is that why you let me go home with him? 'Cause you decided he was a good guy?"

Landon sighs so loudly that I hear it on my end. "That's just it, Sam. I shouldn't be *letting* you do anything. I'm not your mother or your brother or your boyfriend. If you want to have sex with Travis, you should have sex with Travis, and I need to just . . . let it go."

I reach up and rub my forehead. I don't feel hungover anymore, but I could swear my brain is not working at optimum capacity. It's like information is meandering through my synapses, not quite firing in the right directions, and it takes me a while to get what Landon's saying. "But you're my friend. That's part of what friends do. They watch out for each other."

"Yeah, that's what friends do," Landon says. "But friends should also let you make your own decisions."

I say nothing, and the stoplight turns to green, so I press down on the gas.

"Are you going to see him again?"

"I don't know. He wants to but he also kind of made it clear he's not into the boyfriend thing."

I hear Landon hum his agreement. "And you're seeing Jamie today?"

"On my way to pick him up. I'm going to take him to Yellow Springs to see the art."

"Sounds good."

There's dead air again for a while, which makes me even more uneasy than before. Landon and I never run out of things to say to each other, and even if we're silent, it's usually of the comfortable variety. This is definitely not comfortable.

"Are we okay, Landon?"

"Huh?" he asks, then hums again. "Yeah. We're fine. Sorry. Last night was really weird and, uh, I'm just really tired, you know?"

"Well, get some sleep. I'll call you tomorrow, okay?"

He agrees and we both hang up. Just in time, too, because I'm on Locust Street, which is Jamie's street, and I pull into his driveway. Jamie all but bounds out the front door and hops into the car, and I turn to him, amused.

"Good morning," he greets me, beaming, and drops a black peacoat into my backseat. I was right about him looking gorgeous. He's wearing a tight-fitting gray-and-white-striped shirt that I've never seen him wear before, with a vest over that and a pair of combat boots tugged up over his jeans. He looks more like a model than a sophomore in high school, and honestly, I'm not sure even Travis could compete with him at the moment.

"Morning." I reach down to the console and pull up a Styrofoam cup, holding it out to him. "Coffee. You're going to need it, trust me."

Jamie smiles and takes the cup, drinking a bit before fastening his seat belt. He bounces a little in his seat. "So are you going to tell me where we're going, or do I have to guess?"

"Are you up for a long drive?"

"Sure," he says, sipping more coffee, which I'm not entirely sure he needs now. He might be naturally wired. "I told Mom I'd be gone all day, and she's got the night shift anyway. She'll never know what time I got back."

"Good, 'cause where we're going is about two hours away." I put the car in drive and ease it back onto the road. "I thought we'd check out Yellow Springs."

"Seriously?" Jamie whispers with reverence. "I've wanted to go there forever. Did you know there's a potter there who uses a kiln that's over two hundred years old? And one of the watercolor artists there has something hanging in the Louvre? And the glassblower . . ."

I let Jamie talk as I pull onto the highway, and I feel my lips turn up into a smirk. Yes, ladies and gentlemen, Sam Raines is a *master* at planning dates.

....

While I'll admit that the idea of spending two hours in a car with a shy boy made me a little apprehensive, I'll also admit that it was a completely unfounded fear.

Jamie talks all the way to Yellow Springs like I've never heard him talk before. About everything, even the stuff that must be difficult. He tells me more about his father, and his father's disease, and the progression of it over the months before he died. He talks about his mother's job at the hospital. She's a neonatal nurse, which is apparently very rewarding but, at times, the hardest of all jobs at the hospital, and it takes an emotional toll on his mom, and sometimes him in turn. I'd had the impression before that his family didn't have much money, but as I drive he speaks openly about how hard it's been for him and his mom to handle his father's medical bills, and I find myself admiring him for working to pitch in, and for the way he's so unspoiled.

He gets me talking about my parents, and even though I'm used to their quirkiness, he thinks it's a riot. I guess to any normal person, living with two eccentrics–slash–college professors who are hippies that time forgot might be amusing, but to me they're just Mom and Dad. Still, I tell him how my mother gets herself whipped up into a historian frenzy every time she reads a new thesis on the Founding Fathers, and how my dad does his best writing at three a.m., with a bowl of sugared almonds and a cold Magic Hat #9 on hand.

By the time we're swinging around the outer belt of Columbus, we've moved on to music (our taste is different enough to be interesting, but not enough to make me cringe), politics (right in line there), and books (not the same at all, but he promises to try a few of my favorites if I give one of his favorite horror novels a chance). Before we pull into the town of Yellow Springs we've also discovered that neither of us can sing in tune, that we're both suckers for cheesy family sitcoms, and that we don't get the appeal of sushi.

If I had that stupid list that started this whole thing in my hands, I'd be checking each item off, one by one.

Yellow Springs hasn't changed much since the last time I was here, maybe three years ago. It's like Athens, only grown-up. There's a sophisticated feel to it all. The pre–Civil War homes and buildings house art galleries, record stores, jewelry shops, libraries, wine cellars, and antique dealers, and the brick streets are alive with collectors and intellectuals and artists.

I park at the old train depot, which is now a yoga studio, and as Jamie and I climb out of the car, our eyes meet and we grin like idiots. The town feels like a home, a haven, a place where even amateurs like ourselves belong.

"What first?" I say, taking his hand.

"The potter? The glassblower? Maybe we could go into that museum over there, the one with the sculpture outside?"

I look all around myself. I can feel his excitement buzzing like electricity through my hand. And maybe there's some of mine in there too. "You choose."

We start walking, and honestly, I could be happy merely walking the streets all day. Instead, on a cue from a wooden sign, he pulls me a little off the main street through a courtyard with a winding brick path. It meanders around a few shops until coming to a stop outside an old, weathered barn. I've never seen a potter work, not in real life anyway, so I have no idea what Jamie's pulling me toward. Smoke billows in giant black ribbons out of a cylindrical chimney, and through the wide arched doorway of the building I can see flames dancing, orange and red. Even twenty paces away, the heat of the fire licks at my skin.

There's a crowd gathered, watching as the potter carefully uses long tongs to pick up pieces of his delicate artwork and lay them inside the giant stove. The crowd is nearly silent, only a few whispers now and then, and after a while I turn to Jamie. He is rapt, studying the whole process with an eager expression on his face that I've only seen when he talks about going to art school.

"Do you do this?"

"What, me?" he whispers back to me, making it obvious that I shouldn't have used my full voice to ask. "No. This, um, this isn't really my medium, you know? But I'll have to take courses on it at the Institute."

The Institute is the art school of his dreams in Chicago. I admit, the last time I was on the Internet, I looked it up.

Even without knowing much about art, I could tell it was the place to be for serious students. And okay, maybe when I was online I also looked up art schools in New York City. There are some great ones there, you know, if Jamie would want to, say, be a little closer to NYU. For any particular reason. I squeeze his hand.

"Tell me how it works."

Jamie grins at me, happy to have a moment when he can teach, and starts explaining the process of shaping clay and glazing it and baking it. Most of what he's saying flies out of my brain, unabsorbed, the minute he says the words out loud, but I memorize the cadences of his speech, the little pauses and lilts that make his words as unique as he is himself.

Jamie, I decide, would make one hell of a good character for a novel.

When the potter goes inside and the show is over, Jamie leads the way again. We browse through the potter's store, but that leads into another store, and another, and then we find ourselves in a painting supply store.

I can tell Jamie's in heaven, so I hang back and let him browse. He picks out new brushes and colors for himself. When he's done, he has two bags, and his face is pink with excitement.

"You're a kid in a candy store," I tease, and he flushes darker.

"I am. Speaking of, there's an actual candy store across the street. Are you thinking what I'm thinking?"

I glance out the window and across the brick road,

where a store that has displays like the inside of Willy Wonka's factory awaits. "If what you're thinking has anything to do with giant lollipops and chocolate, I'm on board. But then I'm going to need some coffee to balance out the sugar."

I'm doing pretty well considering how much I drank last night, but the caffeine from this morning has worn off, and I could use a three-hour nap. Again I feel that twinge of guilt about Travis as Jamie takes my hand and leads me across the street, but it's forgotten the moment we step inside the shop.

The candy store smells as good as it looks, and even though I don't have much of a sweet tooth, I kind of want to buy one of everything. Jamie struggles with his decision and finally ends up choosing one of my favorite candies for himself—those little German raspberries. I buy a pound and promise to split the bag with him after the coffee.

It's too chilly to sit outside, so we plop down on an old, broken-in couch inside the coffee shop and sip from antique, mismatched china. Jamie digs into the German raspberries and I smile at him. "Having fun?"

"I've wanted to come here forever," he says wistfully through a mouthful of candy seeds. "Thank you, Sam."

"Feels right, doesn't it? This place?" Jamie nods in agreement. "I think I'd like to settle down in a place like this to write after I finish school in New York."

"Yeah. You'd have so many places to sit and scribble. You'd probably be a regular here, and maybe in that little diner we passed by. And I could paint in the courtyards. Or if we bought one of those beautiful old homes, we could make a studio in the attic." Jamie's eyes widen as he realizes what he's saying and quickly backtracks. "I mean, if we both happened to live here. And, um, you know, in the same house or something."

"Jamie," I say, and I reach out to brush my thumb across his cheek, "I think that sounds great."

He lowers his gaze so that he's smiling up at me through his eyelashes. It's so damned cute that I put my arm around him and he tucks his legs up under himself and snuggles into me in return. We don't say much more, and the silence isn't awkward. I just enjoy his company, his smell, the warmth of him pressed against me. But eventually the coffee runs dry and it's time to move on.

"Where next?" I ask.

Jamie pops one more raspberry into his mouth before rolling up the bag. "Where do you want to go?"

"I have to go to the bookstore. That's the only place that's a must for me. But I'm warning you, I'll spend hours there, so let's save it for later."

Jamie peers out the window. "How about we go in there?"

I follow his gaze to a jewelry store window that has displays of lovely sterling silver and semiprecious stone rings and bracelets. I'm not a jewelry guy, but I've noticed that Jamie wears a Celtic knotted ring on his right hand, so I nod.

The inside of the store is almost overwhelming. The

jewelry is grouped by color and it seems as if silver and sparkling stones are dripping from every inch of the walls, tables, and display cases all around. There's an older, round woman with spiky white hair behind the counter, working on twisting silver wire around a large amber stone, and she looks up and offers her help, should we need it. I blurt out how impressed I am before I can temper my awe with a little bit of refinement. She smiles at me over the rims of her bifocals.

"Thank you, dear. I made it all, so if you can't find what you're looking for, I could probably whip something up for you before you skip town."

I thank her, unable to imagine something that's *not* already here that I could request.

I'm lost in the blue topaz section of the store when I notice that Jamie's been paused for quite some time by a particular glass case. I wander over and peer down. The case is full of cross pendants. Some of them are blackened artfully to look like they could be from the Middle Ages, some are bright and shiny; some are thin and fragile looking, while others seem almost muscular, the silver lines wrapping around themselves like thick, sinewy tissue.

"Which one is your favorite?" I ask him, and Jamie puts his finger on top of the case, indicating the cross in the middle. It's a pendant, and one of the few crosses that's not quite delicate, but not overly masculine either. Its metal strands are braided into a Celtic knot that forms the points of the cross, and it's very similar to the ring Jamie wears.

"I didn't know you were religious," I say, kicking myself for not thinking to ask on the way here, when we'd been knee deep in other subjects like politics and future plans.

"I'm not." Jamie continues to stare at the cross, his expression melancholy. "I mean, I'm not anymore. Mom and I used to go to church. Before Dad got sick. Then she stopped going, so we all stopped going. It was hard to get Dad there anyway, but . . . I think she got tired of her prayers going unanswered."

His voice has dropped to a whisper, and I reach down and take his hand, running my thumb over the ridges of his knuckles, trying to comfort him as best as I can.

"It's a beautiful story, though, isn't it?" he asks, turning to me, eyes hopeful. "That there was someone who wanted to save us all."

There's a lump in my throat and I swallow it down and look away from his heartbreaking gaze, back at the cross. I realize then what Jamie's really looking for, and I'm hit with the crushing desire to try to be that for him.

"Yeah," I agree, and am startled that I actually mean it. "A savior would be nice."

Suddenly I can't be in this little shop anymore. It's too crowded, too hot, and I've got to get out.

"I'll be outside," I whisper to Jamie, and have to keep myself from sprinting toward the door. Jamie follows, his brows knitted together in concern.

"You okay?" he asks when we're both outside, touching my shoulder.

"Yeah," I say, because I'm not sure why I'm acting the way I am. I can't explain it to myself yet, so there's no chance of explaining it to him. I only know that I'm overwhelmed by him, by what he does to me and what he sees in me, by the things he makes me feel. "Sorry, you can stay if you—"

"Nah," he says, offering me a smile. "But . . . I am kind of getting hungry."

"Man cannot live on German raspberries alone," I muse, thankful that the heaviness I felt in the jewelry shop is starting to pass. I return his smile and focus on the moment, the here and now. "There's a great little diner down there," I say, waving to a spot a half a block away. "It serves all locally grown, organic food."

"Sounds exactly like the kind of place two aspiring artists should try."

I take his hand again. It's starting to feel weird *not* holding his hand, and I know this day is completely spoiling me in that regard. "Let's go."

....

"Hey," I say, pushing my empty plate toward the edge of the table and reaching for the bill. "There's a place you have to see before the bookstore."

"What?" Jamie asks.

"Not telling. You'll just have to trust me."

He does trust me, following me quietly and without giving voice to the questions I see behind his eyes. The place I'm taking him is far off the beaten path of Yellow

Springs, two blocks away from the center of town, then three more blocks north, buried in the beginnings of a residential neighborhood. We come to a halt in front of a small green house that looks like something Frank Lloyd Wright might have designed, with a stone sidewalk leading up through a pergola to the front door.

"Where are we?" Jamie asks, staring at the house, face scrunched in confusion.

"This is an art museum or . . . I guess they sell stuff, so . . . not so much a museum, but most people don't know it exists. My parents come here when they want to buy something they can really show off." I shrug. "I think it's where Yellow Springs keeps the good stuff."

Jamie laughs—a full, bright, surprised laugh. "Sam . . . you're . . ."

"I'm amazing, go on and say it," I tease.

"I was going to say thoughtful," Jamie says, rolling his eyes, "but I guess amazing works too."

We're greeted at the door by a woman who reminds me of my mother. She's got the same airy feeling, and very intelligent eyes, and a smile that doesn't show on her lips but in her whole body.

"Welcome to the Green House. My name is Ninah and right now I'm enjoying my cup of afternoon tea, which is fortunate for you because it means I won't be hovering over you when you look at these beautiful creations. So I'll be in the kitchen," she waves toward the back of the house, "minding my own business. If you see something you like, feel free to interrupt my tea break. And if not, let yourselves out the same way you came in, and I'll try not to be heartbroken."

Ninah floats away, and I notice that's she's barefooted under her long, patchwork skirt. Jamie and I look at each other, amused and perplexed by her speech. I drop his hand and urge him to look around.

The Green House is composed of only three small rooms, but every spare inch of the plain white walls is covered in art. I wander, keeping on the other side of the room from Jamie so that I don't disturb him. I like what I see, some of it more than others, but I'm not here to buy. I do, however, find myself drawn to bright colors, and to things my uneducated brain can only describe as Impressionist-like, and, of course, to watercolor pieces. Then, in the second room, a painting makes me stop and call for Jamie.

He's in the first room still, and he ducks in, eyebrow arched. "What is it?"

I point, and Jamie comes to stand next to me. The painting is watercolor, bright like I seem to like, and it's of a pretty yellow bird, perched on a branch of a willow tree. The colors run into each other, mixing and becoming one. If not for it being so realistic instead of fanciful, it could be Jamie's.

"It's good," he offers, and his fingers hover over the canvas, following the curve of the bird's back. "I like their lines. Not definite, but precise nonetheless. It looks like it could fly off the canvas."

I keep my eyes on the painting. "It's not as good as yours."

Jamie opens his mouth, tries to speak, and then shuts it again. Then he shakes his head. "No, this"—he looks for the artist's name—"this Henri, he's much better than I am. This is stunning work."

I turn to Jamie, shaking my head. "It's beautiful, yeah. But it's not as good as yours."

"Henri is a friend of mine."

At the sound of a womanly voice, Jamie and I both turn around, startled, as Ninah walks through the door behind us.

I wince. "Sorry, I mean no offense to Henri. He's obviously talented, and I'm not an art critic so what do I know? I just . . . I like his stuff better," I say, jerking my thumb in Jamie's direction.

Ninah leans against the wall, scrutinizing Jamie with a shrewd glare. "You are an artist?"

"I'm an art student," Jamie corrects her with gentle modesty. "Watercolors, mostly. And birds, which is why Sam made the comparison at all, but mine's nowhere near as good as your friend's."

"Let me see."

"What?" Jamie stammers, confused.

"Let me see some of your art," Ninah insists.

"I don't, um. I don't have anything with me."

As Jamie stutters I reach for my phone, tapping through the screens until I get to a picture I took of Jamie's Jubjub, and I hold it out for Ninah to see. "This one is mine, so it's not for sale. But the rest are. Just flick through. He's done a gorgeous phoenix, and a peacock and dodo that look better than I could even dream up in my imagination."

Ninah takes my phone, casting both Jamie and me a dubious glance before looking at the screen.

"Oh," she says after a minute, then taps the phone so that it gives her another picture. Then she starts talking—really talking—to Jamie. Questioning his methods, his instruction, his plans and goals. "And how old are you?"

"I'll be sixteen in March," Jamie says, and I almost regret showing Ninah the pictures. Jamie looks pale, sickly, because this art dealer is inspecting and therefore possibly criticizing his work. "I, um . . . I don't know where I'll go to school yet, of course, but . . . this is definitely what I want to do."

Ninah finally tears her eyes away from the phone, hands it back to me, and settles a focused gaze on Jamie. "How much are you asking for those?"

"What? Asking? Like, to sell?"

Ninah's lips almost falter into a smile. Almost. "Yes. How much?"

"I've, um . . . I've never thought to price them."

"I wouldn't take less than four hundred for each of them here, if you'd be interested."

Jamie reaches for my hand, scrabbling at my side until he finds it, and grips it so tight I have to bite my lip to keep from yelping. "You'd sell them for me?"

"Yes. You're quite talented. And at fifteen, I could throw around the term 'prodigy,' which gets all the art snobs' panties in a bunch." Ninah finally does smile, embellishing it with a conspiratorial wink. "Your friend is right, from what I can tell. You have talent. You should be selling these."

Ninah begins to walk toward the mysterious back room, casting us a pointed look over her shoulder. "Well, come on. Let's talk about your future, sweetheart. I'll make us some tea."

Jamie starts walking with her, turning back to me, eyes wide, to mouth, "Oh my god!" I reach out and touch his elbow.

"Hey, go talk. Unless you need me, I'd probably do more good at the bookstore. And this way it'll be less time that you sit there watching me buy piles of old books. So . . ."

Jamie nods, his happiness shining in his blue eyes. "Okay. Go. I'll meet you there. Sam . . . she wants to buy my art."

I touch my palm to his cheek. "And she's making you tea, so go on. I'll see you soon."

Jamie all but skips away and I watch him go, chest tight with happiness for him, and pride. Then I turn myself toward the front door. I'm not going to the bookstore, though. I lied. At the center of town I turn right, the opposite direction of the bookstore, and toward the little jewelry store we were in before. When I walk through the door and the little bell chimes over my head, the white-haired woman looks up.

"I figured you'd be back. Gonna buy that boy his cross?"

I nod to her because I can't speak. The lump is back in my throat, and I really can't believe I'm doing this; that I'm standing in this store again, and I'm going to buy jewelry for a boy. But at the same time, it seems like the most logical thing ever, because it will make Jamie happy, and that's what I want more than anything right now.

The woman takes the cross out of the case and hobbles back to her desk, ringing it up on an old adding machine. She carefully wraps it in white tissue paper before placing it inside a tiny silver box. As she closes the lid on it, I feel as though she's sealed something else in there with it. Maybe my fate.

"Knew that one was special when I was making it," she muses, almost to herself. "It's just been sitting here, waiting on you, honey."

"And how long has it been waiting?" I ask, almost dreading the answer. My skin is prickly, hot and cold at the same time like I have a fever, and I hate myself for it, but my eyes feel a little watery.

She looks at me over the top of her bifocals and then begins to laugh—a small chuckle that unleashes into a cackle. "You're never going to believe this . . . I made that one on Friday the thirteenth. I hope you're not superstitious."

I laugh too, and she looks at me funny. I don't blame her. My laugh is totally off, almost shrill. I sound like a complete lunatic. "Somehow, that doesn't surprise me. Thank you."

"I hope your boyfriend enjoys it," she says in return, and holds out the box for me to take.

Friday the thirteenth. Meg is never going to believe this.

I mumble my thanks and make a hasty exit. Again, the shop is too small, too hot. I gasp for air on the street, kind of doubled over, clutching the box like it can save me. When my heart rate has returned to normal, I start walking in the direction of the bookstore.

"Sam!" I turn and Jamie's walking toward me, coming from one of the side streets. He jogs to catch up with me. "I thought you went to the bookstore."

"Got distracted," I say, ignoring the box in my hands for the moment. "So . . . ?"

Jamie beams. He's a little breathless, and it's coloring his cheeks a pretty pink. "She's buying ten of my paintings, more if I email her photos of them later so she can see them. And she's thinking seriously about having a show at the Green House for me. How crazy is that?" He pauses, raising a hand to cover his mouth like he's in utter shock. "I could pay for school this way. I never even thought about that before . . . I never considered that I could make money for art school by *making* art, and I wouldn't have . . . I wouldn't have even told her I was an artist if you hadn't been there. I can't believe you showed her those pictures. I can't believe you told her I was better than her friend. I can't believe that I was mortified when you started talking to her!"

I laugh, caught up in his excitement. The smile on his face makes my heart skip along in my chest like you see in cartoons, and we smile like goons at each other for a minute. Then I hold the silver box out.

"I got you something."

Jamie looks down at the box, then up to me, puzzled. "What?"

I shrug, and he shakes his head at me, like I'm beyond help, before pulling the lid off the box and digging through the white tissue. When he uncovers the cross, he makes a strangled little noise in his throat. "Sam . . ."

"I didn't get you a chain. I figured you might like it better on leather or hemp or something. I mean, if you even want to wear it at all. Just because you thought it was pretty didn't mean that you'd actually want to wear it I guess, but if you—"

Then I can't talk anymore because Jamie's kissing me. His mouth is pressed to mine and my words are clogged in my throat and to hell with what I was going to say, anyway. I reach up and take Jamie's face in my hands, kissing him back like I need the air in his lungs, and I don't stop kissing him until I feel his hand pushing on my chest.

"Sorry," I apologize, gasping for air. "I got carried away."

"No, I'm sorry . . . was that . . . was that too soon or . . . not good or . . ." His skin is bright red. "I've never really kissed anyone before."

I smile at him, so big that my face burns.

"What?" he asks, nervous. "It was bad, wasn't it?"

"It was perfect," I say, almost rolling my eyes at myself for using that adjective. "You've never kissed anyone before?"

He looks away from me, fingering the little cross in his hands. "Well, I played spin the bottle in sixth grade, but . . . no, no one else." He looks back up at me, searching my face. "What? Oh my god, why are you looking at me like that?"

"I'm just flattered. Never been anyone's first kiss before."

He looks skeptical. "Are you sure it was okay?"

I answer by wrapping an arm around his waist, pulling him to me, and kissing him. This time he lets me lead, teach, and I slide my tongue between his lips. A hum vibrates in his throat, a singsong little noise of appreciation, and I swear that I could do this forever. I could spend the rest of my days on this street corner, kissing him with every ounce of everything I have, feeling him kiss me back the same way, returning it all.

When I pull away, his eyes are shut and he looks like he's dreaming. "I like kissing," he breathes.

I laugh. "Good. But if we stand here any longer our lips are going to freeze together, and in spite of how nice that sounds in theory, in reality it might be quite painful." I release him from my grip and he kind of stumbles backward, and I have to give myself a couple of points for making him weak in the knees. "It's my turn now, Mr. Big-Shot Artist. We're going to the bookstore, and I'm finding you some suitable literary material to read."

"God help me," Jamie teases, and hand in hand, we set off to the bookstore.

....

Jamie falls asleep on the drive home, exhausted from the excitement of the day. In the backseat of my dad's old car are our purchases: Jamie's art supplies, a half-eaten bag of German raspberries, a silver cross, and a brown paper bag filled with used books. Some of the books are his—classics he's avoided reading for far too long, and a few of my favorite authors—and some are mine. A few of my own choices, but also some bestsellers that Jamie swears by, a handful of Stephen King's finest, which Jamie promises I'll love, and even a graphic novel written by Neil Gaiman. It turns out we both love Neil Gaiman, so we're going to take turns reading it.

I let Jamie sleep and listen to the Cure. It reminds me of Travis, but only in a distant way, and I don't think of him at all on the way home. Instead, for the entire two hours I think about Jamie, about who he is and what he will be, and try to see myself as part of that future. By the time I pull up to his house my face hurts from smiling. I give his knee a gentle squeeze to wake him and he opens his pretty eyes, blinking at me in the darkness until he gets his bearings.

"Thank you," he whispers to me, voice hoarse from sleep. "Today was . . ."

I smile. "Yeah. It was. Can I call you?"

He nods. "I'll be home tomorrow. I don't work until the evening."

"No, I mean tonight. When I get home."

Jamie stares at me, lips twitching into a smile.

"Really? You want to talk to me after spending the whole day with me?"

"I know it's hard to believe, but I'm not irritated by you. Yet."

Jamie laughs. "Sure. I'll be up. Goodness knows I don't need the sleep. Sorry I wasn't much company on the way home."

My thoughts were more than enough company. "It's okay. I'll talk to you soon."

He starts to gather his things from the backseat, carefully dividing our books into separate bags. He leaves the raspberries for me.

"Good night, Sam."

"Night," I say, and lean toward him. He meets me halfway, and this time the kiss is short but deep and kind of sexy, like it holds secrets we're not ready to share yet. Then he climbs out and I wait until he's inside and a light is on before driving away.

That night we fall asleep on the phone together, and I dream about birds flying through a breeze that sounds a lot like soft laughter.

Twelve

It's Tuesday before I hear from Travis again. Well, not Tuesday, technically. Wednesday morning. Three a.m., to be exact. That weird, dark time when people usually, you know, sleep.

My phone rings, and I'm sprawled, facedown, on my bed. My hand shoots out and grips my phone. I pull it to my ear and mumble, "What?"

"What are you wearing?"

Slowly, my brain pieces together that it's Travis's voice. "Travis?" I push myself up on an elbow, look at the red, squared-off numbers on my alarm clock, and try to make sense of them. It's not often I see my clock flash that number. "What did you say?"

"I said, what are you wearing?"

"I have school in five hours."

"You're not answering my question." There's some crunching on the other end of the line, like maybe he's eating Doritos or something. Then he kind of chuckles. "Want to know what I'm wearing?"

I sigh. Despite the fact that it's too late-slash-early and

my head's kind of still in the land of Nod, yeah. I really do want to know what he's wearing.

But that's beside the point. "So you called me in the middle of the night to have phone sex?"

"That's safe, isn't it? Or does that go against your rules too?"

"I don't have rules, that's not . . ." I stop myself. I'm wasting my breath trying to explain the difference to him. Then it hits me. He *called*. "You called me."

"Yeah. So?"

I grin. "Thought you didn't wait by the phone and all that?"

"Who says I was waiting?" I hear the clink of glass. I wonder, exactly, how many bottles of beer he's had, and how much that was a factor in him calling me versus my pure, natural charm. "So . . . what are you wearing?"

I wriggle down underneath my covers and whisper into the phone, "Just boxers."

Travis makes a noise that makes me want to laugh—a ragged, gurgling whimper. Then he says, "It's your stomach, you know?"

"My stomach?" I ask, puzzled. I'm a little rusty at this, but I'm pretty sure this isn't the way phone sex is supposed to go.

Travis murmurs something in agreement. "Yeah, man. I mean, it is, like, this great injustice or something that you're seventeen and have those abs. Y'know? *Seventeen*. It's just not fair."

"Yeah, I, um . . . I do sit-ups. When I'm writing sometimes. Like, when I get stuck and can't think of what to write next. And sometimes before bed."

"Mnnnn, you must get stuck a lot." Travis breathes deep into the phone and I want to laugh again. He sounds blissed out. And I don't mind at all that part of that bliss might be coming from him picturing me naked. "I'm not usually into guys, you know?"

"I thought guys were one of your things?"

"Yeah but . . ." He grunts or something. Not sure if it's because he's frustrated trying to explain himself or if he's moving. I can only imagine he's lying in his own bed, maybe on top of his gray comforter, almost mirroring the position I'm in right now. The thought is, truthfully, sexy as hell. "Not like this. You're just . . ."

"Your type. The geeky writer guy with the quasi 'fro and the decent six-pack."

"Yeah. It's so damn sexy." He pauses. It's quiet on the other end, so I can only assume he's thinking. Or that he passed out. Then, "So when can I talk you into bed?"

I do laugh then, taking care to cover my mouth so that I won't wake my parents. "You can give it a shot anytime."

"Tomorrow?"

"By tomorrow do you mean later today or, you know, like, the actual tomorrow?"

Travis snorts. It's kind of drunken sounding, and I laugh again. "Like, later today. Tuesday."

"It's Wednesday now."

"Whatever, man. Wednesday. Gotta be so picky . . ."

"Wednesday's good. I'll be at the Donkey around three fifteen. Try to talk me into it then."

"Okay, writer boy with the abs." He chuckles to himself. "So . . . boxers, huh? Nothing else?"

"Nothing else."

"Damn."

Even at three a.m., in the darkness and privacy of my own room, I blush. He's thinking about me. *Me.* I almost can't handle it. I tell him, "I should go."

"Yeah, yeah. School night," Travis jokes, and laughs at it. "Donkey. Tomorrow. Writer boy with the abs," he repeats like he's trying to memorize the facts.

"See you then," I tell him, and end the call. I turn my phone off too, just in case. Hot as he is, another phone call at this hour is just too much. I bury myself under my covers and try in vain to sleep.

It's kind of weird, going through school that day, knowing that as soon as the final bell rings I'll be meeting up with Travis. Even though I spend lunchtime with Jamie, and we meet before school by his locker and after school at mine, and he holds my hand like he just can't let go. It's strange, and maybe a little unsettling, and I can't say that I feel great about it. But there are a lot of factors that go into my thinking on this, a lot of things whirring around in my head, and even though it feels wrong, there's something that feels right about it too. Because really, no one is forcing me to make a decision here. There's not even an actual decision to be made. I might as well count my blessings, ride both options out, and see what comes of it. And of course, there's this nagging, persistent feeling in the back of my head that maybe Meg was right. Not about Jamie being perfect for me, but about the Goddess giving me choices. Belief in a goddess notwithstanding, having options isn't something I'm accustomed to, and it's not something I'm willing to give up. Yet.

Landon and Meg come with me to the Donkey. I didn't exactly tell them that I was going to meet Travis there, but they'll find out soon enough. We've just sat down at the bar when Travis comes in, looking like he's just rolled out of bed, which means he's almost sexier than normal.

"Writer boy," he says to me before snaking one arm around my waist and pulling me close to him. Since I'm on the bar stool, he's a lot taller than me, and I have to look up at him.

"Rocker boy," I return, and then he just dives in, kissing me hot and wet and on the shorter side, so that I'm left wanting more.

"Coffee to go. Come on. Let's get out of here."

I cock an eyebrow at him. "In a rush?"

"No, but it's a whole lot easier to talk you into bed when you're already, um, in it." He grins at me, a smooth, sly kind of grin, and that's when I know he's kidding. Maybe.

"Stay here with me. Talk to me. Then we'll see about leaving," I say to him.

He narrows his eyes, gives me a once-over, and says,

"All right. For a bit. But I should at least get to see you without a shirt later. You know, for the effort."

I laugh at that and can't resist kissing him again, this time making it last, before he plops himself down on the bar stool next to me. Meg's elbow lands swiftly in my ribs and I wince, turning to glare at her. She and Landon have twin expressions on their faces. Both are wide-eyed, jaws dropped, and jerking their heads in Travis's direction. I shrug like I have no idea what they're confused about and turn back to Travis.

"So . . ." Travis begins, not at all sure how to start a conversation. "How was your day?"

I smirk at him. "Good. I managed to talk my teacher out of a pop quiz in psychology and there aren't any rumors going around about me, which is more than I can say for most days. How was your day?"

"Just got up." He grins lazily, proving his statement, then signals to Ted. "You want chai?"

"Yes, please."

Travis orders for me. Meg's elbow lands in my ribs again and I stifle a yelp by biting down on my hand. "Travis, you remember Meg and Landon?"

Travis leans back on his stool to see around me and nods once at Meg, then his gaze sharpens on Landon and he nods again, this time a lot more curtly. He begins to drum on the counter with his fingertips, then twists them together, looks around the room, and finally sits on his hands.

"Ask me about my writing."

"What?" Travis says, looking perplexed.

"You want something to talk about, ask me about my writing," I suggest.

"Oh! No, man. It's not that I don't know what to talk about. I've just . . ." He reaches up and scratches at the roots of his long bangs. "I've got a lot on my mind today. Not that I don't want to know about your writing or anything. I'd like to hear about your writing. If, you know . . . if we're just gonna sit here forever."

I have to laugh at that. His bluntness is refreshing on some level. I know exactly what he wants from me. "What's on your mind?"

He looks around himself again, itchy, and I get the feeling he definitely doesn't want to be overheard. I lean closer to him and turn my back fully toward my friends. "I'd rather show you," he whispers, grinning.

"Travis, I already said—"

"No, no. It's not what you think. There's just something I want you to see. In my apartment."

I cross my arms over my chest and hope I'm giving him the best I-don't-buy-it stare I can. "And this thing, in your apartment, has nothing to do with getting me naked?"

"Well," he says, and sticks his tongue out, clicking that metal ball against his teeth, "I wouldn't say it has nothing to do with it. It'll help, yeah, but you won't believe me if you don't see it. Oh, shit, there's Vanessa. I didn't even know she was here. Be right back."

Travis kisses my lips and then slides off the bar stool, heading toward a table in the back corner, where a girl with bright fuchsia hair is chatting with friends. How he missed that hair is beyond me, but now that I'm alone, Landon and Meg pounce.

"What are you doing?" Meg hisses at me, hitting me on the shoulder as she does so. Even with her cutesy hair, she looks a little scary, and for once I think the horned hoodie might not be so far off.

"It's nothing. Just seeing him. Just flirting. It's nothing," I say, but Meg only rolls her eyes.

"Just flirting? So all this talk of you going back to his apartment was—"

"God, can you not, like, eavesdrop?"

Meg grinds her teeth, then hisses through them. "What's going on, Sam? You've been with Jamie a lot at school, and you bought him a cross that was made on Friday the thirteenth—which is a *sign*, by the way—and I know you call him every night."

"So?" I ask. And yeah, I know the answer to my own question, but that's not the point.

"What do you mean, 'So?'" she says, and turns to Landon for help. As per usual, Landon is the calm one.

He offers her a sheepish smile, then says, "Would you give me and Sam a minute alone?"

"Are you kidding me?" she asks, and because Landon's expression is dead serious, she huffs out a sigh. "Right. One of those Penises Only conversations."

Landon shakes his head. "One of those Ex-Boyfriends Only conversations, actually. Please?"

"Oh. Well, in that case . . ."

Landon waits until Meg has wandered over to the corner, taking a particular interest in the flyers advertising student housing, before speaking.

"So, you've decided."

"Not yet," I admit. "I know what's holding me back, I just don't understand yet what's pulling me toward it."

Landon nods, processing that. "Travis is magnetic."

"Just a bit." I glance over my shoulder, making sure Travis is still distracted. "But I don't think that's it. As sexy as he is, I don't think just plain wanting him is the whole reason why I'm considering it."

"Then what is?"

I knit my fingers together and stare down at them. "You know how we were? When you and I had sex, it was so . . ."

"Good?"

I chuckle. "Good, yes. But I was going to say intense. Know what I mean?"

"Of course."

I continue, voice low. "Everything got so intense, we couldn't handle it, Landon. It tore us apart. You remember. We started fighting all the time, and got jealous of the stupidest things. I mean, you thought I was sneaking around on you with Chad Anderson. Remember? And we both know, for a fact, that Chad Anderson is one hundred percent straight, but there we were, screaming at each other anyway."

Landon's scrunches his face. "We kind of lost it there at the end."

"There's no 'kind of' about it. We acted insane. We were too immature." I sigh. "I guess I want to know it doesn't have to be that way. Or, at least, that I can be a grown-up about it, you know? That I won't morph into a clingy, obsessive, lovesick idiot. That I can be chill."

Landon stares at me blankly, and I wonder where I've lost him. I open my mouth, ready to start over with my case, when he leans forward, his voice a whisper.

"So you think sex was the reason why we acted so crazy?"

"Well, yeah. Don't you?"

Landon sits back on the stool. "No, Sam. I don't."

Well, color me surprised. I thought we'd both figured this out. I thought we were on the same page. Hearing Landon disagree with me is just about the last thing I expected, and for a moment I scramble, like I've lost my footing and can't get it back, because the ground is moving underneath me and doesn't show any signs of stopping.

"Then what was it?"

Landon smiles in a way that makes me angry for a second. A Poor Idiot Sam Hasn't Figured It Out Yet smile. "I think we couldn't handle *us*, Sam. You're right. We were immature, but how we handled sex is only one part of it. Our whole relationship was too much. I don't think anyone is prepared to fall in love. Ever. But we did at fourteen. It was way too much pressure. I panicked at every thought of losing you. And I know I acted like I had lost my mind most of the time, but . . . I kind of had, in a way."

This information settles on me, heavy and incomprehensible, and I try in vain to catch up to what Landon's saying. "So when you were paranoid that I was cheating? Or got jealous of how much time I spent on my writing, or how much time I spent on the school paper? That was because you were so in love with me you didn't know how to handle it?"

He nods. "Yes. We were way too young to understand love like that."

"So it was love we didn't know how to handle, not sex."

"Exactly," Landon says. He squints at me. "I kind of thought you'd figured that out."

"I hadn't," I admit, and my mind keeps turning Landon's words over and over again. I can't really understand it, but I say, "I guess it makes sense," anyway, because I don't want to look like an idiot again.

Landon puts his hand over mine. He continues to study me. "So does that change anything? What about Travis?"

"Yeah, what about Travis?" Two arms wrap around me, and I lean back into the embrace. Travis's mouth moves against my ear. "Made a decision yet?"

I flush hotly. "You heard that, huh?"

"Yup."

He lets go of me and I turn around on the bar stool, giving him my best flirty smile. "Come on. Show me this secret thing in your apartment. And then we can talk. And maybe, if you're lucky, I'll take off my shirt."

Travis squints at me. "You're getting a little cocky."

"Hey, *Travis Blake* wants me to come back to his apartment with him, you bet I'm a little cocky."

"You're such a geek." Travis shakes his head at me, like I'm hopeless.

"And I know how that gets you going."

Travis shoots a look to me that would have knocked me dead if, in fact, looks could kill. "I told you that in confidence, asshole. Now let's get out of here."

He pulls me off the stool like he's Tarzan and I'm Jane, and I have just enough time to shoot my friends a look of apology before we're out the door.

....

Travis's apartment is no cleaner than the last time I was here, not that that's a surprise. The first thing he does is dig into his fridge, pulling out a beer. He offers one to me but I shake my head no and he shrugs, twisting off the cap on his own.

He doesn't say a word, but he opens up a manila envelope and pulls out some important, official-looking documents, written in tiny font, with a fancy letterhead.

It takes me a minute but after deciphering some legal jargon I realize what I'm holding: a recording contract. I look up at him, surprised.

Travis waves his hand, saying, "Turn the page."

I flip to the next sheet of paper, and this time it's the same official-looking wording, but a different letterhead.

"Three offers," Travis explains, and takes the papers from me, laying them out on the counter in piles. "Two are indies. Small-time record companies that are a little more . . ."

"Organic?" I offer, but that's not quite the word that Travis wants.

"Flexible, was what I was going to say. They, uh, let you run the show. But there's not much money. I mean, like, not much as far as what we'd make, and not much to produce and market us. But this one . . ." Travis points to a document with a recognizable letterhead, a name that looks intimidating, even to me. "They've got the money. So we'd have the marketing, but you know, we'd hafta do what the suits want."

I stare at him, absolutely blown away. "Three offers?"

"Yeah." He shrugs and takes another swig of beer, but his lips are turning up at the corners and, yeah, he's proud of himself. "I'm gonna be rich and famous. So . . . wanna sleep with me now?"

I laugh. "Travis, you got three offers from record companies. That's amazing. No wonder you wanted to show me this stuff."

"Well, it's kind of your fault."

"My fault?" I ask.

Travis grunts. "Yeah. Uh, the reps were there last Friday, when you came to the show. I played better than usual that night, so this is kinda your fault."

"Trying to impress me, huh?" I tease.

"Cocky bastard."

"Well, you did. And apparently the reps too." I look down at the documents, my eyes skimming over the terms. "Does that mean I'm entitled to a cut, as your lucky charm and all?"

Travis rolls his eyes. "Please. You haven't even graduated to groupie level yet. You want to be a gold digger, you're going to have to do a lot better than taking off your shirt."

Because I can't tell if he's kidding or not, I stare more at the documents, trying not to blush. "So you're going to take one of the indie offers, right?"

"Of course," he says, mumbling into his beer. "Can't let them suck out my soul. Besides, this label, Somewhat Damaged, can already offer us a tour. With some big names, even, as far as indie music goes. It's a good gig."

"Yeah," I agree, and I find myself feeling proud of him. I've only known him for a few days but I can read it, in his eyes and in the way he plays and in between the lines of his speech, how hard he's worked and how badly he wants this. "And later, when you're big, Sony can buy out your contract and *then* you can completely sell out and piss off your fans."

Travis chuckles and takes my hand, pulling me behind him to his room. I feel like I should put up a fight, or at least pretend to, but I don't. Not even when we end up in his bed and he's kissing me slow and sloppy and amazingly good, his body pressing mine down into the mattress of his futon. Just when I'm beginning to wonder if he's going to stop, or if I should make him, he pulls away. I whimper a little bit in protest despite myself, which he chuckles at.

"Wanna talk?"

I throw my head back against his pillow, laughing. "I'd love to talk, although I'm sure you have other plans."

Travis slides off of me and props himself up on an elbow, studying my face. "Maybe, but our plans will meet up eventually. Tell me about your writing."

So I tell him. I tell him about how my parents are both creative in their own ways, how they encouraged me to make up stories as a youngster and I got addicted. I tell him about how I work, about how much it means to me, about how hard it is. And I tell him about my hope of getting into NYU, about the writing samples that are sitting on my desk at home, waiting to be mailed out all over the country to various creative writing schools. He lets me talk, uninterrupted, and listens to every word like he does, sincerely, want to know.

Then, when I'm finally quiet, he asks, "Do you write lyrics?"

I snort. "God no. I'm not at all musically inclined. I held a trumpet in the marching band for one year."

Travis stifles a laugh. "Held a trumpet, huh?"

"I wouldn't call what I did playing."

Travis laughs out loud then, scratchy and sexy. "You write poetry, right? I bet you could write lyrics. Try it."

"What?" I ask, but Travis is already up, crossing the room to an acoustic guitar he has sitting on a stand in the corner. He grabs it and sits on the edge of the futon, strumming a few chords. After a few adjustments with the pegs at the ends of the strings, he turns to me. "Lyrics. Try it."

His fingers begin an intricate dance over the strings,

and he repeats a pretty little riff over and over.

Any words in my head seem useless compared to that.

"Just . . . make something up?"

"Yeah, man. Like your stories. The best songs always tell a story."

"I can't sing," I say, embarrassed.

"Then don't. Just talk."

Talk. Huh.

I sit up and cross my legs under myself, facing him. Then I close my eyes and listen. I've written stories while listening to music before, but never *to* music. It's a bit strange, a bit awkward, but the notes of his guitar are insistent, waiting on me. The tune reminds me of something ancient, of a far-off land with lush fields and rolling hills.

I start timidly, using the age-old first line of fairy tales. "Once upon a time, in a far-off land, lived a handsome prince."

"Eh." I open my eyes, and Travis is pulling a face. "Not a prince."

"A knight?"

"Nope," Travis answers, still plucking the strings in time. "Try again."

"A princess?" I ask, the pitch of my voice going up high.

"You'd better not be calling me a girl."

"Oh, so this song is about you, is it?"

Travis meets my gaze, confident and smoky. "Isn't it?"

"Who's the cocky bastard now?"

"Better start telling a story, my hands are getting tired."

"Fine," I huff. "Once upon a time in a far-off land, there lived a god of music. This god was so talented that all of the other gods fought for the privilege of listening to him play his . . . magical lute. And not only was this god talented, he was pretty—"

"No."

I smirk. "He was gorgeous, and some of the other gods were jealous."

As I talk, Travis begins to shift his fingers, changing the chords slightly, and I follow, chasing after his movements with my tale.

"One day when the god was walking around on Earth, he saw a handsome mortal, who could not sing and could not play the lute, but wrote the most incredible stories, and the god fell in love."

Travis raises a brow at that but continues to play his song, and I continue weaving the story.

I don't know how it happens, but soon I'm lost in Travis's music and in the fantasy we've created. I'm no longer sitting in a tiny apartment in Athens, Ohio, but in a world where gods and mortals mingle. At some point, the real-life Travis is replaced by a down-tempo recording of Liquid, and he gives me a notebook and a pencil, but I couldn't tell you when. All I know is that I'm writing like I haven't written in years, and the story has morphed into the modern day, of a rock star who falls for a music critic, and the words won't stop.

At least, they don't stop until I feel Travis's lips on the nape of my neck. I'm flipped over on my stomach, scribbling away, giving him complete access to me, and the story is forgotten momentarily as the metal ball on his tongue glides a stripe over my spine.

I make an embarrassing, needy sound and stretch my neck out for more.

He keeps kissing, licking, and nipping all over my skin. I break out into goose bumps and shudder, and I have to remind myself to breathe. Travis stretches out next to me, half on top of me, his mouth unrelenting.

"Good?" he asks, and all I can do is whimper in answer. Then his hands are on me, turning me over on my back gently, and he's kissing my mouth. "I got kind of jealous of your story," he mumbles against my skin, and I want to kiss him back, but he's moved on to my neck again, this time working on the little dips under my collarbone. Landon always said that was my favorite place to be kissed and holy Moses is he right.

Then Travis is pulling me up, hauling me off the mattress, and pulling my shirt over my head. I feel at once exposed and free, but all too alone. So I take the hem of his shirt in my hands and take it off of him. His entire chest is covered in tattoos, all symbols and designs that seem a little familiar, and make me curious as to their meaning, but then I reach out to touch one of them and feel the heat of him underneath my palm, the stretch of his skin and the hard swell of muscle, and I don't care anymore.

"Travis," I breathe, as he ducks his head to kiss over my chest. His hands are on my stomach, exploring and teasing the skin there, tracing the neat line of hair below my belly button.

"So gorgeous," he murmurs, and then he's back, kissing my mouth again. My arms pull him in closer, and he settles his weight on top of me and *oh my god*, I want him to keep going.

But in spite of all that want, when he reaches for the button on my jeans, I suck in a breath and tense. Travis pulls back, searching my face. He must not like what he sees because he slides off of me and pulls me close to him, so that my head is resting on his chest.

He's quiet, and I let myself just listen to his heartbeat for a minute before saying, "I'm sorry."

"Don't worry about it," he whispers gently, which makes me feel even worse. For the second time in a week I'm in Travis's bed, wanting nothing more than to curl into a ball and cry. But I can't do that. I can't act any more childish than I already have. Then Travis's fingers slide through my hair and he says, "Find some answers?"

My face is burning with embarrassment. It's hot against the assorted symbols painted into his skin. "Yeah. Maybe."

"I'd love to know."

I turn my face into his chest and inhale. He smells like leather and that spicy scent he always wears, but a little bit like Dial soap too, and it makes me smile in spite of everything. Because somehow Dial soap seems so human, not like something a gorgeous, musical god would use, and that's comforting.

"I love how you make me feel. I've never wanted anyone like this." I pause to think, and then add with a chuckle, "And I really love the way you want me."

Travis chuckles too. "But?"

I lift my head up and look down into his amber eyes. "I think I want to mean something to you. And I want to be sure that you mean something to me. I know that's not the way you are, but . . ." I bite my lip. "I think it might be the way I am."

Travis looks at me for a long moment before reaching up and taking my face in both of his hands. He blows out a breath and gives me a sad smile. "Yeah, I kinda figured. But . . ."

"But?" I ask.

"But I think that maybe you and I could be good friends." He shrugs and drops his hands away from my face. "I mean, I really like you. It's weird. I felt like I was pulled into your orbit or something. Like, I don't know, magnets or some shit."

"Maybe magic," I say. Magic with a *k*. I settle back against him and close my eyes.

"Hey. I know it's really none of my business, and I'm probably the last person on earth that should say it, but . . ."

I poke him in the side. "But what?"

"That thing I heard Landon tell you. That maybe you two messed up your relationship because you were so in love?"

My face grows hot. "You heard that part too, huh?"

"I heard the whole embarrassing conversation, my

friend." Travis sniffs. "Anyway. You shouldn't believe it."

I raise my head and look at him. "I shouldn't?"

"No," he says, and for maybe the first time, I can tell he's completely serious. No jokes. "Sure, you two could have screwed it up because you were young, but don't confuse acting like a jealous asshole with love either. If he was accusing you of cheating, that's not love. That's fear and insecurity and ego, man. And there's no room for that in real love."

I blink. "I don't think I can handle any more of this day. First Landon drops a bomb on me, then I get a lecture from Travis the love guru."

"It's not a lecture. Just advice. And I'm older and wiser."

"Older, anyway."

Travis gives me a playful punch on the shoulder. "Listen to me, whippersnapper. I'm not lying. I don't want you thinking love can screw up a relationship. Sex can. Jealousy can. Being possessive and controlling and manipulative can. But not love."

I know Travis is right, which is why Landon's explanation didn't make sense. I know it because when I think back to that day on the park bench, when I told Landon that I couldn't be with him anymore, it wasn't really because of the intensity of our relationship. That was a symptom of something else. It was because Landon wouldn't let me breathe. He was jealous of everyone and everything around me, including my writing. That wasn't love. Landon may have loved me, but that's not what he was showing me when he was being controlling.

"Now you're quiet. Did I make you upset?"

"No," I say. "It's just that I feel like I'm Goldilocks. I don't want what Landon and I had. That was too much. But you're . . ."

"Not enough."

I nod, embarrassed again. Travis sits up, and I do too. He pulls me close to him, and I let him comfort me. And even though I sort of mean my next words, I really am just kidding. Mostly.

"It's okay. I get it. You're going to be a big star. Can't have anything tying you down."

Travis grins. "It'll be insane. I'll have Victoria's Secret models lined up."

"And Calvin Klein models, with better abs than mine."

"That too."

I laugh. "That and you really don't want to hurt anyone you'd have to leave behind, do you?" Travis shrugs me off and all I can do is shake my head at him. "The badass rocker with the big heart."

"If you ever talk, you're gonna be so bad for my reputation," he grumbles. "Should have you sign a nondisclosure agreement. I'm sure the label has one . . ."

"I'll take it to the grave," I promise. "So what now?"

"Now," Travis begins, "we try this friends thing and you tell me about Jamie."

I must look horrified, because Travis rolls his eyes at me like I'm an absolute child. "Oh, come on. You brought him up when I asked about a boyfriend. You like him."

I relent with a sigh. "Yeah. I do. He's incredible, Travis. Shy and sweet, but so talented too. He's an artist and he really gets me, and my writing, and the way he looks at me . . . like I hung the moon in the sky . . ."

"So . . ."

"So?"

Travis leans forward, keeping our gazes locked. "So why waste time with me? Or anyone else?"

Travis has a point.

"You're entirely too honest."

"And right," Travis adds. I roll my eyes.

"If we're going to share, you should tell me about Lindsay."

"What?" Travis says, but he obviously knows who I mean. For the first time, I watch Travis's skin go red with embarrassment. I reach out and run my finger across a particular tattoo on his chest.

Travis looks down at his tattoo, like he's forgotten it's there. "Of course you'd notice that, wouldn't you? You observant little jerk. Lindsay," he begins, scratching his nails over the name like it itches, "is the reason why I don't do relationships. Need to get this damn thing removed."

"Tell me about her."

"No."

"I'm trying this friends thing."

"Touché." Travis stops rubbing the inky signature of a girl from long ago. "Yeah. Okay, deal. You don't have to be home for a while, do you? 'Cause this could take a while."

I have no idea what time it is. I lost all sense of it when I was writing my fairy tale. I look around and find Travis's only clock, which is a digital number held up by a Frankenstein action figure. It's not even nine yet. I promised I'd call Jamie tonight, but he doesn't go to sleep until late. I have hours.

"Tell me," I urge.

"Just remember, you asked for it." He sighs. "So Lindsay was the girl who left me at the altar . . ."

....

It's nearly eleven by the time Travis drops me off at home. He pulls up to the curb, and instead of getting out, I just stare at my house for a while. Then I unbuckle my seat belt and turn my whole body toward Travis.

"So, friends?" I ask him. And as much as I know friendship is all I should want, there's a part of me, a tiny part, that hopes he'll decide to fight for more. But he's not going to. For my own good.

"Yeah, friends." Travis runs his tongue ring over his bottom lip and looks at me in a way that could only be described as predatory. "But that doesn't mean I won't try to sleep with you anymore. Or that I'll keep my hands to myself. Especially if I'm drunk. Or if I've been performing. Or if you're wearing a tight shirt."

I laugh, and he chuckles along with me. Then, when we've quieted, I lean forward and kiss him, long and sweet, on the lips. I don't even fight a sigh as we pull apart. "Pity. I think I could have fallen for you."

"And I would have run," Travis says, and I can't help but notice his voice is kind of sad when he says it. Then he gives me another short kiss. "Ask Jamie out tomorrow. Don't wait any longer. You've got your answers."

I smile. "Yeah. I do. Thanks."

"Hey, anytime you need answers, I'm here. And I mean that. Especially if it involves making out." I roll my eyes at him even though I can hear the notes of sincerity in his tone. "And hey, come see us play Saturday. We're having a little party to celebrate. My lucky charm should be there when we sign the contract."

"Wouldn't miss it," I say, and somehow find the will to get out of the car. I watch him drive away, already missing the heat of his lips on mine, then I let myself into the house and call Jamie.

Thirteen

Jamie's in the middle of painting some tropical-looking bird when I see him at lunch. He's got yellow paint on his earlobe, and it makes me wonder how long it's been there, or more specifically, how long it's gone unnoticed.

I don't interrupt him but I do slide my arms around him and hug him from behind. He keeps painting, but cracks a smile all the same, and leans back into me.

"Wanna eat?" I ask.

He's obviously in the artist zone because he swishes his brush in the air toward one of the tables, where a half-eaten piece of cold pizza sits.

"Wasting away for art then? I admire your work ethic."

Jamie laughs and leans out of my embrace, tucking the paintbrush behind his ear. Which explains the paint on his lobe. "I can eat if you want. This little bird was calling to me. I think it might be some kind of songbird, I don't know. I'll have to look it up."

"You and your birds," I say, but I say it with affection. "Ever paint, like, kittens or something?"

Jamie wrinkles his nose. "Nah. They don't have wings."

"So you'd paint a pterodactyl?"

"Ha. No. Just pretty, feathered wings."

"Shallow."

Jamie laughs again and we head to the table. He picks up his pizza and inspects it, probably for paint, before taking a bite. "Aren't you eating?"

"Yeah, I think Meg has my lunch, though. I really just came in to see you and to, um, ask you out."

Jamie chews slowly and then swallows. Then he sniffs at me. "I already have plans for tomorrow."

"Oh," I say, disappointed, even though that's not exactly what I meant. I meant to ask, *Will you be my boyfriend?* "What kind of plans?"

"I don't know, but I've got them," Jamie says, and turns to me, giving me a dry look. "Or at least that's what I'm supposed to say since you waited so damn long to ask me out again."

My mouth drops open. "Are you serious? You're pissed that I didn't ask you out before now?"

"Yes. According to *Cosmo* you should have asked me out by Tuesday," Jamie says, so seriously my heart starts to pound, and then he collapses into a fit of giggles. "Oh my god, your face."

"You little jerk. I thought you were for real."

He continues to laugh, sucking in air between fits. "Serves you right. Last Saturday was awesome, Sam. Really, you should have reserved me for every weekend for the next month after that."

I let myself laugh at that, even if my heart is still beating in an unsteady pace. "You're right. I really should have. Actually, that's kind of what I'm hoping to do."

Jamie, who had bitten down into his pizza again, freezes and stares at me. "What?" he asks around a mouthful of cheese and pepperoni.

"I'm asking you out. I mean, I'm asking you to be my boyfriend. Not just to go out on another date. I kind of do want to reserve you for every weekend. Like that old Beach Boys song about going steady and not leaving your best girl home on Saturday night or whatever that was." I wince at myself. Whenever it truly counts, I can't be smooth to save my life.

"You want me to be your boyfriend?" Jamie asks.

"Yeah. I mean, I know it was only one date, but . . . it was a really good date."

"Really good," Jamie agrees. Then he finally chews his pizza. "So does this mean I have to wear your class ring on a chain around my neck?"

"And my letterman jacket," I say, and Jamie snorts. As he leans backward, revealing more skin around his neck that his T-shirt had hidden, I see that he's already doing something better. "You're wearing the cross."

"What? Oh, yeah." Jamie looks down, even though he can't quite see where the cross hangs from a thin hemp cord from that angle, then reaches up to run his fingers over it. "So maybe I can skip the letterman jacket?"

I lean over and kiss him. Just once, quick and chaste, because who knows when his art teacher could walk into the room, and I do not want to spend my Friday afternoon in detention for PDA. “So tomorrow, then?”

Jamie blinks, his eyes focusing on me slowly. He still hasn’t quite gotten used to this kissing thing, and I don’t think I’ll ever get over his reactions to it. “Yeah, um. Tomorrow’s good. I mean, I didn’t actually have plans . . .”

A moment passes, where we just smile at each other like goons, and that makes me feel happy and grateful at the same time. Grateful to have found him, for the crazy spell that might be why I did, and to Meg and her goddess.

“It feels right. We feel right.” Jamie looks down at his hands. “I know. I’m fifteen and this is my first relationship ever. What do I know, right? But it feels right to me.”

“No, I agree. Jamie . . . I think I was supposed to meet you,” I say, and cringe at myself. “That sounded absolutely insane. Sorry.”

Jamie takes my hand and traces his thumb over my knuckles. “Not any more than what I just said.”

I smile before kissing him again, just one more time. “So it’s settled? You and I are . . . ?”

“We definitely are,” Jamie says, and this time he kisses me with a lot more enthusiasm than should be allowed at school.

“Well then, I’m going to go eat and tell my friends I’m going steady with the cutest guy in school.”

Jamie cracks up at that. “Okay. Call me tonight?”

“You bet,” I say, and leave him with his songbird.

••••••••••••••••••••

I'm in the passenger seat of Landon's car, on the way to Meg's and then to the Blue Gator after that, to see Travis's band and celebrate their signing with the rest of his friends.

That means it's Saturday, a whole two days since I asked Jamie out, and I haven't actually told Landon yet. I guess I figured Meg would tell him for me.

Okay, I was *hoping* Meg would tell him for me.

"I asked Jamie out," I say, and because I'm so chicken, I look out the window as I talk. "And as far as I know, he doesn't have a boyfriend in Paris or anything, and, you know, he seems to care about me, so this just might work."

"The Perfect Ten?"

I chuckle a little. "He certainly has all the things on the list. And then some. He likes *The Breakfast Club*, so it's a start."

I feel Landon's eyes on me, so I finally turn my face to look at him. To my relief, he's smiling, and I feel a little silly. What did I expect? Of course he's happy for me. This isn't freshman year. We're not dating. He's not going to throw a fit like he did about Chad Anderson. He's going to be happy for me, because we're friends and that's what friends do.

"Of course you forced him to watch that."

"Hey, he forced me into watching *Texas Chainsaw Massacre*. I had to keep a light on while I slept last night."

Landon snorts. "He gets major kudos that he convinced you to try it. I couldn't even get you to watch *The Dark Crystal*."

"Shut up, those dragon things were terrifying."

"They were *puppets*, Sam." Landon turns down Meg's street and the Honda hums along the brick road. "So, two movies, huh?"

My stomach tightens. He's not really asking about the movies. Landon and I must have watched a thousand movies while we were together, but I couldn't tell you what they were about. Even the basics. We were too . . . *busy*. "Two," I answer. I wait for him to look at me to add, "And we really did watch them. Mostly."

"Hey, you don't have to explain. It's none of my business."

"Then why ask?"

Landon is quiet, and we've arrived at Meg's house, so he pulls over but doesn't honk to get her attention. "Just being nosy, I guess," he answers after a minute.

"Don't worry, Mom. I'm taking it slow."

Landon looks at me, trying to read me. I keep my face emotionless.

"Because you're still scared it will mess things up?"

"Because I'm scared *I'll* mess things up." I bonk my head back against the headrest a few times for good measure. "He's so great. Too great."

"I'm glad to hear it," Landon says. He looks away, then he puts both his hands on the steering wheel and honks the horn. I'm not expecting it and I jump.

Meg bounds out of the house, clad in combat boots and fishnets, which means her parents must be out or sleeping or something. She throws herself into the backseat and we're off.

The Blue Gator is one of the cooler bars in Athens. It's huge and wide open in the middle, so there's plenty of space for dancing, even if a band is playing on the stage. There's a balcony that wraps around the entire room, so you always have a good view. I've only been here once before, about a year ago, when Landon and I went to see a band that wasn't famous and turned out to not be that good, but they'd opened for some great bands like the Raconteurs, so we were expecting greatness.

This isn't a ticketed show, so the bouncers at the door want ID. I just smile and say, "I'm Sam Raines," and feel like the most fabulous, famous person in the world when they step aside and let me and my friends through.

The place is packed. The stage is set up for Liquid to play, and I can see several familiar guitars waiting on stands for Travis. Travis himself is leaning up against the bar, talking to a few women who are looking at him like they'd like to devour him, and I turn to Landon.

"Looks like Travis is already having a good night."

Landon eyes me. "You sure you're just friends now? Not a little jealous?"

I turn back to watch Travis. One of the girls laughs a little too loud and lays a hand on his chest. I know exactly what he feels like under her hand—warm and solid and smooth. "Maybe a little," I admit. "Come on, let's get a drink."

Before I can even reach the bar, though, Travis has caught me up in his arms, and I lean into him out of reflex. His mouth meets mine and *damn*, the man can kiss. He swirls his tongue around mine once, twice, and presses himself into me farther before finally releasing me with a laugh. “Sorry, friends now. I forgot. We *are* just friends, right?”

The look in Travis’s eye is wicked, naughty, and just a little bit hopeful. I give him a soft smile. “Just friends. I’m a taken man now.”

The smile that widens on Travis’s face almost makes it worth it to me that that was our last kiss. Almost. “You asked him out?”

“Thursday.”

“You’re a fast worker. I like that.” Travis winks at me, and then, like he’s used to people waiting on him hand and foot, he wiggles a finger at the bartender and motions to me. Seconds later, I have a drink in my hands. “It’s not a Black Widow, I promise.”

Travis winks again and I take a sip. There’s no guesswork in this drink, no illusion of a sober future—this drink is nothing but whiskey.

“I have to go. We’re going to play a few before we sign the contracts. Reps from the label are here to cart my soul off to L.A. as soon as I sign in blood, and they’d like to get a move on. This whole clean-air, small-town atmosphere thing is making them dissolve.”

I laugh and reach down, squeezing his hand. “Don’t forget me when you’re rich and famous.”

“Of course not. I could never forget a boy with those abs. Sean or Steve, or . . . was it Seth?”

“Ha, very funny.”

"Save me a dance?" he asks, and doesn't wait for my answer. He snaps his fingers at Vanessa and Brendon, who immediately drop what they're doing to follow him to the stage. He may not be the lead singer, but he's the leader of the band, and it suddenly hits me that if they succeed in this at all, it's because of his drive and his brains.

Huh. Maybe he really could have been a Perfect Ten.

I make a mental note to talk to Meg about her religion more.

While Liquid plays, I dance with Meg and Landon, mostly the meat in their sandwich. Okay, so I don't really dance, more like I hop up and down. Sam Raines is not the best dancer in the world. Landon can dance, though, like, *really* dance, like he's one of Beyoncé's backup dancers or something. I swear that's half the reason that he's popular. If he's on the dance floor at a party, everyone's watching. So I hang back and do my thing, watching Landon and watching the crowd with awe. All of these people are here, supporting Travis and his band. A huge burst of pride surges in my chest as the band signs the agreements with their future record company. The entire crowd cheers and it's such a cool feeling, to feel a part of something right at its inception. Someday, when Travis's walls are crowded with awards and platinum records and magazine covers, I'll be able to say that I was there the night it all began.

When it's all over and the record execs whisk the contracts away, Travis appears at my side again. I am flattered down to my bones.

"Don't you want to go spend some time with Vanessa and Brendon?" I ask.

"You promised me a dance. Then I'll do whatever. I've got all night."

The song the DJ is playing is slow, down-tempo electronic rock, almost like he wants to blend with Liquid's sound. I hand Landon my drink before heading to the floor with Travis. We move just as slow, our bodies tight together, my arms around his waist.

"We have to leave in a week. They want us in a studio before the end of the month."

I pull back from Travis and look up at his face. "That's soon."

"It is. Sooner than I'd planned. I've got to write a lot this week, but I've got a lot I've been saving that I'm dying to record too. We'll see."

A week. That's not quite long enough to have a friendship, even. I rest my head on Travis's shoulder and say into his ear, "That's just . . . really soon."

"I know. But I'll be back. Sometime in January, maybe sooner. Whenever we can get the tracks laid down right. Then we can try this friendship thing. But first . . ." Travis's hand cups my chin and he holds me still like that so he can kiss me on the lips. "That was the last kiss. I swear. Don't wanna mess things up with your boyfriend, old buddy, old pal."

I chuckle sadly. January seems so far away. "You should go talk to those girls again," I say, already missing him.

"The slutty-looking ones?"

"Yeah, those are the ones." I snort.

"What would I want with them?" Travis says, that wickedness dancing in his eyes again.

"Something that a friend can't give you," I say pointedly, and glance back at the group of girls in question.

"Yeah," Travis muses, looking at them too, then he turns back to me with a sheepish grin. "Guess I'm settling for second best tonight. I'll call you before I leave, okay?"

I watch him make his way through the crowd back to the girls, and in seconds they're laughing at something he's said, pawing at him at every opportunity. The jealousy in me has waned a little, made small by how proud I feel of him, and the certainty of knowing he's going to be an awesome friend. This is how it should be, I suppose.

"Want to dance?"

I turn and Landon is holding out a hand to me, an expectant grin on his face.

"Of course."

Dancing with Landon is different from dancing with Travis. Even though Landon's practically a professional, he lets me lead, following each sway and dip of my body. It's fun, more fun that I remember it being, easy and carefree. I can do anything, goofy or ridiculous, and he just follows me, laughing along, no questions asked. Even the moments where it must be obvious that he's outshining me—when his hips do something so fluid it's mesmerizing, or he turns so quickly I know I would have fallen on my face—I don't feel the least bit self-conscious, or like I'm not good enough. And when a slow song comes on and it's time to stop laughing, he just slides himself into my arms. We fit so well, and my hands flatten over the small of his back, pressing him close. It's a weird thought, but for a second I wonder if our bodies remember each other, if my skin remembers his skin, my nerves his nerves; if our pulses find the same rhythm again.

"You okay?" he asks.

"Yeah. I'm happy for him."

Landon's quiet at that, then he turns his head so that his mouth is close to my ear. "I'm having fun."

I bring him just a little closer to me, his body stretched and leaning against mine as we sway. Yes, Landon's a friend, but there's something about this, this moment with him so close against me like he used to be all the time, that makes me feel like I'm doing something wrong. Something a little sinful. And I know I'll never tell Jamie about it, just as I'll never tell him Travis kissed me good-bye.

"Me too," I say, and we keep dancing.

It's well past midnight when we leave. Meg's been all around the room, dancing even with Travis, but Landon and I haven't moved far from our original place. And when he drops me off at my house we don't say anything about it to each other. Not a word, because like so much else between us, there's nothing to say about it. It is what it is, and that's that.

....

At some point during the next week, Jamie stops going to the art room during lunch to paint, and starts showing up at my table. Meg beams at him, flashing a row of white teeth, picks up her books, and makes room. Just like that, he's in our circle. When Landon skips out on band and joins us, he sits next to Meg instead of me, and just gives Jamie a little nod.

"Fisher, nice to see you."

Yeah, Jamie's definitely in.

What's really awesome, though, is that the next week, Jamie's friends join us too. Kit and Meg get along like they were twins separated at birth, bonding over their mutual interests in making their parents crazy and boys that don't treat them right. Sean, Jamie's other best friend, is completely chill. He's a lot like Landon in a way. Not nearly as social, but completely laid-back. He just kind of laughs along with everyone and when he does offer his opinion or crack a joke, I can see why Jamie made him a best friend. He's wicked smart and probably keeps secrets like some sort of CIA agent.

One day, after Meg and Kit get up to return their cafeteria trays and Sean mumbles something about a missing homework assignment and stalks off, I lean into Jamie and say, "Does it creep you out a little?"

"That our friends are exactly alike?" I snort in response, and Jamie just laughs. "Yeah, a little."

But it's good. It's very good. And it makes Jamie feel even more right than before.

Jamie even starts coming to the Donkey with us after school, and it's like he was part of our little group all along. He lets Meg explain things about Wicca and pretends to agree, even though he shoots me questioning looks over the top of her head, and Landon begins to use him as his source of sophomore gossip.

A thought or two about Travis sneaks in, but only to wonder about how he is—I am purely Jamie's boy now. But Travis does call, just once, before leaving. He says they're ready for the studio and as casual as he tries to act about it, I catch the tremor of excitement in his voice. He asks about Jamie, and all I can say is, "He's perfect, Travis," and I think I truly mean it.

That Friday, after our daily trip to the Donkey, Jamie walks with me back to my house so that I can pick up a car and drive him home. Landon, our usual ride, had some sort of meeting after school, debate or something, but that's okay. It's more time with Jamie. And it will be the first time my parents have met him. I admit, I've been hiding him away a little bit. I guess after Gus and my mom got on so well, I couldn't quite bring myself to introduce them to Jamie, but it can't be helped now.

My mother takes one look at him and recognizes a kindred. "Ah, the prodigy!"

Jamie winces with embarrassment, and I mouth a "Sorry!" to him as Mom scoops him into a hug. "So talented. I couldn't get over the painting you gave Sam. I could stare at it for hours."

"Bring it down, Mom," I say. Obviously, it was too

much to hope for that she would just hand us the car keys and we could be on our merry way.

She lets Jamie go, but not without offering him food first.

"A sandwich? Cookies?"

"Mom. The keys."

"I'm sorry, am I embarrassing you in front of your boyfriend?"

"Yes."

"So it's official, then, huh?" My mother clasps her hands together, hopeful.

"You didn't tell her I'm your boyfriend?" Jamie asks, pouting, playing like he's hurt.

"Oh my god. Keys. Please?"

Mom hands me the keys to her Prius and pats my cheek. "Don't be out too late. Your father is planning major revisions tonight and he can't have you barging in, interrupting his flow."

Jamie finds the whole discussion wonderfully ridiculous and snickers all the way to the car. "Your mom is great."

I roll my eyes. "Get in. And stop encouraging her, would you?"

"What? She's fun." We pile into the car and the Prius silently makes its way down the road. Jamie watches me intently. "So your dad is back?"

"For now," I say. Truthfully, I haven't seen him enough to notice. He came home from New York two days ago with his latest manuscript marked up in so much red it looked like it was bleeding, and he hasn't come out of his office since. "I think he's going to help me edit my writing samples for college applications soon."

If he remembers, anyway.

It's like Jamie reads my mind because he says, cautiously, "Well, I'm no writer, but I read a ton. If you want an extra pair of eyes, I'd love to read your stuff."

I look away from the road to look at him. "Really? That would be great."

"Of course. That's what boyfriends are for, right?"

"It's probably written in the fine print."

Jamie laughs and I park the Prius in his driveway. I lean over to kiss him good-bye but he puts two fingers on my lips, stopping me. I make an undignified sound that might be the kind of sound a puppy makes waiting on a treat.

Jamie's smile is one part amused and one part triumphant, and I scowl.

"Why don't you come in?" he asks after making me wait a few more seconds than I like.

In. He's never invited me in before. My palms start sweating instantly, like the giant geek that I am.

"I . . . um . . ."

"Mom has the late shift tonight. She won't be home until almost midnight."

"Okay." I stare at him.

"So. We'd be alone."

"Alone?"

"Yes. Unsupervised. No chaperone. Completely scandalous."

"You're teasing me."

"You just seem so confused about what I'm trying to say."

I laugh, embarrassed, and cover my face with my hands. "Not confused."

"Shocked, then?" He wiggles his eyebrows in a way that reminds me of Landon. "I only *look* like an angel, you know."

I laugh so hard at that I get tears in my eyes. As out of character as it is for Jamie to comment on his looks, that doesn't make it any less true.

"Are you sure?" I ask him.

"Yes," he says, and to his credit, there's no hesitation. He cocks his head at me. "But maybe you aren't?"

When I don't answer right away, Jamie settles back into the car seat and stares out the window.

"Jamie . . ."

"It's okay, Sam," he says, but his voice is tight so I think it's probably a lie. "I wouldn't be sure about me either."

"It's not that," I say. I put a hand on his knee and he looks at me, finally. "I'm sure about you."

He just looks at me, with those pale blue eyes all wide and hurt, and that's all it takes for the whole thing to come tumbling out of me in a big rush. I tell him about

Landon, about how he and I behaved together and how for the longest time I blamed that dysfunction on us getting physical so soon, never realizing that we just had an incredibly unhealthy relationship, period. I even tell him about what Travis said, although I don't tell him it was Travis who said it.

"And regardless of knowing the difference now, I guess I'm still a little scared. Okay, a lot scared. Because I would never want us to be the way Landon and I were. I like us too much, Jamie." He folds his hand over mine. "I like how we talk and joke around and care about each other's art. If I ever get so jealous of you painting that I ask you to stop it, or get so jealous of every guy that looks at you, I don't know what I'd do."

Jamie is looking at me, but it's like he's not seeing me. His eyes are focusing on something different, like a memory. "Sam, I have a question."

"Okay."

"Was it ever you that acted controlling? Or was it just Landon?"

I think about it for a moment. "Unless I'm not remembering right, which is a possibility, it was mostly Landon."

"And you recognized that there was something wrong about it, even if you didn't get the root of the problem exactly right."

"Yeah."

Jamie cups my jaw in his hand and forces me to keep his gaze. "Then why on earth do you think you'd do these things to me? You need to stop blaming yourself for what was mostly Landon's problem."

I open my mouth to defend Landon, but Jamie isn't done.

"And furthermore, I'd never do those things to you. Do you know how much I love it that you write? And so what if you take a lot of time to do it. That just gives me time to paint. We both have things we love to do, Sam, and yeah, those things require some time apart, but that just means that we have incredible experiences to share when we see each other again. It makes us both better people."

A whole minute passes before I speak. "You really love it that I write?"

Jamie's smile is big. Genuine. "I do."

The list, and the hopes I'd sent out to the universe or the Goddess or whatever, pop into my head. I'd put "talented" on there. I guess what I should have also put down was "appreciation for my own talents too." Regardless, the Goddess seems to have thought ahead for me.

Maybe I owe Meg another meal at Seven Sauces.

"And you'd really help me with these samples for my college applications?"

"Of course."

"Good, because I think my dad is going to forget."

Jamie nods. "Sounds like he's busy right now. So come in. I'll read them and tear them apart for you," he says, eyes dancing with humor. "If you can handle it."

"You can't be any worse than my father," I say, and

it's a joke but it's also true. I glance over at Jamie's house, considering. Jamie notices.

"We can stay at the kitchen table and I swear I won't make a move."

Which reminds me of Travis a little, and I laugh. It's a little soggy sounding. Imagine that. Someone shows me they care and suddenly I'm a crying fool.

"Deal. Jamie, it's really . . . I mean, Landon wouldn't have . . . and it's awesome that you . . ." I give up. "Thanks for doing this."

"I told you. That's what boyfriends do. Or they should," Jamie says, and I pick up what he's laying down: Landon should have treated me better.

"You sure you've never had a boyfriend before?"

"Never, but I feel like I've been training for it my whole life." Though his voice is light, there's a seriousness in him that I can see and sense. His eyes are focused, sharp, like his Jubjub bird. I recognize that feeling, down to my bones. I open my mouth to say something, I don't know what, but Jamie speaks again. "You know how you said you thought we were supposed to meet?"

"Yeah?"

Jamie lifts a hand to his throat, fingers the knotted cross lying there. "About a week or so before you came to Seven Sauces, I prayed for the first time since Dad died, Sam. I prayed to find someone. And I know I'm going to sound crazy . . . like a religious freak or a superstitious idiot . . . but . . . it can't be a coincidence, can it?"

My whole body tingles, every hair rising up, my

nerves on high alert. I could swear there's a buzz or a hum in the car.

I shake my head. "No, Jamie. I don't think it's a coincidence. Because I don't think you're a freak or an idiot for saying that. Anyone else might, but you've met just about the only other person in this podunk town, besides Meg, who doesn't believe in coincidences."

Jamie kisses me then, and there's another hum, though it might be a feeling more than a sound. He pulls away briefly, then kisses me again. "One more. Improves the odds that I'll actually behave myself inside."

He winks, which is about enough to make me throw any self-control I have out the window, but thankfully when we go inside he does behave, and I leave a few hours later knowing how to fix my stories.

Fourteen

"Well, what do you think?"

I'm sitting at the little desk in my room, turned around in my chair so that I can look at Landon, who is surrounded by about thirty of my best writing samples. It's Sunday afternoon and he'd called, bored out of his mind, wanting me to come over. But I'd been putting off sending in college applications long enough, and if I wanted to get them all done before Christmas break, I didn't have much choice but to work on them now.

So he'd come over here, grudgingly without any pot because my parents were home. (Don't get me started on the hypocrisy of that. Goodness knows they did their fair share in college, and probably before and after. Hell, they probably do it when I'm not around. But can their sweet baby boy indulge? Noooo.) I'd set him to work too, reading through all my samples for his opinion.

"I don't even know, Sam. You know I've never been good at giving you criticism."

Not exactly true. More like he never wanted to. But

I press him, because this is far too important right now. "Come on, Landon. Help."

"They're all good," he says. "You've changed a lot of them since the last time you had me read them. For the better."

I grin. "Jamie helped a lot the other day."

Landon looks surprised at that. "Well, it's better than what I could have done. You should ask your dad, not me. They're up to his level now."

"I want a layman's opinion," I say, which is kind of a lie. I really want Dad's opinion, but that will have to wait. If I get it at all.

"I am *extremely* layman." Landon picks up one of the stories again and holds it out to me. It's the story about the music critic. I grin.

"Jaime really liked that one too."

"I can see why," Landon says, nodding. He begins to gather up all the other papers that are burying him but continues talking. "There's something about the way your writing sounds in that. Not that the others aren't good, but that one sounds the most like you. When did you even write that? I've never seen it before."

"Last week. With Travis. He, um . . . he played guitar while I wrote it. Put me in some kind of trance."

Landon sits up, papers gathered in his hands. He arches a brow. "Sounds sexy."

I know that my face relaxes into something like a dreamy grin, and I hate it, but whatever. "It was. It felt very, um, intimate, I guess."

Landon snorts but he doesn't quite meet my eye. Instead, he concentrates on all the papers in his hands. "Where are you applying, besides NYU?"

"Iowa, University of Michigan, Cornell . . ." I reach into my memory for more names. "Brown."

"Cornell? Brown, really?" Landon asks, clearly surprised, then he backtracks. "Not that you're not smart enough, I just can't picture you at an Ivy League."

"I know, it's a little bit weird, but they have great creative writing programs. And Dad says that the connections alone would be worth the admission." I shrug at him. "Where are you applying?"

"I don't know yet."

"Landon, most schools want applications in by the beginning of the year."

"I know." He sets the papers aside and picks at a loose thread on my bedspread. "But I don't have any clue what I want to do, so I can't choose a school anyway."

And for the first time, it hits me hard: I may not have my two best friends with me next year. I expected it with Meg. For as long as I can remember she's talked about how she's going to go to Hocking College to get one of their forestry degrees, so she can commune with nature professionally. I knew she wouldn't be with me in New York or wherever I end up.

But Landon . . . I guess I always figured he'd go with me wherever I went. I never even considered the possibility that we wouldn't live in the same place. Not once.

The thought makes me feel like I've had too much

coffee—jittery and unbalanced, and so I blurt out, "Apply to NYU."

Landon chuckles sadly. "And what? Brown? I'm not smart like you, Sam. Hocking probably won't even let me in."

I'm about to argue with him, to tell him that he's smarter than I am in so many ways, but my phone vibrates in my pocket and the Cure's "Lovesong" plays loud and clear through my jeans.

"Sorry, it's Jamie. Hold on."

I answer the phone and turn away from Landon, who is lying back on my bed and staring up at the ceiling now, looking forlorn. I try to concentrate on what Jamie's saying, but his voice isn't nearly as persistent as the urge to crawl next to Landon and comfort him. I never could tolerate it when Landon seemed sad.

Jamie tells me he got called in to work and won't be home until eleven thirty, and I promise to stay up for his call. He asks me what I'm up to, and I tell him I'm doing college applications. He laughs evilly and says he'll leave me to have fun with that, and I hang up.

Landon sits up, studying me. "You didn't tell him I was here."

"Didn't I?" I ask. "Guess it didn't come up."

He studies me more, enough that I grow fidgety under his gaze. It's not like I was hiding it from Jamie, but, friends or not, it's a little strange to say to my boyfriend, "Oh, my ex? Yeah, he's just lying on my bed right now. No biggie." Especially since I'm fighting the urge to snuggle up to Landon on said bed. Even if I just want to cheer Landon up, that won't sound good no matter how you spin it.

"I should go," Landon says, and I'm relieved to hear him say it. I probably should invite him to stay for dinner because neither of his parents cook, but I don't find the voice to ask him.

"I'll walk you out."

I follow him to his car and we both lean up against it, quiet for a minute, before Landon says, "Thanks for killing the boredom."

"Hey, thanks for your help."

"My opinion about anyone's writing isn't help, trust me, but . . ." He gives me one of his trademark quirky smiles. "Send that one out. I think it's your best." Then his grin fades. "I'm glad Travis could inspire you that way."

"Oh, he didn't really," I say, and it feels kind of like a defense.

"Sure," he kids me, and opens the door. "See ya."

Back inside the house, my mom comes out of the kitchen, a wooden spoon dripping something red as she walks toward me. "Did Landon leave? I was just about to invite him to dinner."

It's true, Gina Raines loves just about everyone she meets, but she's always had a big soft spot for Landon. She mothers him even more than she mothers Meg, and Meg's practically her adopted daughter. In fact, I clearly remember that one of her biggest smiles was for Landon, the first time I invited him over after our breakup. It was like the prodigal son had returned.

"It's okay. He needed to get home."

For the second time that day, someone studies me a little too intensely for my liking. "Is everything okay?"

If only I knew.

I sigh. "Something just feels off, you know? And I don't know why or if I'm just imagining it."

Ugh, I wish I hadn't said anything, because now not only is she studying me, she has this insulting look of pity on her face too. Then, to add insult to injury, she reaches out with her free hand and ruffles my hair. "I'm sure you'll figure it out soon enough, Sam. Now wash up. Dinner's done."

"Okay. Hey, Mom?" She stops her trek back into the kitchen to turn around. "Will you read something later? Landon said it's the best thing I've ever written but I'm not sure."

"Of course. Did your father look your samples over?"

"No. He's been so busy with his own work," I say. "I hate to bug him."

Mom sighs, and I sense that whatever she says next isn't going to be good news. "He's going to have to go to New York again, Sam. Interviews, awards, a few marketing meetings. He can't get out of them, as much as he'd like to."

"How long?"

Mom shrugs. "I'm not sure, but he'll be back a few days before Christmas. I made him promise that." She gives me an apologetic smile. "I'll make sure he reads your stories. I promise. He can read them on the plane, if nothing else."

My mother is about the only person on earth who could tear my father away from a manuscript and live to tell the tale, so I know she'll manage it, and I'm extremely grateful.

"Now come on. I put tons of ketchup on the meatloaf. You'll love it."

She ruffles my hair again as she makes toward the kitchen, but this time I don't mind it so much.

....

It's the last day of school before Christmas break, snow is falling lightly outside the classroom windows, and I'm staring at my book because my brain is already on holiday mode.

"Mr. Raines."

I look up from my weathered copy of *Diary of a Superfluous Man* to see that Mrs. Palmer has stopped the discussion—if you can call it that; it was mostly Joel trying to flirt his way to an A—because a runner from the office has just delivered a note. She frowns at the note, then at me, and my heart sinks. Notes from the office can be great news, or they can be horrible news, like telegrams from the military.

"It looks as though you are wanted in the guidance office."

I grab my books and take the note from her waiting hand before exiting the classroom. Guidance is a hallway and a half away, and as soon as I round the corner, I get mugged.

No. Not really.

But Meg does fly at me out of nowhere, scaring me enough that I drop my books and let out a girly screech.

"What the hell is wrong with you?"

She's giggling like an idiot as I pick up my books, then she shushes me when I try to ask another question. "Sorry. Kit was working in the office today and did me a favor. I need major advice and we can't talk about this at lunch. Too much corn."

Corn. I snicker. In middle school we'd invented a top-secret code to let each other know that our parents were in the room when we were on the phone together. That way the other would know that we couldn't talk about the important stuff. Corn equals ears. We were so clever.

She loops an arm through mine and we make our way to the auditorium. We don't make a peep as we take a seat in a middle row, like we're the first ones to arrive to a show.

Though neither of us act, Meg and I both love the auditorium. She loves it because she swears it has some kind of energy. I love it because unless there's a rehearsal, it's usually the quietest place in the school, even more so than the library. I love writing in this space.

"Here," Meg says, thrusting her phone in front of my nose.

I read what's on the screen. It's a text from Michael, clearly meant to be suggestive, although all it does is make my stomach queasy. I cringe and give her the phone back. "So his parents are out of town this weekend?"

She nods, then bites her lip, her eyes pleading with

me. "Bringing his sister back from college for the holidays. Cover for me? Please? I can tell my dad we're having one of our famous movie nights."

"All night?"

She shrugs. "At least until really late. Please, Sam? You know they'd freak if they found out his parents weren't home."

"So he's not even going to spring for a hotel room?"

She glares, and I sigh, hesitating with my answer. I've lied to her parents before, that's not unusual. But only for small things, little white lies like, "No, Mrs. Oliver, there won't be any drinking at the party" or "We want to watch one more movie, can Meg stay out later?" or "Yes, Mr. Oliver, I'll try harder to pray away the gay." I've never covered for her like this, when she's sneaking off to be with Michael the Douche. Alone.

"So, does this mean you're really going to . . . ?" I can't force myself to say the words.

"Maybe?" she says, shrugging. "I still haven't decided. That's why I wanted your advice. How did you know you were ready with Landon?"

I shift in the theater seat. God, I'm going to hate this conversation, I can tell. Everything from the fact that Meg's considering having sex with that idiot to bringing up the whole thing with Landon. It's like all my least favorite things combined.

"I'm not sure we were." I force a laugh at my own joke, but Meg's still staring at me with her big trusting eyes, expectant. I sigh. I never could resist her puppy dog looks. "I was in love with him. I couldn't imagine my first time being with anyone else."

Meg turns her gaze to the empty stage, considering my words. The bell rings but we don't budge; we have an office excuse.

"I love Michael," she says finally.

"Why?"

Meg shrugs. "Why did you love Landon?"

"No, don't avoid the question. Why do you love Michael?"

"He's sweet. Romantic. Attractive." She chews on a hangnail. "It's like your list. You had all these things you wanted in a person, right? I guess Michael would have a lot of things on my list, if I had one."

"And what about loyalty?" I ask.

"What about it?" she fires back.

Her peachy cheeks change into an angry red, but I go on. "He asked you out and then, what? A week later he cheated on you with Ellie Graves—"

"We weren't really going out yet."

"A technicality," I say, ready to pull from the long mental file of Michael's other misdeeds. "How about last year when he broke up with you for two days for that slutty sophomore? Or the time he left you crying at Mark Ramey's party because you refused to go upstairs with him? Or just a couple of weeks ago when you read his texts to another girl?"

"We talked about all those things and it's fine. That's what people who are in love do, they work things out." It's kind of a below-the-belt jab at me and Landon, but I let it slide because if she's truly considering having sex with Michael, she's clearly not sane. "Why do you hate him so much?" she asks.

"I already told you!"

"All of that stuff is about me, though."

"Exactly!" I practically yell. "I don't give a shit that he's a homophobic jerk, or that he wears football shirts every day, or that he uses enough cologne to choke a cat. I hate him because he hurts you all the time."

I know I've hit a nerve, a big one, because her red face turns downright purple. "He loves me—"

"I'm sure that's what he told you," I say, my voice pissy and sharp.

Meg sucks in a breath and then grits her teeth. "At least I've been with him for two years and I know who he is. It's not like I went home with some rock dude that I'd only known for a few hours—which I lied for *you* about, by the way."

"Travis is irrelevant."

"Why is he irrelevant? Just because I'm a girl so I'm a slut if I want to have sex?"

"You know I don't think that," I growl at her.

"Oh, so it's just because you're the amazing Sam Raines that you get a free pass?"

I set my jaw. "You know that's not true either."

"Then explain to me, oh wise one, why Michael is such a bad guy for texting someone else, when you've been doing the same thing to Jamie?"

"That's not exactly true and I told you why," I snap. "He's not good enough for you."

"Right," she says, and sinks down into her chair, kicking at the row of seats in front of us. "Sorry that Michael's not a beautiful French boy, or a sexy guitar player, or a painter who looks like an elf. But he doesn't have to match your stupid list, just mine."

I pull at my hair in frustration. "Fine. Lose your virginity to a guy who treats you like crap. It's your life."

"Why not? It's exactly what you did."

"Landon and I were not that bad."

"You were, Sam. You just didn't see it." She collapses back into the auditorium seat beneath her. "God, you're being such a freaking hypocrite."

"Yeah, well, you're being a bitch."

Shit. Now I've done it.

Her face crumples and tears well up in her eyes, and even though it's still too fresh for me to grasp it, my heart starts to ache. But Meg's too proud to let me have the satisfaction of seeing her cry, so she stands and walks out of the auditorium, the door slamming behind her.

I curse at myself, and the word echoes around the empty theater.

Then I text Landon.

I don't know how he gets out of class but he's charming like that. Within a minute he's in the seat next to me, listening with a look of pure concentration on his face while I tell him everything, his hand gripping mine.

"She brought up you and me, as if we were anything like her and Michael."

Landon nods. "Yeah. We were a completely different type of dysfunctional than they are."

I laugh a little at that, then we both fall silent. Landon strokes his thumb over my knuckles.

"I know this is about Meg, but . . ."

Landon's voice is unusually soft and kind of strained. I wait as patiently as I can for his next words.

"Do you really think we were so awful together? I mean, it wasn't all bad, was it?"

"Us? Nah," I say, smiling. "We weren't all bad."

"Good," Landon says. "I know we made mistakes. I know we have a lot of issues about it, but . . . I thought there was a lot of good too."

"There was, Landon. Of course there was. And the good is still here between us. The good survived."

"Thanks, Sam. I needed to hear that." Landon gives my hand a squeeze, then lets go. "For what it's worth, I'm really sorry I wasn't a better boyfriend."

"We had a lot to learn," I say, shrugging. "I think I'm learning."

I consider telling him what Travis said, about how jealousy doesn't come from love, but maybe that's not my place anymore. Maybe he needs his own Travis to say it. Or better yet, his own Jamie to *understand* it.

Then, though his pretty eyes seem a touch sad, Landon rests his head back against the theater seat and gives in to one small laugh.

"Ugh. Michael? The girl has no taste."

"Yeah. We haven't been a good enough influence on her."

"Obviously not." Landon stands, pulling me up. We pause in the aisle, grinning at each other. Then Landon's whole face softens. "Give her a break, Sam. She says she loves him. Love can make you stupid. And crazy."

I take his meaning and sober a little. "I know. She'll get over it, won't she?"

"Most likely. But it might take another dinner at Seven Sauces."

Landon winks at me because the jerk knows he's right: there's another chocolate torte in my future.

....

By the time I head to lunch that day, the sky has unleashed a winter storm and slushy, gray snow is covering everything. It's ugly, and messy, and not at all the pretty kind you see on Christmas cards. To make matters worse, they decide that keeping us here at school would be safer than sending us home in it, so we don't even get out early. I should take it as an omen that this day is just going to get worse, but I don't. I make my way to the art room, hoping to catch Jamie for a bit before I find Meg to apologize.

I try to cheer myself up as I walk, thinking about my plans with Jamie over break. Christmas is in four days, and my birthday four after that, and for the first time since freshman year I'll be sharing both with a boyfriend. Jamie has invited me over to his house for Christmas dinner, and we have plans to spend my birthday in Columbus, shopping and eating at a restaurant neither of us can really afford. To top it all off, I called Ninah for help with Jamie's Christmas present, and she emailed me a list of art supplies that Jamie would need—art supplies I was sure he didn't have yet. They've been arriving piece by piece on my doorstep every day, sent in small and large cardboard boxes from supply stores peppered across the country. I can't wait to watch him open them all up, to see the smile on his pretty face get bigger and bigger with each one.

But Jamie isn't in the art room when I get there. I remember that he said something about a project the art club was doing for the thespians, something about painting their scenery, but I can't remember when he said he'd be doing that. I was too busy trying to steal another kiss while the teachers weren't looking.

I'm about to leave and head to the stage to look for him when my eyes focus on an easel in Jamie's corner of the room.

The easel has been the honored place of the phoenix for weeks, since its large canvas is too wide for a space on the wall, and I know Jamie's been working on it steadily, adding small details and swoops of color here and there until he feels right calling it done.

This canvas, however, looks nothing like the phoenix. It's black, or nearly so, covered in thick, ropey strokes of paint. They're scattered, in no particular pattern—a blob here, a drip there, an angry slash on top of a jabbed splotch. Reds, yellows, and oranges peek out from underneath the tar-like paint, as if scared of the darkness covering them. It's the phoenix all right, but it's been mutilated, destroyed.

My stomach ties itself into a sick knot and I wonder who could have done this to such a beautiful painting. A jealous senior? Some ignorant bigot wanting to teach the homo a lesson?

Light footsteps draw my attention from the phoenix as Jamie steps into the art room. I glance at him before turning back to the canvas. "What happened? Who did this?"

"I did."

Jamie's voice is whisper-soft but thick, as if something's caught in his throat. I turn to look at him in question and see what I didn't notice before from a single glance. He's crying, or has been. His porcelain skin is blotched with red, his long eyelashes coated and sticky with wet, and white paths trace their way down his cheeks. The knot within my stomach coils tighter as fear and worry for him fill me.

"What? What's wrong? What happened?"

He doesn't answer me, and he doesn't come any closer. He merely stares at me, eyes shiny with tears. "Who's Travis?"

Travis.

The room spins as answers to that question fly in circles around my head. Terror seizes me, runs cold and poisonous through my veins, causing my heart to freeze inside my chest.

"Travis is a friend," I hear myself say, and my voice

thumps around inside my ears along with my blood.

"A friend, huh?" Jamie laughs once, a tinny sound without resonance. "Because it sounded like he was much more than that when I heard you and Meg arguing earlier."

Oh no. He heard that whole argument? I frantically try to remember what, exactly, Meg and I said, but I can't. "It's nothing. I didn't—"

"Sure. You didn't. You just went home with him and Meg had to cover for you because you were *out with a friend.*"

"Okay, he was more than that for a while, yeah. But nothing really happened. We decided we were just going to be friends and then I asked you out."

"How long?" Jamie asks, and there's an accusation behind his voice.

"How long what?"

"How long between when you decided just to be friends with Travis and when you asked me out?"

"Oh, um . . ." I grope for words and will myself to think, but nothing's making sense. It's all jumbled and I can't untangle it and I feel like I might break apart because of the way Jamie's looking at me. It's like he hates me or something. I've never seen him look at anything or anyone with hatred, and how did I get here, that he's looking at me that way?

"Let me see if I can help you remember," Jamie offers in a not at all friendly voice. "Was it after Yellow Springs, then?"

"Yes, but . . . we weren't officially together."

"Yeah, that's a really convenient loophole, isn't it?"

"It's not a loophole, it's fact. I never said—"

"No, you never said, you're right," Jamie spits. "You just took me to a place I've wanted to see for years and bought me a silver cross and let me kiss you like some foolish idiot who has no idea that you're hooking up with some musician."

"Jamie, I wasn't lying to you. That whole date all I could think about was how perfect you were, how great we were together. I didn't think about Travis at all, and I'd seen him the night before. Doesn't that tell you something?"

"Oh, the night before, huh? From him to me in an hour or less. Actually, that does tell me a lot about you," he snarls, and I realize then that I just dug a bigger hole for myself. "I should have known. I mean, you were dating Frenchie when you asked for my number."

I shake my head. "That's not fair."

Jamie snorts. "Did you do more with Travis than kiss?"

"What? No . . . I . . . no."

"Your hesitation makes me have absolute faith in your answer, Sam."

"It wasn't like that, I swear. I got drunk and he took care of me. That's why Meg had to lie for me. I swear it."

"You were drunk and he took care of you." Jamie snorts and rolls his eyes. "He sounds like a real gentleman."

"Travis is beside the point. What I'm trying to say is that, yeah, I had a thing with him, but I told him I just wanted to be friends." I look at Jamie, whose gaze is too angry and intense, so I look up at the ceiling instead, and damn it if there aren't tears in my eyes. "I wanted to be with you."

Jamie shakes his head, and his anger seems to dissolve. In its place is defeat. "Seems like it. You tell me you worry that sleeping with me will mess us up, give me that whole Landon sob story, but you're just fine spending the night with him, apparently."

"I was confused, Jamie. I was trying to figure some things out." I leave it at that because it seems like, at this point, telling him that part of the truth could only make things worse. "That's all it was. And really, nothing happened. I'm not lying. You have to believe that. You mean so much to me. Travis . . . Travis was nothing compared to that. You're all I want, Jamie. Yellow Springs meant a lot to me too, okay? Everything has."

He shakes his head again, and I almost wish for his anger back, because it's better than the awful, torturous hurt in his eyes. "Really? So you haven't seen him again since we've been official?"

I hesitate again, and it's just long enough that he knows the truth, even if I tried to lie. I confess. "Once. He had a party."

"And?"

I hate myself, genuinely hate myself, because the next words I have to say are really going to hurt him.

"He kissed me."

Jamie nods, like it's no surprise that I'm the world's

biggest asshole. "And I'm sure you didn't kiss back, right?"

I don't answer that. I don't need to. Then he points to the door. "Get out."

I hear myself beg, "Don't. Everything with Travis is over. Please believe me."

"Why should I believe anything you say?" Jamie asks, then does something that is far worse than his anger, far worse than his crying. He walks around me to the phoenix's canvas and stares at it. Then he reaches for a brush on the table to his right, and it's covered with black, oozing paint.

"No!" I say, horrified. He pauses, the brush in midair. "I'm sorry about Travis, but don't break up with me. I was just stupid. It's you, okay? Only you."

It occurs to me in that moment how much I sound like Gus, and I'm even more disgusted with myself, if that's even possible.

Jamie bites his lip and shakes his head, then pushes the brush against the canvas like he wants to cut it, push through and lacerate the thin material until it's nothing more than shreds.

"Please leave."

His words come out weak, strangled, barely spoken. He continues to slash the brush across the canvas, though, spelling out all the anger he can't voice.

I reach out and place my hand over his and the brush stops its massacre.

"Don't," I say. I know he's right and I know I'm wrong and there's nothing I can do now but beg and pray and hope he'll forgive me, but I can't let him do this. "Don't ruin any more, Jamie. I'm not worth it."

"I know," he says, and even though I deserve it, even though I agree, that goes straight to my heart like a knife.

I walk toward the door, but before I leave, I turn to look at him. He hasn't moved. His hand is still poised over the canvas, a horrified look on his face as if he's just realized what he did to his beautiful artwork.

"I'm really sorry I hurt you," I say, and he drops the brush into the cup of paint and buries his head in his hands.

I leave him then, and walk numbly back in the direction of the cafeteria. I'm seconds away from crying, from screaming, from beating my fists against the wall in hopeless rage, so I walk faster. I have to get out. I have to get far away from this stupid school and let it go. Scream and cry and hit something hard.

"Sam," says a voice from behind me, and I barely acknowledge that it's Landon. I hear him jog to catch up to me and he plants himself in front of me, unmoving. "Hey, what's wrong? What happened? Meg's still angry?"

Tears are coming, threatening and blazing hot, and I shake my head at them, or maybe at Landon. "Jamie . . . found out about Travis . . ."

"Oh." I hear Landon's pity and his concern ringing through his voice, and his arms wrap around me for a hug.

"No, don't. You hug me now and I will lose it. I'll lose it in front of the whole school and I can't lose it in front of the whole school. I can't . . ."

Landon immediately lets me go and I can feel his eyes on me, even if I'm staring at the ground and trying to hold in my tears. "What can I do?"

"Can I have your car?"

He pauses, thinking. "Can I drive you somewhere? I don't think you should drive like this. Not with this snow."

"Please, Landon."

He hesitates for another minute before digging into his pocket and pulling out his car keys. "If I don't hear from you within an hour, I'm going to send out a search party. And I'm going to call your mother. Please, Sam. Drive carefully, okay? Don't go too fast. And don't take any of those damn back roads. Stay on straight stretches of highway, please?"

I promise him I will, take the keys, and run out the door of the school. Within minutes I'm flying down the highway, the windows rolled down even though it's the middle of December, the radio blasting indie rock anger as loud as I can push it. I don't stick to my promise. After a few miles on the highway I pull off onto a country road, and after a couple more miles I pull off the road completely, under an old rusted train overpass.

When I was a child, maybe six or seven years old, my mom and I had taken this country road out to an Amish farm, where we'd picked our own strawberries and grapes, paying for them by the bushel. But on the way home, a deer had run out in front of our car, and even though Mom had slammed on the brakes, she'd hit it, full on. It fell right in front of us, right underneath this old overpass, and we both climbed out of the car, ignoring the huge dent it had made in our old brown Volvo, to lay a comforting hand on its broken body as it breathed its last breath. Mom and I both cried after that, holding each other for what seemed like hours, mourning the loss of something so beautiful and innocent. It seems like an appropriate place to stop today.

I get out and sit on the hood of Landon's Honda and let myself cry until I'm dry. Then I get up, wipe my face clean, and start the car. I don't take it back to the school, which would have been convenient for Landon, but I'm not exactly thinking about his needs. I'm not thinking too clearly at all. I park it in front of my house, go inside, and crawl into bed. My dad is in New York, and Mom won't be home for hours yet, and I'm exhausted.

I fall into a shallow sort of sleep, and when I wake it's dark outside and the car is gone, so Landon must have walked over to pick it up. And he must have said something to my mom because they let me sleep and don't knock on the door. I catch my mother, sometime after midnight, peeking in to check on me. I pretend to be asleep as she wanders up to my bed and kisses my forehead softly, like she used to do when I was little. She doesn't wake me in the morning either, and I spend the day in a bed surrounded by presents meant for Jamie, meant for my boyfriend, constant reminders of what I've lost.

Fifteen

I wake up to my mother's voice, which sounds far too bright for the gloomy winter's day outside. Of course I can only assume it's gloomy. I haven't been outside lately, much less even walked to the window. But the light coming through my pulled blinds is dim at best, and even under my down comforter I feel a little chilly.

It's been a couple of days, maybe three, since Jamie broke up with me. I've been sleeping so much it's hard to tell, to be honest. Mom comes in from time to time to offer food or attempt to get me moving. Dad came in when he got back from New York to say hello and drop off a few books his editor recommended for me. For the most part, though, my parents have left me alone to wallow in self-pity. And I am having a spectacular wallow. All I can think about when I'm conscious is the look in Jamie's eyes as he told me to get out, so filled with dark contempt, and it's only made worse by the slow, torturous reckoning that I'm never going to kiss him again and I don't deserve to.

My mom's voice drifts through the door again like

chiming bells, and it dawns on me that she's not talking to me, or my father for that matter. Then I hear Landon's soft laugh and I put two and two together. Before I can even think about getting out of bed to put on a fresh shirt or brush my teeth, Landon cracks the door open, just wide enough to fit his head through, and gives me a weak smile.

"Am I allowed in?"

I almost consider saying no. I haven't been out of this bed for possibly three days and I must look (and smell) like crap.

"I'm gross," I say in lieu of a protest.

"I know. I can smell you from here." Landon's grin is warm and so welcoming that I can't resist smiling back. He sets a large cardboard box on the floor as he enters. He leaves the door ajar, remembering my mother's rules about having boys in my room, even though it's been years since that mattered with us. "How are you?"

I sit up and Landon takes a seat next to me. "Hurting," I say, even though that one word can't possibly cover the anguish that's made itself at home in my chest since Jamie said those painful words.

"Gina said you haven't been out of bed in a few days. She's worried." He reaches over and seeks out my hand on top of my comforter and rubs his thumb along my knuckles. "Me too."

"Did she ask you to come over?"

"Nah. I figured it had been long enough that you might be ready for a friend now." Landon shrugs and swoops his thumb over my knuckles again.

I watch his thumb move. "And Meg?"

"Meg will be over tomorrow."

"She's not mad anymore?"

Landon makes a face. "I wouldn't say that, but she's not pissed enough to stay away while you're doing the breakup hermit thing. She really did want to come over but her parents won't let her out of the house. They have to go to Christmas Eve Mass or something, although I'm pretty sure that's not for hours yet."

"It's Christmas Eve?" I ask, and the realization that it has indeed been three days sobers me a little, brings a tingle to the edges where it had felt so numb.

"Yep. Very important day for Santa Claus. And apparently Catholics."

"Far too holy of a day for Meg to soil herself with the likes of us," I say, and chuckle. My throat feels rusty with it.

"Precisely. Can't go gallivanting about with us heathens on high holy days. Pretty sure that's grounds for excommunication." He laughs with me, and it feels so good to hear that sound. Then, after a long pause, Landon says, "Were you in love with him?"

I pause before answering. "It hurts like I was."

"Close enough, maybe?" Landon offers.

I use one of my father's favorite sayings. "Close only counts in horseshoes and hand grenades."

"And sometimes carpentry," Landon adds, and then gives me a smile that barely turns up the corners of his mouth. "And love, perhaps."

"He was kind of wonderful, you know?" Despair colors the edges of my voice dark. "Everything I wanted."

Landon leans away from me and fidgets with his clothes, first smoothing a wrinkle in his dark jeans, then tugging down the hem of his gray sweater. "He did seem to be your Perfect Ten."

"So why did I screw up?"

"I don't know." Landon's pale gray-blue eyes are warm, sweet, almost prettier than normal. At least I think so. It's been a long time since I really looked closely at his eyes. It's really been a long time since I've pulled my head out of my ass and really looked at anything, to be honest.

"I was being an asshole."

"Maybe. Or maybe two really hot guys both wanted you and you had trouble deciding between them." Landon shrugs. "Which isn't an asshole move. Maybe a horny teenage boy move, but not an asshole move."

I chuckle because there's a lot of truth to that, but then I sober again. "I made that stupid list, though. I know what I want. Or at least I thought I did. And then I basically did to Jamie what Gus did to me. What's wrong with me?"

"Nothing's wrong with you, Sam."

"I lied to Jamie."

Landon nods. "Yeah. But he should have given you another chance."

"Yeah?" I ask, incredulous. "Would you have given me another chance if I'd cheated on you?"

"Yes," Landon answers without hesitation. "Because I was so stupid in love with you. But also because you're awesome. You're a Perfect Ten. Jamie should have realized that."

I stare at him, taken aback and flattered. I shake my head at him. "You're just as delusional as Meg. No wonder you took her side the other day."

"I didn't take her side. I just understand." Landon shrugs like it's no big deal, what he just said, but he's blushing. The blush deepens as he adds, "For what it's worth, I think Jamie should have fought for you. A real Perfect Ten would have."

I consider that. Landon might be right; a real Perfect Ten might have given me another chance. Then again, would I have even noticed Travis if Jamie was really the Perfect Ten?

The whole thing makes my head hurt on top of an already hurting heart, and I rub at my temples.

"I want a break," I blurt, and Landon raises a brow at me. "I don't want to think about that stupid list for a while because I've got no clue what I want, or what I don't want, or whether he measures up or not, or whether he should have given me a second chance, blah blah blah. I just don't know anymore. All I know is that I hurt Jamie. And I miss him. And this whole thing sucks and it's really kind of sucked since I first started it, with Gus and Travis and Jamie and *ugh*! I don't want to do this anymore. It hurts."

Landon nods and I can tell he understands. "Okay, then. Take a break. Be single for a while. Are you hungry?"

It's kind of whiplash-inducing, but I've always been

thankful for Landon's no-nonsense approach. He just accepts things and rolls with it.

"Starving," I reply. I've eaten sandwiches and other things my mother has brought me, but not anything substantial enough for a growing boy.

Landon nods. "Okay. Why don't you shower and I'll go find food? Then after you eat we can watch bad TV all day long."

"Sounds great," I say, and it does. I throw the covers off of myself and stand, stretching. "What's up with the cardboard box?"

"Oh," Landon says, and shrugs. "I figured I'd box up all this stuff you were going to give to Jamie for Christmas and, uh, dispose of it."

I sniff, amused. "Gonna burn it in some Wiccan ritual?"

Landon covers his mouth because an irreverent snicker escapes his lips. "I was just going to give it to the Salvation Army. But maybe a ritual burning is more fitting?"

I shake my head. "Nah. Good karma might undo this stupid spell more than burning paintbrushes, and goodness knows we need to end it."

Landon gets up and sets the box on the bed, eyeing it once before squinting at me. "You sound like you believe the spell worked."

"I'm not saying it worked, but don't you think it's a little fishy that three impossibly gorgeous boys mysteriously came out of the woodwork after that?" I can tell Landon's trying to hold back a laugh and I roll my eyes.

"What? All I'm saying is that maybe Meg doing some sort of spell to end it doesn't sound like a bad idea to me. Just in case."

Landon snorts and then orders me to go shower. I take a long time, standing under the water until my muscles relax completely and my skin is all wrinkled up. I even shave. When I get out, I dress for comfort—wool socks, flannel pajama pants, and an old Denison sweatshirt of my dad's. The box is gone, along with all of Jamie's presents, and I follow the sound of laughter to the kitchen, where Landon and my mom are putting together plates of food. I sit on a stool at the counter.

Mom winks at me. "Good to see you've rejoined the living."

"Nursing a broken heart takes time," Landon says.

Mom hums. "Yes, but even the most heartbroken of all of us need to eat on occasion. And shower."

Landon snorts at my mom and shoves a plate across the counter for me. It's my favorite—chunky peanut butter and homemade strawberry jam, with the crusts cut off like I loved when I was a kid. I'm almost positive it was my mother who cut the crusts off, but if it was Landon I wouldn't have been surprised. There's a healthy dose of potato chips and sliced apples on my plate too, sprinkled with salt, and I truly do feel like a kid again. A kid who needs someone to take care of him and cut off his crusts. But it feels wonderful, not insulting, and warmth spreads through me, taking away the chill that's been settled in my bones for days.

"I seem to remember seeing something about a *Star*

Trek marathon on the sci-fi network," I say casually, and accept the glass of milk my mom hands to me. I catch Landon's eye. "If you'd like to watch that, I could go for it. But I know you hate *Star Trek*, so it's okay if you don't."

"I don't hate it, I just don't worship it like you do."

"It is completely deserving of worship, I'll have you know," I argue around a mouthful of peanut butter. "Whole languages were invented because of that show."

"Oh yeah, and I'm sure Klingon is extremely useful in the real world."

"We both study a dead language and you want to argue with me about usefulness?"

"Touché." Landon swipes a chip off my plate, even though there's still a pile on his, just to feel like he's winning something, I'm sure. "*Star Trek* it is. Anything is better than *Sixteen Candles* for the millionth time."

"We can watch *Labyrinth* after," I offer. "And maybe *The NeverEnding Story*."

"Ha! We'd need a full week of my favorites just to make it even."

I nod and then say, with as much gratefulness and pride-swallowing as I can muster, "Then consider it a thank-you."

Landon, to my surprise, flushes and glances at my mother for a second before shrugging it off. Then he says simply, "I'm sorry he hurt you, Sam."

I don't miss the quick hug my mother gives to Landon before we make our way back to my room. I don't miss her whispering her own words of thanks into his ear either.

On any other day, I might be upset that they've obviously been talking about me and planning things behind my back, but today I'm just grateful.

Two hours later, while Commander Riker and Deanna Troi are having one of their exciting moments of sexual tension, Landon lies down beside me, his head in my lap, and for a second it feels like we're back in freshman year, hanging out like we used to do. Together. I comb through his hair with my fingers, smiling when he keens like a cat against me.

Who needs love, anyway? I ask myself. Maybe it's much better to have friends who think the world of you, enough to conspire with your mother when things are going wrong and to sit with your stinky self when you're sad and cut the crusts off your sandwiches. Maybe especially friends who don't mind a little snuggling when there's a boring TV marathon on.

Maybe not having a boyfriend won't be so bad at all.

····················

Sometime in the middle of the night, my dad wakes me with a gentle nudge. I sit up, squinting at him in the weak light. "Dad?"

"Hey. Do you have a minute?"

"It's the middle of the night, Dad," I say. That's my father, odd as can be and socially awkward to boot. "So no. No plans right now."

"Good. Follow me."

I get out of bed with a stretch and a yawn and follow

him to the other side of the house, where his office, a converted sunroom with just enough space for his antique desk, is brightly lit by a couple of lamps. It's a mess in here. Several boxes are piled on the floor, filled with manuscripts new and old, and the single bookcase is piled with books instead of neatly arranged, and there are so many that the shelves are bowed. He uses a few of his literary awards as paperweights, keeping some of the piles of loose papers on his desk in control. I notice he's been smoking, which I hate because (a) cancer, and (b) that means he's feeling really stuck if he's resorted to smoking. There are several butts in the ashtray, one still lit and resting carelessly among the others.

As Dad sits behind his desk and starts riffling through the mess, I try to make conversation. "So how was New York this time?"

"Hmm?" He pushes the ashtray aside. "Oh. It was tolerable, I guess. Lots of meetings when I should have been writing instead, but a decent bagel and schmear selection."

This is why my father is so good at what he does. Writing is all he wants to do, even with the distraction of a decent bagel.

"Here!" he proclaims, producing familiar pages from the bottom of one of his piles. "Your samples for applications. I took a red pen to them, but really, they don't need much."

I take the pages he hands to me and look them over, incredulous. There are some editing marks, a few sentences crossed out or circled here and there, but nothing major.

"Really? You don't think so?"

Dad pulls at his hair, which is curly like mine but longer, grayer, and slightly thinner, which means it looks a bit like Einstein's. Which maybe isn't a compliment.

"No, they're quite good as is. If you don't mind me saying so," he begins, and I nod my permission, "the one about the musician is your best. I would advise you to send that one."

"Thanks. Jamie really liked that one too."

Dad bites at a hangnail. "I'm sorry to hear he's not around anymore. Your mother said he was a lovely person."

"It's my own fault," I say.

"All the same," Dad says. "I'm sorry that you're hurting, Sam. I know it's not your first breakup, but it never gets any easier. And I'm sorry I wasn't around for it."

I don't know why but my father's one simple apology lifts a ton of weight off me.

"You really like my samples? I mean, they're just stories."

"Everything is just a story, Samson. It's the way you tell it that makes it worth telling." He smiles at me, revealing perfectly straight teeth that are just a little too big for his mouth. Another thing we have in common. "I wrote a book about a man who rides the subway all day long. Nothing happens in it, at all. But people love it because of the telling. And you, my son, are great at telling. You have a style that is very uniquely yours, and I'm so proud of that. I've been so afraid that you would follow my path instead of your own, but it's clear to me, you've found your own way."

There must be something in my eye because my view is suddenly all watery. Damn it.

"I hope NYU agrees with you."

"If they don't, they're wrong." My dad's toothy grin flashes again. "I'm sorry I woke you up. I didn't realize how late it was."

As if to prove it, he pulls out the cigarette butt, long ago burnt out and all ash, and looks absolutely bewildered that it's not lit anymore.

"I didn't mind," I say. "You should get some rest, though. Take a break. It's Christmas."

He nods. "I will after this scene," he says, which roughly translates into "I'll sleep when I'm dead" for my dad.

I leave him bent over his manuscript, squinting at his words like they're completely foreign to him. When I get to my room, I take one more look at his edits to my work before putting them underneath my bed for safekeeping.

Merry Christmas to me.

....

When I wake again it isn't Landon by my side, or even my mother. It's Meg.

"Merry Christmas."

I sit up immediately so that I can hug her. She hugs back and clings to me, her soft hair against my face.

"I'm such a jerk," I say.

"I'm the jerk. I shouldn't have brought up Landon. I know it's a sore spot."

"No, I was being a hypocrite and an idiot and—"

"You were being a good friend," she interjects, and draws back to smile at me. "Other than calling me a bitch."

I wince. "Yeah, that was definitely a jerk move."

She makes a *pffft* sound. "I've been called worse."

Meg leans over and takes a plate off of my bedside table. It's piled high with my mom's chocolate chip cookies, and she holds it in front of my face. I take one. "Your mom's on a baking tear so I'm staying all day."

I laugh. "But it's Christmas. Aren't you supposed to be in church?"

"Nah. I'm all churched out and my parents didn't feel like arguing in front of the family." She inspects the pile of cookies for the one with the most chips, and takes one from the bottom. "Besides, I think I filled my quota of family time Friday night. I helped Mom dust off all her saint figurines. That's a few hours of my life I'll never get back."

"Friday night, huh?"

"Yeah," Meg says, spraying some crumbs on my bed. I couldn't care less. "I'm a wild one, I know."

"I just thought you had plans with Michael."

"I did, but then you and I fought and I was worried about you and whatever. I can lose my virginity after prom, like everyone else." I study her, and she shrinks a little under my stare. "Okay. I don't think I'm ready, all right? And get this. My mom actually lectured me about waiting for marriage while we were cleaning, as if she could read my freaking mind. And it was all creepy and Catholic-y but she said a few things that made sense too. And so did you, so . . . I guess I'm keeping this virginity thing for a while."

I smile, proud and relieved. "And Michael? Is he okay with that?"

She beams. "He said he'd wait forever if he had to because I'm worth it."

I'm relieved to hear that, and it's kind of sweet. Sickeningly sweet. Maybe Michael's not a completely horrible person.

"So . . ." Meg takes another cookie because the first one has mysteriously disappeared. "What do you want to do today? And the answer is not 'Sit around moping in my PJs.' Not at Yuletide, sir. The God is reborn and we need to celebrate."

The God is reborn. I have no idea what that means. Jesus was born on Christmas, sure, but just the once, and that's not Wiccan anyway. Whatever. Meg's here, we're not fighting, she didn't have sex with Michael, and it feels great to smile.

"How about you help me undo the spell and then we open presents?"

She freezes midchew. "What? You can't undo the spell."

"Why not?"

She opens her mouth to say something, shuts it, then

opens it again. "Because I don't know how."

I smack my forehead with my palm.

"What?" Meg asks, chewing again. "I'm new at this. I mean, I can look it up in my books, but do you really want to undo it? The Goddess might have the best saved for last."

I give Meg a wry look. "Gee, it's worked out so well with Gus and Travis and Jamie, I just can't wait to see what's next." Meg rolls her eyes at me but I ignore it. "Besides, I'm on a break. No more guys for a while. I need to fix my list before I date anyone again. At least."

"Fix your list? What's wrong with it?"

I take the plate of cookies away from her because she's about to eat another, and I know she'll regret it. "I've just been thinking that maybe I wasn't in the best state of mind when I made it, so maybe I put a few things on there that shouldn't be on there."

"You mean since you were completely desperate and pathetic?"

I glare. "I mean since I was kind of shallow. Like, maybe instead of putting down *Thick hair* I should have put down something a little more substantial. That's all I'm saying."

Meg nods, leaning closer to me, eyes narrowed in concentration. "Okay, I like it. Go on."

"Like Gus. He wasn't faithful. I mean to me, but not to his stupid French boyfriend either. So maybe—"

"Maybe all these guys are the Goddess's way of teaching you something!" Meg concludes, and she's got the spirit if not the concept.

I run with it. "Yeah. Like now I know that I want someone faithful, and someone dependable, and someone who isn't going to give up if I screw up once."

Meg sticks out her bottom lip. "Maybe Jamie will get over it and ask you back out."

"I hope so," I say, and my chest tightens because it's so true. I can proclaim I want a break all I want, but if Jamie wanted me back I wouldn't hesitate. I'd go straight back to him, do not pass Go, do not collect two hundred dollars. I look at Meg hopefully. "So you'll help? Maybe if I rewrite the list—"

"Nope. It won't change the spell. But it's working anyway, don't you think? Just not in the way you'd planned. Trust Her. Figure out your new list, take a break, then *boom!* She's going to hit you with Mr. Right. The Perfect Ten. I can feel it. Can't you feel it, Sam? The Lady of the Moon is *working*."

I have to admit, Meg's faith in this is kind of endearing. Not just her trust in a goddess she's never seen, but her trust that things are going to work out for me. So I don't roll my eyes like usual at her Goddess talk. Instead I reach out and tug a lock of her strawberry-blonde hair like I used to do when we were kids, when I wanted to get her attention or wanted to make her smile.

"Thanks, Meghan Grace."

Maybe I'm so sentimental because we fought, or maybe it's because it's Christmas, but when I thank her, I'm thanking her for just about everything she's ever done. It's so sappy and nauseating, but I mean it.

I think she gets that, because she leans forward and gives me a kiss on the forehead. "I love you, Sam."

"Love you too."

She wrinkles her nose. "I hope that means you got me that spell book I wanted for Christmas."

"Spell book? I thought you wanted *The History and Dogma of the Catholic Church*, volumes one through ten. Crap. I hope I still have the receipt . . ." She sticks her tongue out at me but she's already up and skipping off toward the Christmas tree, where her present waits.

I follow slowly, and get into the living room just as she's tearing off the wrapping paper from her spell book. She lets out a squeal of excitement before digging under the tree to find her present to me, which she hands to me with an order to open right this very minute because I'm going to die when I see what's inside.

But what's inside doesn't really matter to me. I have her, and Landon, and even though my heart is broken, it's going to be a pretty good Christmas.

Sixteen

The next month passes by like a glacier—every day just a slow-moving, cold, colorless, and uneventful blob, making it impossible to tell one day from the next. Well, almost uneventful. There are only a few things that make all of January even worth mentioning.

The first is that I give Jamie his Jubjub back.

I haven't seen him that much. It's as if he's made it his mission in life to avoid me. Once, he came around a corner in the hallway, saw me, and fled in the opposite direction. Another time I went to the auditorium to work on my writing samples and he was painting the sets, and the expression on his face was bad enough that I felt like I'd broken his heart all over again, which broke mine all over again, so I left. I saw him out too, at the Donkey. I saw through the windows that he was with someone. Another guy. I don't know if it was a date, but Jamie was smiling. I hated that someone else was making him smile. I hated knowing that if he saw me, the smile would go away. I didn't want to face either of those things, so I didn't go inside.

His friends hate me, obviously. Landon warned me that pretty much all of the art club would have liked to have a public stoning of me, so now I go out of my way to avoid their table at lunch. It's an extra lap around the cafeteria, but at least I'm too far away to be reached by flying food.

I haul the Jubjub into school, but since I have no place to store it, I go to the art room first thing in the morning. Half of me hopes Jamie's there so that I can see him and maybe say I'm sorry again. The other half hopes that he's nowhere to be found and I won't have to cower with my tail between my legs.

He's there, though, adorable as always. He's got on a sweater that seems a few sizes too big and a winter hat that looks hand-knitted and more for style than function. He's taking a picture of one of his paintings with his phone, and after it snaps, he sees me standing in the doorway.

He looks as if he'd like to run. Or scream at me. Or maybe cry, I can't tell.

Or maybe I'm giving myself far too much credit and he really just wants me to leave him alone.

I hold up the painting. "I'm just here to give this back."

Jamie stares at the Jubjub as if it's the first time he's seen it, or perhaps as if he's a little scared of it. Like it might fly off the canvas and nose-dive in his direction.

Since he doesn't move and doesn't say anything, I'm left with no option other than to put it on the work table that's in between us.

"It's beautiful," I say, looking at it one last time. Jamie's looking at me. "You should sell it. I'm sure it would go for a lot of money. Or maybe you should send it to the Institute. I'm a little biased, but I think it's one of your best."

He doesn't say anything at all, and I'm rambling so I need to get out of here. Fast. Otherwise I'm going to break down right in front of him.

So I turn to leave, and it's then that I look at the painting he'd taken a picture of. It's new, so new that some of the paint still looks wet. The painting is nearly all gray, in different shades from light silver to dark smoke, and in its center is a dove, suspended in the clouds. The dove isn't flying, though, not like the birds Jamie usually paints.

It's falling.

Its right wing is twisted, pointed in an unnatural angle, broken. The bird is struggling, trying to right itself with its one good wing, all in vain as it plummets toward earth.

But the worst part isn't that the poor creature's wing is broken. It's the look in its eye—raw, aching pain and hopelessness, as if it's almost relieved that the ground is rising so fast to meet it.

I look at Jamie and he turns away like he just can't look at me. Or won't.

There's so much I want to do. I want to pull him close and hold him tight. I want to tell him I'm an idiot and make promises about how I'll never hurt him again, if only he gives me another chance. I want to kiss him once for every tear I've caused, and then a thousand times more to make up for it.

But Jamie probably wouldn't want any of those things. He just wants me to disappear. So instead, I say, "See you later," like an idiot and make toward the door.

"Are you sure you don't want it?"

I stop, hesitating because I'm not sure. I really want that painting. It's beautiful and it means so much to me, just like Jamie himself. But just like Jamie, I don't deserve it.

"You should have it," I say in answer, and leave him there, standing next to his broken dove.

....

The other important event comes a week later. I look up from my calculus exercises to see Landon hovering in the classroom doorway.

Landon has truly been trying to salvage his grade point average so it's alarming to see him skipping a class. I grab my books and head to the front of the room, where Mr. Byers is grading last night's homework at his desk.

"Mr. Byers, may I go to the nurse? I feel really queasy."

It's kind of a lame lie, but the great thing about being a "good kid" is that when you need to lie, most adults are willing to believe you. Then I'm out the door and into Landon's arms. Landon hugs me so hard that I know something bad is coming, something really bad.

"What, Landon? Are you okay? Are your parents all right?"

"It's Meg," he says as he pulls away. He wipes at his

temples, which I can see are beaded with sweat. "Hurry. I don't know what to do."

I have to jog to keep up with him, and we run down the long corridors of the school until we're almost in the music wing, to the bathrooms right between the cafeteria and the doors out to the student parking lot. Meg's curled up on her side underneath the sinks, hugging herself tight, mascara and eyeliner dripping down her face in sad, curving paths. I kneel on the floor in front of her.

"Meg, what's wrong?"

She doesn't answer, just shakes her head and continues to cry, so I lay a hand on her shoulder and look up to Landon for help.

"She was running an errand for Madame Vinson and caught Michael with Gillian Carlisle."

"Right in the middle of the hallway," Meg whimpers.

"They were making out in the middle of the hallway?" I ask, and want to say something about how tacky that is, never mind that Landon and I thought nothing of playing a little tonsil hockey at our lockers after school. Besides, the point is that the bastard is cheating on Meg. "Did he see you?"

Landon answers. "She kind of . . . went off. The entire foreign language hallway and the English hallway heard. Which is how I found out."

"My throat hurts," Meg says, and I can only assume she means from the screaming.

"Gillian Carlisle?" I ask, incredulous. I knew Michael had no taste, but this is just ridiculous. "But she's so slutty."

"Exactly." Meg sniffles. "And I'm not."

"Should have known the line about waiting for you was too good to be true."

"And I fell for it. I'm such an idiot."

I don't agree with that assessment, at least not yet. There's something I want to know first. "Please tell me in all the yelling you did at Michael that you actually broke up with him and told him you never wanted to see his ugly face again?"

Meg looks up at me, blinking through unshed tears, and shakes her head with a whimper. Then a sob escapes her, and all bets are off. She loses it again, sobbing and yelling and sometimes wailing, the way Italian widows do at funerals. So I drop my books and crawl underneath the sinks with her so that I can wrap my whole body around hers. She curls into me and continues to yell out nonsense, or hateful things at Michael and Gillian, and as she cries I feel Landon's hand on me, steadying me as I steady Meg.

When she pauses, I say the only thing I can think to say. "You're better off without him, you know that, don't you?"

Meg shakes her head again, and then she says, "I know you don't understand it, but I love him."

I know she loves him. I know because he's the only guy I've ever heard her talk about beyond a flip "He's cute." I know because she's put up with his bullshit for a solid two years now and forgives him for everything. I know because in spite of her proclamations that sex is a natural instinct, her Catholic beliefs still linger and even considering it with Michael was a huge step. I know she loves him because he's become the person who makes her smile, who can always cheer her up, and whom she wants to talk to, when I used to be that sole person for her. And I've been jealous of that. Perhaps too jealous.

"I know."

She stills in my arms and then, after a moment, twists around so that she's on her back, looking up at me with bloodshot eyes. "Why do I love him so much when he keeps hurting me?"

I know exactly the feeling she's describing—an addiction. How the sweetest, tastiest fruit in the world can be poisonous, how the thing you love most can be the most harmful. I can't help but glance at Landon, meeting his eye for one awful, aching second before saying, "You have to let him go, Meg. He'll never make you happy."

There's a sudden shuffle and I look up. Landon's on his feet. He doesn't look at me when he says, "I'm going to go get my keys. Let's get out of here."

"Landon," I start, but he's already gone. I push off the tile floor, untangling myself from Meg with a whispered apology and a promise to be right back, and run after him. He's halfway down the hallway before I catch up to him. "Landon. I'm sorry. I didn't mean that to sound so—"

"So what? Pointed?" he snaps, rounding on me. He turns his head away quickly but it's too late, I see the wetness in his eyes. "Go back to Meg, Sam. Help her."

"No, listen. I didn't—"

"Stop," Landon hisses at me, and when I reach out to touch his arm he dodges me. "Just leave it, okay? Go back to Meg."

He sprints away from me, and I curse at myself before going back to Meg. She's up and about in the bathroom, splashing her face with cold water. She turns around, giving me a sheepish smile as she tears off a paper towel and dries her face.

"He's pissed at you."

"Yeah. I didn't mean it to sound like I was talking about him."

"You didn't?" she asks, not all that innocently, but I don't get to defend myself because Landon is back, keys in hand. He looks only at Meg.

"Where do you want to go?"

Meg turns around and blots her eyes in the mirror, sopping up traces of errant mascara. She's looking more like Meg, not just because she cleaned up, but because there's a light there in her eyes again, one that was too dim minutes ago. "Let's go to the cemetery. I want to do a ritual."

Landon's eyes go wide. "Are we finally going to get to use a voodoo doll?"

Meg groans, a kind of soggy sound. "I wish. Unfortunately, we Wiccans vow to do no harm. I just want to ask the Goddess to make me strong enough to let him go."

My chest tightens when she says it, and I feel that urge to punch things again, preferably Michael's stupid face. But Landon, who is far more passive than I am, rolls along with it. "What do you need? Candles? Incense? A, um . . . spell book thingy?"

Meg lays a hand on his arm, touched by his effort. "Just a white candle and a lighter. I've got both in my book bag. Let's go."

In five minutes we're parked at Saint Catherine's, on the hill where I worked my magic with the list in October. We scramble through the snow until we're at the top, behind the mausoleum with the stained-glass Jesus. Meg has a thin pillar candle, white as the snow around us, and she grips it in both hands, turning to us so that we make an awkward little circle. Landon is refusing to make eye contact with me still, and every time he looks away from me, my stomach twists into a tighter knot.

"What do we do? Don't you need a spell or something?"

Meg's lips curve up at Landon. "The great thing about Wicca is that you don't need any fancy spells or words if you don't want to. You just have to speak from the heart. Cheesy, I know."

"Okay," I say, trying to get into the spirit of things. "So how can we help?"

"Grab the candle," Meg instructs. "And get rid of the doubt, okay? I know you think this is all nonsense, but it works for me, and I need you with me on this."

"I'm with you," Landon and I say in unison, and for the first time since I made that comment to Meg in the bathroom, he looks at me. To my relief, his eyes are soft.

Not angry, but not happy either. He jerks a shoulder at me as if to say, "Whatever." Then we grab the candle, and it's just a touch too short for all of us to get our hands around it, so we end up basically joining hands in a web between us. Then Meg starts to speak.

"Earth, air, fire, and water, elements of the Goddess, purify this circle and make it a welcoming place for the divine. I ask that when the circle is ready, the Goddess attend."

There's no wind like there was for my spell in October, but there's something far more meaningful. I close my eyes and feel it—a stillness, a calm, a little stir. When I open my eyes, Meg's watching me, a knowing smile on her face, and we both glance at Landon, who keeps his eyes shut. Meg continues.

"Goddess, you are the power that gives life and brings death. You are the start and the end. You bring both love and heartache. Help me to understand that losing Michael is part of the never-ending cycle of life, death, and rebirth, and help me to be reborn. Help me to learn the lessons you are trying to teach me. Help me to understand the roles everyone must play as I journey down this path. Help me to be reborn with clarity and openness, so that I can love again."

The talk of rebirth and the cycle of life reminds me of Jamie's phoenix, and I see it so vividly in my mind's eye that it's more an apparition than a memory. I see it living, breathing, stretching its wings into the sky with new feathers, new life, a burst of ashes in its wake. And I don't know if Meg meant to make these words so strangely appropriate for me as well, but regardless, I find myself whispering them back to myself, voice catching and hovering on the phrase "so that I can love again."

Meg's hand tightens around mine, then Landon's, and I open my eyes to see both of them looking at me. Meg then turns to Landon and says, "I'm going to light the candle. I want us to send all of our negative feelings into it and fill it up. We'll let it burn down to our fingers or until it goes out on its own, whatever comes first, and when it goes out, all our negative energy will go out with it, okay?"

Landon and I nod, and Meg lights the candle. I stare at the flame, thinking of all the utter crap I've been through this year, and even before that, and do my best to visualize putting it into the candle. I put in my loneliness, the hurt I felt over Gus, the stupid `decisions I made with Travis, and the heartbreak I feel over losing Jamie. I put in all the leftover feelings I have about Landon too. At least all the bad ones, like hurt and resentment and fear. In the end, it feels like I'm pushing those thoughts away, and when the candle flickers from the unbalanced grip we've got on it and goes out, drowning in its own wax, there's a sense that those thoughts are gone with it. Gone. Not forgotten, but gone.

I want to explain it away, to tell myself that it's all mind tricks and easy meditation, but there's a part of me that knows it's not as simple as that.

Meg whispers a thank-you to the Goddess and releases the elements from our little circle, then drops our hands so that she can put the candle back in her bag.

Landon and I let our hands fall to our sides but don't let go.

I can feel the warmth of his skin through his knitted gloves, and he weaves his fingers between mine. My hand is tucked under his, just like we did a million times as freshmen. Even when Meg zips her bag and hoists it on her shoulder, then walks toward the car with a knowing little smile, he doesn't let go. He walks slowly, holding back until Meg is way ahead of us.

"I'm sorry about what I said," I say.

"I was a bad boyfriend," he says in response.

"You weren't," I start to argue, then amend that. "At least, you were no worse than I was."

"No. It was me, Sam. I was jealous and possessive and . . . at times not even kind. There was a fight where you asked me to just be kind to you, and I couldn't even give you that."

I glance over at him, see his memories there in his eyes, see what it was like from his side. "You were scared."

"To lose you? Yes. Terrified. My mistake was believing that I was acting that way because I loved you so much. And I did love you, Sam, but that's not why I acted like that."

Interesting, because that was my mistake too.

"But I understand all that now. And I'm still insecure, but at least I know that about myself and . . ." Landon shrugs. "I've changed. I mean, I think I would be a better boyfriend now."

I stop walking, pulling him to a halt as well. "What are you saying?"

He takes my other hand in his and squeezes them both. "You know that thing that Meg said in the ritual? About keeping open?" I nod. "I know you're giving yourself this break and you want to figure some stuff out, but I think you should be open too. And not just to new stuff. Maybe some of the old stuff isn't so bad either."

I stare at him, puzzled. "I'm not sure I follow . . ."

"I'm saying don't count me out." Landon smiles, one of his rare shy ones. "I know I don't have a lot of those things on your list. I'm not as stylish as Gus, or as hot as Travis, or as talented as Jamie. But I make you laugh, and I'm a good friend, and I do have pretty eyes."

I laugh a little, but to be honest, I'm a bit too overwhelmed with what he's saying and it comes out all weird.

"And I'm in love with you, and that has to count for something, right?"

That completely levels me, and I hear myself suck in a breath. "What? Again? But . . . when did you . . . ?"

Landon chuckles a little, as if he can't believe how clueless I am. "I never fell out, Sam. But I screwed up. Majorly. And I figured you'd never give me another shot. But then when you started talking about changing your list I knew I had to take a chance, because if thick hair gets crossed off the list and you put 'batshit insanely in love with me' in its place, then I'm closer to being your Perfect Ten. And maybe you'll consider me again."

I'm so floored that I can't say anything in response. I can't even think. My face is frozen in what I'm sure must be the stupidest, most stunned expression in history. Luckily, Landon doesn't seem to want words from me.

Instead, he kisses me.

My reaction is automatic—a habit, a replaying memory. I lean into him, wrapping him up in my arms just like I used to do. His lips are as warm and inviting as I remember, maybe even more so now, but the rush of love and want is different. I still love him, and yes, my body is burning for him, but it lacks sharp edges, lacks the urgency. I'm not just kissing Landon now, I'm kissing the boy who hurt me irrevocably before but also helped me heal; I'm kissing the boy who once held my vulnerable heart in his hands and both cherished it and bruised it. I'm kissing my best friend.

When he pulls away, he stays close so that I feel the heat of his cheek next to mine, the subtle scratch of light stubble against light stubble, and I can't help myself: I sigh.

I hear Landon do the same, and he's smiling bright and proud when I open my eyes.

"So you'll consider it?" he asks.

My lips, my skin, my hands—they're all tingling and warm from his touch. It's nice, and familiar, and wonderful. And wow, I love that feeling. I want to keep feeling it.

Which is why I hear myself say, "Yes."

Seventeen

Perfect 10

1. Sexy
2. Talented
3. Style
4. Nice eyes
5. ~~Thick hair~~ Loyal
6. Sense of humor
7. ~~Attractive~~ Understanding
8. Ambitious
9. Fun
10. ~~Good taste~~ Batshit insanely in love with me

I stare at the list, trying to determine if this is it, the final copy, or if I still need to make some changes. It kind of feels done, but then, the original list felt that way too, and look where it got me.

"Is this all I should change? I mean, should I keep fun on here? Or sexy? Or nice eyes?" I look across the lunch table at Meg. She's staring at her Cheez-Its, as she has been for nearly the entire lunch period. I wave my hand in front of her eyes. "Earth to Meg . . ."

Meg barely acknowledges my presence. "He's over there with that slut."

I don't turn in Michael's direction because I know I'll just walk over there and punch him if I see him. "It's better than being here, wasting your time. Come on, eat. And help me with this."

Meg stuffs about nineteen Cheez-Its in her mouth and chews until she has enough room to talk. "This blows," she says.

I sigh and push my list aside. Meg's problems are bigger than mine right now; the list can wait. "Truly," I agree with her.

"I keep expecting him to meet me between classes like we used to. And did I tell you I waited at my locker for him this morning for, like, a whole five minutes before I realized he wasn't coming? It's scary, Sam." She swallows the blob of orange. "I think I'm delusional."

"Nah, I was like that after Jamie broke up with me," I say, and the memory stirs up the dull ache that's persisted in my chest since. I rub at it like an idiot, like that will stop the pain, and resist the urge to look over at the artists' table, where Jamie is sitting for once. "I was like that with Landon too. I still wanted to call him and stuff. It's just habit, you know?"

Meg pushes her lunch bag toward me, making a face. It seems a shame to let good chocolate go to waste, so I take out her cup of pudding and dig in.

"So . . . how did you break the habit?"

I lick pudding off my fingers and think about it. "I don't know," I admit. "I guess I just kept reminding myself I couldn't call, and then eventually I didn't try anymore."

Meg doesn't look any happier at that explanation. "And how long did that take?"

Months. It had taken me months. In fact, I'm sure I was still fighting the urge to call Landon when he showed up on my doorstep with the rose.

I shrug and then lie through my teeth. "A couple of weeks, maybe."

That, at least, makes her smile. "So you don't feel the urge to call Jamie now?"

This time I don't bother fighting it, and I cast a glance toward the artists' table. Jamie's sitting next to Kit and smiling at something she's saying. He must feel my eyes on him because for just a second he looks in my direction and his smile falters when he sees me. I turn away.

"No," I tell Meg. I think I've lied to her in this conversation more than I have our entire friendship. "So, the list?"

Meg's apparently ready for a change of topic because her face brightens and she reaches for my notebook. "Yeah, yeah, the Perfect Ten." I watch her eyes work over the items on my list. "If you really want my opinion—"

"I do."

"You have to keep sexy on there. I mean, you took off attractive, so you've got to keep something like that. And

I'd keep fun, because without that, the whole list is kind of a bust, don't you think? I'd keep nice eyes too. Windows to the soul, like that cute Catholic boy said."

Then she pushes the list aside, leans her elbows on the table, and studies me with amusement.

"What?" I ask, laughing a little at her expression. It makes me feel slightly uncomfortable, like she knows things I don't know.

"Landon has nice eyes."

I flush. "Yeah, he does."

"And he's sexy as hell and funny and he's got a great sense of style."

"Yeah," I agree, and then blink. "Wait, you think Landon's sexy?"

It's Meg's turn to flush, and she steers the conversation expertly away from my question. "It's all so romantic, isn't it?"

"What is?"

"Oh, come on, Sam!" she exclaims, then picks up my list, pointing to it. "You do a spell to find the perfect person for you, and you go through all this drama to figure out what you really want, and he's been here, right under your nose the entire time. It's like a movie. I'm telling you, the Goddess knows what She's doing."

I wish I could agree with that. I wish it more than anything. But honestly, since I told Landon that I'd consider trying again, I've done nothing but wonder if that was the right decision.

I pluck the list out of Meg's hands and look at it, hoping I can get some kind of answer from it. "You really think Landon is all of these things? What about number eight?"

She snatches the list back and searches for number eight. "Ambitious? Great Goddess, Sam. How blind are you? Why do you think Landon's actually been going to classes?"

I stare at her, clueless.

Meg shakes her head at me. "He's trying to get his grades up so that he'll have a prayer of getting into NYU with you."

"He applied to NYU?"

Meg nods, and that floors me. But the thing is, I should feel flattered and relieved that Landon is trying to get into NYU, and I don't. Instead it only makes me feel nervous.

"He's really in love with me, isn't he?" I ask quietly. "He never stopped?"

Meg smiles wide. "He never stopped."

"And you've known this whole time?" I ask Meg.

"He told me after the whole thing with Jeff." I start to ask about that, but she shushes me. "Nope. He'll have to tell you about that. Not my secret to share. But yeah, I've known for sure since last summer. I thought you'd figure it out when he was acting like a jealous freak about Travis, but I guess you were too, um, *distracted*."

I can't help but chuckle. "Distracted is a nice way of putting it."

We both grow quiet, and I study my list again. Meg's right. If I count Landon's attempt to boost his grades as ambition, he's a Perfect Ten. And he wants a second chance with me. We fell in love once, and we could fall in love again, right? Especially since we've both changed for the better. It could work this time.

So why don't I feel sure?

I'm about to ask Meg that question, but then the table shakes and Landon's sitting next to me. His eyes are sparkling with mischief and, wow, they're pretty. He definitely has number four going for him.

"Hi," he says.

"Hi," I say back, and then we both stare at each other for a few moments, like two middle school kids at their first dance, giggly with nervousness and unsure of what to say.

"Oh for the love of Isis. You've seen each other naked. Are you really going to be this awkward?" Meg groans, burying her face in her hands.

I flush. Landon just grins wider. "Want to do something tonight?"

"Yeah," I answer, and I'm a little surprised to find that I mean it.

"Okay. It's a date then." He grabs a few Cheez-Its from Meg's bag and pops them into his mouth. "Gotta get back to band. Is seven okay?"

"That's fine."

"Good," Landon says. "See you then."

He leans toward me a little, and for a second I think he might just kiss me right there in the cafeteria. I glance at Jamie but he's not even looking at us, and I'm relieved.

Landon doesn't kiss me, though. He just squeezes my hand and then he's off, jogging back to band, since he's turned into the kind of person who cares about school when I wasn't looking.

Meg's beaming, dancing in her seat. "Sam and Landon, sitting in a tree, K-I-S-S-I-N—"

"Oh my god, shut up."

She cracks up. "Whatever. It's so perfect, isn't it?"

I don't answer that. I can't. So I deflect like a freaking pro. "Or maybe you want to live vicariously through me since Landon is . . . what was the phrase you used? Sexy as hell?" She narrows her eyes at me and it's almost scary enough to make me stop snickering. "Maybe he's *your* Perfect Ten."

A Cheez-It bounces off the bridge of my nose. I laugh a little with her and then grow quiet, studying my list again. I feel Meg's eyes on me, regarding me closely.

After a moment, I look at her and ask, "I'm doing the right thing, aren't I?"

"Giving Landon another chance, you mean?" I nod. "Of course you are. He's one of your best friends. He knows you better than anyone. And the list, right? The new list, I mean. He's everything you want. Everything you've *learned* you want, I should say. Right?"

"Yeah, he is."

She leans across the table, close enough so that she can whisper. "Besides, it's so obvious there's still something there. Everyone can see it."

I think about that, the way everyone always assumes

that Landon and I are together, or that we still have a lot of feelings for each other. There must be something there that everyone else is seeing. Hell, I've felt it myself, like at Travis's signing party when we were dancing, or when he looks at me with his pretty eyes, or yesterday, after Meg's ritual, when he kissed me. There was definitely something there.

I smile at Meg, relieved. "Yeah, I think maybe there is. Yesterday, when he kissed me at the cemetery . . ."

"Good, huh?" she asks, wiggling her brows.

I chuckle. "Yeah, it was. Familiar and wonderful and . . . it's Landon, you know?"

"I know," she agrees. "You'll fall for him again and things will be perfect. The Goddess led you straight back to him. It'll work. Just trust Her."

For some reason, I look back toward Jamie's table and I'm startled to realize he's looking at me. Meg follows my gaze and turns back to me, her face twisted with worry. "You are over Jamie, aren't you, Sam?"

I stare at her, but before I can answer, the bell rings and I'm saved. I jump up, gathering my things. "I have to get to class."

"Sam . . ."

"We'll talk later, okay?"

It's an empty promise, because I don't know what I'd say even if we did talk. I don't think I can begin to sort out everything that's going on in my mind, not anytime soon, anyway. I think she knows it, because she doesn't try to stop me as I walk away. I go to my next class, then another, and then another, and then home to get ready for my date with Landon, Meg's question hanging over me the whole time like a storm cloud.

....

For our date, Landon doesn't take me to our old standby, Casa, or even to Seven Sauces or Toscanos. Instead we drive all the way out to Trimble, which is an even more hillbilly town than Athens, and to a little diner that looks like it's straight out of the fifties. Lucy's, it's called. I raise a brow before we get out of the car, but Landon only winks.

"Trust me."

When we get inside and are seated at a booth, Landon orders chocolate shakes and two of the daily specials for us from a woman whose voice sounds like she smokes two packs a day. She returns with shakes served in a glass, with the extra in the metal mixing cup as well, piled high with whipped cream and a cherry. It's so thick I have to use my spoon, and it's love at first bite.

I sigh dreamily.

Landon laughs and pops a cherry into his mouth. "Told you to trust me."

I should have. The waitress yells at the cook about our order, Buddy Holly is singing on the speakers, and there's a jukebox in the corner. It's kind of weird and cheesy, in the way that Landon and I both love, so of course he would be the one to take me here.

"How did you find this place?" I ask.

"One day in the summer. Went exploring," he says, as if that's an adequate explanation.

I shake my head at him, amazed. "Just full of surprises, aren't you?"

"Of course." He dips into his own shake. "Just wait until you taste the meatloaf."

The conversation flows after that, as it always does with Landon. We gossip, we tell jokes, we share our concerns about how Meg's coping with the breakup.

It's fun, being here with him, and it's nice. I'm not nervous like I would usually be on a first date. It's just me and Landon, hanging out, being us. It's only when the waitress brings us half a coconut cream pie (literally—either she likes us or it's a week old; we decide after a slightly crunchy bite that it's the latter) that the conversation lags. And it's then that I ask about Jeff.

Landon looks uncomfortable for a split second, but then forces a smile. "I dated him over the summer. I told you. It didn't work out."

"Because of me?" I ask, then wince at myself. "Sorry. That was arrogant of me."

"It's not, and yes, because of you. In a way." Landon pushes his milkshake out of the way so that he can lean across the table and speak softly. "I mean, I was so hung up on you, and I guess I was tired of it. So I thought maybe if I just tried with Jeff, then maybe I'd fall for him and get over you and everything would be happily ever after, you know? But it kind of backfired."

I scrunch my brows together. "What do you mean?"

Landon shrugs. "He was so *not* you that that's all I could think about. I kept thinking stuff like, *Sam would have laughed at that* or *Sam would have bought me the right size shirt* or *Sam would have known that I hate marshmallows.* It really just convinced me that you're the only one I wanted."

That flatters me beyond belief, and I have to admit, I feel kind of victorious that this Jeff dude couldn't compare. I smile into my empty milkshake glass.

"I love you, Sam. And I know you can't say it back yet, but I think you will. Soon."

He's so earnest that I can't help but go all mushy inside. It feels wonderful to be loved and wanted, and I want to return those feelings so badly it hurts. And maybe he's right, and Meg too. Perhaps the Goddess and the list led me straight back to him. Perhaps we are perfect for each other. Perhaps if I just give this time, I'll feel all those things for Landon again.

I just need to stop feeling all those things for Jamie first.

"Ready to go?"

I nod that I am, and Landon throws money on the table. We leave and get into his car, but before Landon buckles his seat belt, he shifts in his seat so that he's facing me. I know what's coming. I've seen that look on his face a million times. When he leans toward me I don't hesitate. I want to kiss him. I want his lips on mine and I want to know what I'm feeling for him. But most of all, I just want to feel something at all.

And I do feel something, it's just not what I was hoping for.

It's good, though. Very good. Landon hasn't forgotten what I like. He knows that I love to start each kiss slow and work up to a faster pace. He takes his time teasing my mouth with his, easing my lips apart with his tongue, drawing me in bit by bit. His hands cup my face like he always used to do, and mine slide around his back, pulling him closer like they've always done. He even tastes like he used to, a bit like vanilla and smoke and something even sweeter underneath, a taste that is all Landon, something I could pick out of thousands. It's nice.

But his kiss doesn't leave me breathless like Gus's kisses. It doesn't make me crazy enough to set aside my sanity, like Travis's did.

And most of all, it doesn't fill me up like Jamie's kisses did. It doesn't make me feel like I could just burst from all the happiness and warmth inside me. I feel all this love coming from Landon but I'm just . . . empty. There's nothing to give back, nothing pouring out of me in return. Not like I had with Jamie.

I put a hand on Landon's chest and push him away gently. He pants a little, trying to catch his breath, and leans his head back against the seat. He looks higher than he does after we've smoked. He looks happy, and that makes me even sadder that I don't feel that way in return.

"Wow," he breathes. "I've missed that."

I do my best to smile back at him. "I should probably get home."

"Or . . ." he starts. "We could go back to my house. My parents are out of town. Again."

I freeze, panicking a little, scrabbling for an excuse.

Luckily, Landon doesn't read me correctly. He gives me a sheepish smile. "Yeah, you're right. Let's not rush it this time, eh?"

I breathe out, relieved. "I think that would be best."

Landon nods and turns the key. We drive home, both of us quieter than usual. Landon hums along with his stereo and keeps his hand on mine, but my mind is miles away from his little Honda. All I can think about is what Landon said about Jeff, how Jeff only proved to him that he still wasn't over me.

He kisses me once when he drops me off at my house and I promise I'll call him the next day, smiling brightly. But as I'm unlocking my door, tears come, fast and relentless.

Landon's my best friend. He's my Perfect Ten. He's the one the whole silly list and spell led me toward. But he's not the one I want.

He's not the one, I realize with a start, that I love.

I'm in love with Jamie. Oh my god, I'm in love with Jamie. And I think that maybe I've known that for a while now, somewhere deep down. Maybe that's why I felt like I had to buy him that cross. Maybe that's why I can't feel anything when Landon kisses me. Maybe that's why I was able to turn down someone as incredibly sexy as Travis Blake.

I turn around once I get the door open and speak to

the cold, dark night air. Later I'll be embarrassed about this, I'm sure, but right now I'm too sad and confused and frustrated, and I'd like to give that Goddess of Meg's a piece of my mind.

"Seriously, what kind of lesson is this, huh? What exactly am I supposed to do now?"

The answer comes in the form of a small gust of wind, just enough to lift up a few of my curls and make me cold. It's definitely not enough, not when I'm going to have to break my best friend's heart even though he's a Perfect Ten, and the guy I really want thinks I'm the world's biggest asshole.

"You're going to have to do better than that," I mutter, and go inside to have myself a good cry.

Eighteen

I am such a freaking coward that I avoid both Meg and Landon all weekend long. Even Monday morning, I dash to my locker and then to my first class so that I don't have to see them, and then in Latin I make vague promises to Landon through notes passed by Rachel Gliesner and fly out the door so quickly that I'm sure I leave a trail of smoke behind myself.

I even skip out on lunch because I just don't know what to say to Meg yet. I don't know how to tell her that I'm going to have to hurt Landon, and I'm half-afraid she'll try to convince me to keep trying with him.

I go to the auditorium. Although I'd like to say I was just searching for some peace and quiet, peace and quiet isn't what I'm searching for at all.

The door closes behind me with a loud *thunk* and Jamie turns around, looking out over the theater seats to see who the intruder is. Even at this distance, I can see the pain in his eyes when he sees me standing there, and I immediately regret the decision to come here.

"I'm sorry. I shouldn't have . . . I'll leave," I offer dumbly.

Jamie's shoulders sag. "It's okay. It's a free country. Do what you like."

"No. I shouldn't have disturbed you. I'll go."

"Don't," Jamie blurts, cringing at himself as the word echoes around the theater. "It's okay. Just stay."

It reminds me of how he asked me to stay the first time I saw him paint, and that makes my heart do a little tap dance inside my chest. So I nod and join him up on the stage, sitting on the edge while I watch him work. Soon he gets lost, the way he always does when he paints. I think he even forgets I'm there, which makes it slightly less awkward that we're not talking. He has his back toward me, painting a big section of scenery that looks like a dinner table in the middle of a log cabin. It's a big canvas compared to what I usually see him work with, and he has to stretch up on his tiptoes and use wide strokes. He's wearing a tight black shirt and it's mesmerizing the way his back muscles move, the way his forearms flex and his hand grips the brush. I'm so fixated on it that when Jamie curses loudly, I actually jump.

"What's wrong?" I ask, alarmed.

Jamie steps back from the scenery, shaking his head at his work. "It's all wrong."

I push myself off the floor and stand next to him. He's finished the table, and added in bowls of food and spoons and little details like wrinkles in the tablecloth.

"It's great," I say, not knowing how something that good could be all wrong.

"It's crap." Jamie points his paintbrush at one of the bowls. "That one has to be 'just right,' and it's not. Not even close."

I study the bowls and then I get it. One bowl is steaming, the other is not, and the one in the middle . . .

"Goldilocks and the Three Bears?"

"Yep. The winter children's play. And they're not going to have any scenery because their artist sucks."

I turn to him, brows furrowed, because I've never heard him be so hard on himself. That's not Jamie. Jamie can be humble and way too unaware of how talented he is, but he's never mean to himself.

"It's good," I say, a bit forcefully.

"No, it's not. I can't get it right. I'm not used to this paint, or painting on wood. I'm supposed to be some freaking prodigy but all I can do is stupid watercolors of birds. And I'm not even good at those lately." He throws his paintbrush down on the stage floor and it leaves a grayish track of paint as it skids to a halt. Then he closes his eyes and it's like he's talking to himself. "I can't do this. I still haven't finished five of the paintings I promised Ninah and I just can't do it. Nothing looks right, and the damn birds won't fly."

That breaks my heart all over again, and the responsibility of it is crushing. But I'm not sure I could fix this, even if he'd let me try. And who could blame him if he didn't?

"Your birds are beautiful. And so is this."

Jamie shakes his head. "I'm messing everything up."

"You haven't messed anything up at all," I say, and I can't fight it any longer. Ever since the moment I saw him on the stage I've wanted to be close to him. I've wanted to hold his paint-stained hand again, make him laugh again, and wrap my arms around him and feel him ball up my shirt in his fists, holding on to me as if I could make everything better.

But now, with so much pain and fragility in his eyes, I can't hold myself back anymore. I have to touch him, because even if I can't mend him, I have to do *something*, futile as it is.

So I pull him into my arms and bring him close and, to my surprise, he lets me. He feels exactly like I remember, thin but soft, and he smells like chemicals and paint. It's wonderful.

He buries his face in my neck and whispers, without any malice, "I wish I could hate you."

I want to say something, but I don't know what. Maybe to tell him to go ahead and hate me because he should, maybe to say I'm sorry again. But instead of all of that, what actually comes out of my mouth is this: "Just keep painting. It's 'just right,' Jamie. It really is. And your birds are perfect, okay? They're perfect."

He pulls away from me, studying me with his big blue eyes, and a smile slowly stretches across his lips. It's a relief to see that smile, and I let out a breath I'd been holding far too long.

"I, um . . . I have something I want to give you," he says shyly, and disappears behind the scenery, reemerging a minute later with an envelope in his hands. He holds it out to me.

I take it, giving him a questioning look before breaking the pretty seal on the flap and opening it.

Inside is an invitation, a little card that has a few of Jamie's rough sketches of birds on it, with classy, antique-looking lettering stating the dates of his art show at the Green House in Yellow Springs. It's this Friday night.

"Ninah sent these out all over the country. I'm so nervous I've been throwing up every morning." He laughs a little at himself, and I go back to looking at the invitation. Even his rough sketches are good. It's going to draw a big crowd, I'm sure, and that crowd will be full of all the right kind of art snobs, people who will buy his work and give him connections.

"I'm so proud of you," I tell him. My throat feels tight with it when I speak.

"It's because of you that Ninah even knew about my work at all. I don't know how to thank you," he says to me. "Please come."

My eyes snap up from the invitation, meeting his. His are hopeful but duller than I'm used to.

"Don't thank me, Jamie. It's your talent that did this. You would have had this, regardless of my big mouth."

"So you'll come?"

I don't answer that. "Do you really wish you could hate me?" I ask instead, because it's the only thing I can think about.

He doesn't answer my question either. "I can't hate

you." He tries to smile but fails. "Ninah really liked my dove."

I nod. I know why. The dove with the broken wing might be completely different from Jamie's other work, but it's been one of his most honest.

"I wouldn't miss it," I finally answer, and Jamie really does smile then, his pale blue eyes a little watery. "Mind if I bring Meg?"

Jamie doesn't get a chance to answer because just then the door in the back of the auditorium opens.

I raise a hand to shield my eyes from the bright stage lights and look out over the seats. It's Landon, and he's making his way toward the stage. His face is blank but I see what he's feeling in his eyes—not anger or confusion, but worry.

"Meg said I should try to find you here," Landon says as he climbs up and joins us on the stage. It figures that Meg would have known where to look. Landon turns to Jamie and says, "Hey, Jamie," in this weird, stiff tone. It's not exactly friendly, but it's not mean either.

Jamie merely nods back.

"Well, you found me," I say as lightly as I can. "Jamie and I were just chatting."

"Sam was trying to convince me that my scenery doesn't look like crap," Jamie provides. I look over at him and he gives me a tight smile. "Which is nice of him. Completely wrong, but nice."

"I'm not wrong. It's good," I say seriously, and as I say it, I feel a hand slip into mine. I look down and follow the arm back up to Landon, who is looking at me proudly, as if saying to Jamie, *Yep, he's all mine.*

I watch as Jamie's gaze drops to where our hands are joined. His smile falters for a second before he forces his mouth back into it. Then he looks at me. His eyes aren't bright and hopeful anymore. They're filled with the same sort of contempt I saw in them when he broke up with me, and all the hope I'd been gathering for the last half hour disappears, leaving me even emptier than before.

"As I was saying, Meg can come to the show," Jamie says, voice flat. Then he adds pointedly, "And your boyfriend too, if you want. I should get to class."

Jamie takes off, grabbing his book bag and leaving all his art supplies behind in disarray. A door off to stage left slams, and then it's just silence. I stare after him, numbly.

I drop Landon's hand. No. More like I shove it away and move a few steps back from him. "I thought you said you'd changed."

Landon stares at me, confused. "I have. Why? What's wrong?"

"If you've changed, then why did you do that?"

"Do what?"

"Hold my hand like that. Right in front of him. I thought you said you weren't going to act possessive anymore."

"That's not why I held your hand, Sam." This time, Landon takes a step backward, away from me. I expect him to be mad maybe, but instead he just looks confused. "I held your hand because I wanted to. Because I thought you wanted to, too."

I can only stare at him in silence.

"Sam, you want to hold my hand, don't you?"

I don't answer again, and Landon's confused expression turns into something closer to pain, and I hate it. I hate seeing that hurt, and I hate knowing I'm causing it.

"Sam . . ." Landon says again. This time his tone is desperate.

I take a trembling breath. I can feel him looking at me, expecting an answer, and I have to give him one. But I can't lie, not even to make him happy, and I can't make this any easier on either of us.

"I really, really want to want to hold your hand," I say.

"But you don't."

"But I don't," I say slowly, knowing that I'm breaking his heart as I say it. "I'm sorry, Landon. I'm . . . I was in love with Jamie. I still am."

To my surprise, Landon nods in understanding. "I thought you might be. I just didn't want to see it." He shrugs. "But I'm your best friend. And your ex. I know all the signs of Sam being in love, even if it's not with me."

"I didn't realize until the other day. Not really."

"It doesn't matter." Landon shrugs again. "You'll get over him, Sam. Eventually. And then you'll fall in love with me again."

"I'm not going to get over him. At least not anytime soon."

"I can wait. I already have."

My heart breaks even more for Landon. "Don't wait on me," I say. "You're my best friend and I love that. And

I'm not sure I'd want to change that, even if I wasn't in love with someone else."

"You feel something for me. I know you do. I see it sometimes when you look at me. You can't tell me you don't."

"Of course I do. I love you, Landon. Just not the way you want me to. I wish I could change that, but I can't."

Landon's eyes darken as that sinks in, like clouds gathering before a storm. He stares at me. "So that's it? You just want to be friends. There's no chance."

"I don't think so," I answer, and he closes his eyes.

"I don't want to be friends."

That grabs my heart and twists it. "You don't want to be friends?"

"Not just friends," he says. "You're the one for me, Sam. You're my Perfect Ten. I don't understand how I'm not yours too."

"I'm not a Perfect Ten," I argue. "Not even close. I'm a know-it-all, and I'm selfish and self-involved, and extremely shortsighted. You know that's true."

"I don't care about those things!" Landon says. "You're perfect for me. You're all I want. And I am all of those things on your list."

"I know, but . . ." I stop myself, trying to keep myself together a little, "It was Jamie I fell for. But I'll get over him. And you'll get over me. And we'll go to NYU together and—"

"It doesn't work that way!" Landon pulls at his hair as he yells. "This isn't one of your stories where everything ends up happily ever after! I don't know if I can ever get over you, okay? And I don't think I can be around someone who doesn't love me when I'm so, *so* in love with him."

I stare at him, unable to understand what he's saying. I wipe hot tears off my face. "So you don't think we can be friends anymore?"

When he doesn't answer and his eyes just get darker, I shake my head. Emphatic, futile denial. "No. Please. I don't want to lose you because of this."

Landon exhales, nodding. "You are shortsighted."

Then he begins to walk away and I panic, calling after him. "Landon, please . . ."

"I have to go," he says, and turns around. But he's not looking at me. He's looking out into the harsh theater lights. "Good luck with Jamie. And NYU."

He leaves without another word, the door slamming behind him just like it did with Jamie. It's like a death knell for our friendship, and I sink down until I'm sitting on the stage floor, hugging myself as the sounds of the slamming door and my sniffles echo around the auditorium.

I don't know how long I stay there, but it's a while. Long enough that I can curse myself for all the stupid, selfish things I've done the past few months, long enough to curse that ridiculous list and spell that started this whole thing, long enough to curse the lonely desperation that drove me to it. And what was the point? Here I am, sobbing on the stage in front of Jamie's pretty scenery, heartbroken, and what do I have to show for it? Nothing but more loneliness. Right back where I started.

Except that now I've lost a best friend.

I still have one, though, and she appears in the auditorium and wraps me up in a hug. She says nothing. I'm sure she's already heard the story from Landon. All she does is sit next to me and hold me until I've cried myself dry. Then she hands me my coat and gives me a smile.

"Come on, Samson. Let's take a walk," Meg says, and leads me out of the school and toward the cemetery, letting me lean on her every step of the way.

....

There's a sort of mutual understanding that we go to the hill, to the mausoleum that has become the place where all the important stuff happens. There's no question that this is an important thing, and so as soon as we cross through the cemetery gates, we both turn in that direction.

We sit on the mausoleum steps. The marble—or granite or whatever it is—is freezing under our butts, but to be honest, I don't really notice.

"How mad is he?" I ask when I find my voice.

"He'll get over it."

"How mad is he?" I repeat.

Meg sighs. "Pretty mad."

I look down at my hands and wring my fingers together. "He said he didn't want to be friends anymore. I've lost him."

Meg looks like she might cry, but she shakes her head

once, emphatically. "I don't think we're ever going to lose Landon, Sam. I think we're stuck with him forever."

I chuckle at that, soggily, then I rest my head on her shoulder. "Are you mad at me too?"

"Why would I be mad?"

"Because I hurt him."

"Nah. You didn't do it on purpose."

"I really wanted to fall in love with him again."

"I know you did," Meg says.

"I'm in love with Jamie."

"I know you are," Meg says, and I feel her kiss the top of my head.

We sit like that for a while longer, not saying a word, just listening to each other sniffle and breathe. Then an idea strikes me and I stand up so fast that I almost knock Meg over.

"Sam?"

"Do you have matches? Or your candles?"

She scrunches her face up in confusion. "No. Just my lighter. Why?"

I pull the Perfect Ten list out of my back pocket and unfold it, holding it up in front of her face. "I'm getting rid of it."

She shakes her head. "That won't do anything. I told you, I don't know how to end the spell."

"You said Wicca was about speaking from the heart, right?" She nods. "Then I'd like to say a few words."

"But you don't even believe in this," Meg says. "I know you don't."

"I had enough hope that it seems something worked the first time, didn't it? I met new people who wanted to give me a chance. Maybe that was your goddess, or maybe it was just that I finally tried. Either way, it worked. And I've got enough hope now that maybe I can end this whole stupid thing and stop hurting people I care about."

Meg stares at me for a long moment. Then slowly, hesitantly, she reaches into her coat pocket and withdraws her sacred heart lighter. But before she hands it over to me, she says, "Okay, I can see why you'd want to end the spell. But why destroy the list? You went through a lot to get it right."

"And it's good that I did. But it doesn't matter."

Meg sucks in a breath like I've uttered a blasphemy. Perhaps I have. "What are you talking about?"

"The list doesn't matter, Meg. Some guy could be perfect for me. He could have beautiful eyes and ambition and talent and he could love me more than anything on earth, but I might not be able to love him back," I say.

"Like Landon."

I nod. "Like Landon. Then again, I might fall for someone else instead. Someone who might not have all the things on my list, but will seem perfect to me anyway."

"Jamie?" Meg asks, and when I say yes, she rolls her eyes and snatches the list from my hands, holding it in front of my nose. "Jamie has all the things on this list, Sam."

"No, he doesn't," I argue. "He doesn't have the most important one. 'Batshit insanely in love with me.'"

"Are you for real? Sam, Jamie's painting birds with

broken wings and trashing his masterpieces and you think he doesn't love you? That's the very definition of batshit insanely in love." Meg shakes her head at me. "Goddess, you're hopeless."

I ignore that. "He may have been in love with me, but it's too late now."

"Well," Meg says, relenting. "That may be true."

I nod. "And that's another thing. I fell in love and then what did I do? I screwed it up. Spectacularly."

Meg reaches for my hand and squeezes it. "No one can blame you for getting stupid over a hot, soon-to-be-famous musician. I know Jamie was mad, but he should have given you another chance. I was in total agreement with Landon about that."

I look down at my list, eyeing the word *understanding*. "Yeah, maybe he could have had a bigger dose of number seven, but I could have had a bigger dose of number five myself."

Meg raises a brow.

"Loyalty," I say, and she snorts. "I could have fallen for any of them, Meg. Gus, or Travis, Landon again, even. But it was Jamie I fell for, for some reason. He's the one my heart chose. And I took him for granted."

"So what now?" Meg asks.

"I burn this and tell the Goddess thanks and that I've learned my lesson and that next time She sends someone perfect for me I won't mess it up." Meg laughs at that, then I add, "And then maybe you can help me do a spell to get over Jamie?"

"If there was a spell that made you get over people, I'd have done it for Michael a long time ago," Meg says, and she gets a little teary as she says it.

"We're a sad pair, aren't we?"

She chuckles sadly. "Yeah. But we've done what we can. We asked to be open again and to be strong enough to let them go. The Goddess might help, but we have to do our part too. And make sure we don't harm the innocent in the process."

I take her not-so-subtle meaning. "What can I do about Landon?"

"Give him time, Sam. Let him get strong too."

"When did you get so damn wise?" I ask her, grinning.

"It's a witch thing," she says, and laughing, I pull her in for a hug.

We dance around a little, relieved to hear each other laugh, and when she pulls away she finally gives me her lighter. "Burn it. Speak from the heart."

I take the lighter and look over my list one more time. "Hey, got a pencil?"

Meg produces one from her coat pocket like she was waiting on me to ask. I kneel on the mausoleum stairs and scratch out all the items on my list, except for number ten. Then I add one so that it looks like this:

Perfect 10

1. ~~Sexy~~ Batshit insanely in love with him

2. ~~*Talented*~~
3. ~~*Style*~~
4. ~~*Nice eyes*~~
5. ~~*Thick hair Loyal*~~
6. ~~*Sense of humor*~~
7. ~~*Attractive Understanding*~~
8. ~~*Ambitious*~~
9. ~~*Fun*~~
10. ~~*Good taste*~~ *Batshit insanely in love with me*

Meg grins at me. "Who's the wise one now? I'm telling you, we should form a coven."

"I tell you what, if Landon magically—or magic-k-ally—pops out from behind the mausoleum and says he's forgiven me, I'll consider it."

In spite of myself, I cast a glance in the mausoleum's direction, which earns me a hearty laugh from Meg. Then I feel her hand on my shoulder. "It won't be today. But you'll see him soon enough, I promise."

I can do nothing but hope she's right, and so I flick her lighter until I get a flame and hold it up to the edge of my list. I drop the paper to the marble stairs as the flame catches, and as we watch it burn to nothing but ash, I thank the Goddess for everything, the good and the bad.

There's no gust of wind this time, no sign that the magical world has heard my words, but someone has, and that's really all that matters. Meg's hand slips into mine and we turn our backs to the mausoleum and walk away.

Nineteen

"Mom, you cannot give me a casserole to take with us."

"It's a two-hour trip to Yellow Springs. You're bound to get hungry."

I rub my temples. "Then we'll stop somewhere on the way, I promise."

"At least take the cookies."

"Mom . . ."

Meg takes the plate from my mother's offering hands and gives her a bright smile. I shoot her a look and she lifts her nose in the air. "What? I'm not turning down cookies. Besides, I won't twist your arm to eat them. More for me."

"At least someone appreciates my baking," my mother sniffs.

"Everyone appreciates your baking, love, especially me," my dad says, patting a small gut that is a testament to his words. He wraps his arms around my mother from behind and squeezes. It would be cute, if I had time to contemplate my parents' show of affection. Dad rests his chin on Mom's shoulder. "Look at our son, Gina. Crashing his true love's art show to win his heart back. If only I wrote romance novels."

"Dad," I warn. I count backward from ten. Slowly. "Meg, can we get a move on? It starts in a few hours."

Jamie's art show is tonight at seven. It's almost five o'clock and we obviously haven't left yet. We haven't even made it off the front porch.

"Somebody's anxious," Meg says, and she and my parents all exchange a knowing and completely irritating smirk.

"Yes, I am. And if you're not in the car in one minute, I'm leaving without you."

Meg opens her mouth to say something sassy back but then freezes, staring off in the distance behind me. I turn around.

It's Landon.

It's been four days since I've seen him, though some of that is my fault. The day after I told him I was still in love with Jamie, I told my mom I didn't feel good and stayed home from school. The day after that I tried it again, and she merely kissed me on the forehead and told me it was okay to take a couple of days off if I wasn't feeling up to going to school.

Getting your heart broken hurts, but losing your best friend? It's hell.

When I did go back—today, actually—I didn't see him at all. That didn't surprise me. He knew my schedule as well as I did, and he'd know exactly how to avoid me.

As he comes up the front walk I can see that he's carrying one white rose.

"Um, Allen? Meg? I think I'm going to need some help putting this casserole away, since you're not going to take it," Mom says.

"Yes. It does look heavy," I hear my dad say, and Meg adds, "I'd love to help you with that, Gina," and they quickly disappear into the house, and that is exactly why I love them all.

"Hey," Landon says as he steps up onto the porch.

"Hi," I say, and although I have no idea what he's going to say to me, I'm so happy to see him that I can't be nervous about that.

He hands me the rose. I take it, sniffing it once before smiling.

"So I've been thinking," he says. "About your list and Jamie and you and me and everything. And you know, whether it's chemistry or fate or some Wiccan goddess, we can't really choose who we fall in love with. It just happens, whether they fit your list or not. You fell for him, and not me, and that's not your fault. So I shouldn't really hold that against you."

I smile, glad that Landon figured out the same thing I did, and I look down at the little rose in my hands. It's so pretty—intricate, really. The petals fold around each other in layer after delicate layer. It reminds me of me and Jamie, the way it was cut right when it was blossoming. And it reminds me of Landon and me too, because it seems so fragile.

"You really tried for me, I know you did. You wanted to give me your heart. It was just already gone. And I know you tried so hard because you do love me. Just as a friend, sure, but you loved me enough to want to try, and I'm really glad for that."

"I do love you," I say, drawing my gaze away from the rose to look right in his eyes. "I love you so much. God, Landon. The past few days I felt like I was going insane without you."

"I know. That's why I'm here. I felt the same way."

"What? You mean you want to be friends still?"

Landon holds out a hand, quieting me. "I kind of have this whole speech thing prepared, so if you could just let me spit it out . . ."

I nod and bite my tongue.

"I'm really sorry about the other day. You know how I am when I'm angry. I don't really think. I still have a lot to learn about anger management. But I just wanted to forget about you, you know? Never see you again so I wouldn't have to hurt all the time. And when I got home and realized I'd told you I didn't want to be your friend anymore, it hurt worse than anything I've ever felt. Worse than when we broke up, really. Then I started thinking about the list and how it's not your fault that you love him instead of me and all that. But you know what I thought about the most?"

I shake my head.

"I thought about how much it would hurt to not see you every day and talk to you every day. And that hurt a lot more than a broken heart." He smiles. "Turns out that even if I love you so much I can't be around you right now, I love you too much to lose you forever."

He reaches for my hand, and I give it to him, letting him squeeze it. "So you're still going to be my friend?"

"Yeah, if you want me."

"I do."

He nods. "But not right now."

My smile falls and I look at him, confused.

He squeezes my hand again and lets it drop. "I need time, Sam. You hurt me. I need to get over that. I need to get over you."

I understand that, so I nod. "But then you'll be my friend again?"

"Of course. You can't get rid of me that easily."

I smile. "Meg said she figured we'd be stuck with you forever."

"She's right," Landon says, smiling too. "And I promise it won't take me six months this time. I'll be back wreaking havoc in your life again by spring break, I can feel it."

"I can't wait," I say, and we smile at each other. Then Landon pulls me into his arms, giving me a rib-crushing hug.

"Me either. Get to the show. I'm making you late."

"We were already late before you showed up, don't worry," I joke, then I add, "You can come if you want."

"Thanks, but I really, *really* don't want to. Eventually I won't feel like hexing Jamie with some awful curse, but today is not that day." Landon pauses, considering. "Hey, you think Meg knows any hexes?"

He's kidding, and that is a great sign that he's already moved on to laughing about things. I hug him again, one more to last me through the weeks ahead.

"Take as long as you need. But not too long. I miss my best friend."

"Bye, Sam." He gives me a kiss on the cheek before he walks away. I watch him go, already feeling a little less empty than I did minutes before.

Meg steps out of the house, smiling at me. "Everything okay?"

I tuck the rose behind my ear and take my car keys out of my pocket, jingling them in her face. "I'll tell you on the way. Now let's hit the road. I've got to go get my Perfect Ten back."

....

"Samson! I'm so glad you're here. Jamie will be too. Come. Come! It is such an exciting night!" Ninah makes a grand gesture, ushering us into the gallery. "If you'd like a glass of champagne, find one of the boys in a tux. I promise I won't alert the authorities."

She winks at us, and then leans close to my ear to whisper, "Talk to him, love. Tell him he simply must finish that phoenix."

As she drifts off barefoot into the crowd to hobnob with art people, Meg raises a brow.

I ignore it. "Champagne?"

As if I have to ask. An adult just offered us alcohol. And champagne at that. It's all so sophisticated.

I leave Meg to find one of the boys in tuxes. The place is packed, much more than I ever imagined an art show to be, and everyone's dressed to the nines. I'm thankful my mom insisted I wear my corduroy blazer and my best sneakers.

Jamie's art is hanging from invisible wires, creating a labyrinth of floating walls around the room. It doesn't take much studying to realize what Ninah has done: the birds are flying, hanging in midair as is befitting to them. The art snobs are gathered in little groups every few paces, discussing the work in hushed, reverent tones. I catch a few whispers, enough to know that Jamie has impressed them and that very few of them will be able to resist the chance to scoop up one of his paintings before he's well-known.

I see someone in a tux carrying a tray of golden flutes and I make toward him. I pass the dodo painting as I walk and just happen to glance down at the small card that has the asking price written on it and just about have a heart attack.

Jamie's never going to have to work at Seven Sauces again, that's for sure.

Then I see him.

He's in the next room, talking with an older couple and gesturing to different aspects of a peacock's iridescent tail. He looks happy. He looks gorgeous. He's wearing a navy suit that's cut perfectly to fit his trim body, and a light blue tie that makes the blue in his eyes look electric.

I walk into the room, champagne forgotten, and he sees me. There's a hint of a smile, the slightest nod before he goes back to chatting with potential buyers. I walk through the room slowly, looking at each of the paintings. Most of them I've seen before, which is a good thing because I'm not really paying attention to them now. I can feel Jamie watching me, though his light voice never stops explaining his methods.

I move on to the next picture and freeze.

It's the Jubjub, and hanging like this in midair, it looks more alive than ever. It's breathtaking.

I lose myself in it for a while, and then Jamie is standing next to me. It's like I feel him before I see him, like every cell in my body is aware that he's close and wants to get closer.

"Lewis Carroll said that the Jubjub lives alone but in a perpetual state of passion," he says.

I swallow thickly. "It must be very lonely."

"It is." He clears his throat. "You came alone?"

"Meg's here," I answer. "Landon . . . I'm, um. We're not together."

"I know," Jamie says. "He told me."

Landon told him. That makes me feel warm all over.

I turn so that I can see him. He's studying his work. I wonder if he sees how beautiful it is, or if he's wondering if it's good enough.

"Ninah said I have to tell you to finish the phoenix."

"It was the only one I didn't finish for her. She's a tough boss." Then he looks at me, his eyes all soft and warm. "She shouldn't worry. It'll rise again. Phoenixes always do."

I let myself sink into his gaze for a wonderful moment before I have to stop and remind myself that I'm the reason why he has to redo that painting at all.

I focus on the Jubjub instead, and it's then that I realize that this painting doesn't have a price tag.

"How much do you want for it?" I ask. I know the Jubjub is easily worth double what he's asking for the other paintings, and I know I don't have a chance in hell of buying it, but I have to know how much someone is going to spend to get the privilege of having this on their wall.

"This one's not for sale."

"It's not?" I ask numbly, still staring at the painting.

"No. It belongs to this guy I fell in love with."

My heart beats a crazy, erratic rhythm in my chest. "I hope he wasn't a jerk who broke your heart, then."

"Well, he was kind of a jerk, but maybe I should have given him another chance. And, honestly, I've been miserable without him."

"He's been miserable without you." I reach down, tucking one of Jamie's hands into mine. "And he loves you too."

We smile at each other, then turn back to the painting, but we don't let go of each other's hands. I can feel happiness coming off of him in waves and I know he's not criticizing his work. At least not this time.

"You should know," I start, "my dad agreed with you about my writing samples. He liked all of them, which was just crazy, but he said your favorite was his favorite too. That's the one I ended up sending out."

He smiles. "Glad I have the same literary taste as the great Allen Raines. And that he read them for you."

I nod. We both know how much it meant to me. "And it worked. I got into NYU."

"Your dream. That's perfect, Sam."

Perfect.

The word makes me think back to that night in October, standing in a cemetery with my two best friends, asking for what I thought was perfection. I know all about perfection now. I know how it can be found everywhere, in anything. There's perfection in learning from mistakes, perfection in learning to let go, perfection in second chances and trying again. There's also perfection in things that change, and in things that never will—like loyal, loving friends.

But most of all, I know now that perfection isn't the kind of thing you can plan. It isn't the kind of thing you can ask for either, because no one knows what perfection really is until they experience it. Perfection is in the unexpected. In the surprises. In the things you have to lose before you can understand.

But I don't tell Jamie all of that. At least not yet. "New York is so far away, though," I say to him instead.

"It is." I look over at him and he's smiling a little, just the slightest curve of lips, as if he's in on some joke that

I'm not getting. "But I hear it has a few good art schools, and that some artists even enjoy living there."

I frown. "But that's two years away. What'll we do until then?"

"We paint. We write," he says, and his pretty blue eyes are sparkling with hope. "We remember how to fly."

And then Jamie kisses me.

It's unexpected. It's surprising.

It's perfect.

THE END

Acknowledgments

This book was a long, eventful journey, and I'd be remiss not to thank the people who have helped it along the way.

To my parents, for their continual love and support.

To my very first readers, Ann Skinner, Erin Detwiler, and Melissa Lawson, thank you for reading this before it even got good.

To Amy Rosenbaum, whose love for this little story brought so many good things to my life, thank you. To the Southern Ohio Writer/Reader Collaborative, thank you for being the critique group of my dreams. Somehow you make me look forward to getting my ass kicked once a month.

To Sarah Prashaw, Kristy Mishler, Jenn Hoey, and Kate Nondahl, because our daily group emails provided both a place to vent and a good laugh, as needed. Oh, and Kate Nondahl, thank you for talking it out. This book and everything else.

To Jacqueline Pierce—your friendship has gotten me through all the highs and lows, darling. Thanks for being my cheerleader. To John Finck, who has read this book as many times as I have, thank you for your faith in me, for always pushing me to make it better, and for being the best critique partner and friend a girl could ask for. To J.H. Trumble—I wouldn't be here without you, in so many ways.

Brent Taylor, friend, agent, champion. I'm going to say it one more time: you were born for this. Thank you so much for believing in this book for so long, and I'm so glad I could write something worthy of your belief.

To Ken Wright, thank you for giving this book a home, and for falling in love with it not just once but twice. To Alex Ulyett, thank you for seeing the potential in this book and helping me realize it. You always knew exactly what this story needed, and knew exactly how to get me to wrap my stubborn head around it. You are truly magical. (Magickal?) To the whole team at Viking Children's, thank you for the enthusiasm, thank you for your dedication, thank you for all your careful planning, hard work, and patience, and thank you for the most amazing cover ever created.

You are all unicorns, and Sam and I are lucky to have you.